T0274512

Fracturing Fate

Books by Sasha Alsberg available from Inkyard Press

Breaking Time
Fracturing Fate

The Androma Saga by Sasha Alsberg and Lindsay Cummings

Zenith
Nexus

Fracturing Fate

SASHA ALSBERG

inkyard
PRESS

Recycling programs for this product may not exist in your area.

ISBN-13: 978-1-335-45375-4

Fracturing Fate

For questions and comments about the quality of this book, please contact us at CustomerService@Harlequin.com.

Inkyard Press
22 Adelaide St. West, 41st Floor
Toronto, Ontario M5H 4E3, Canada
www.InkyardPress.com

Printed in U.S.A.

To Marcia Longman and JD Netto.

This one is for you.

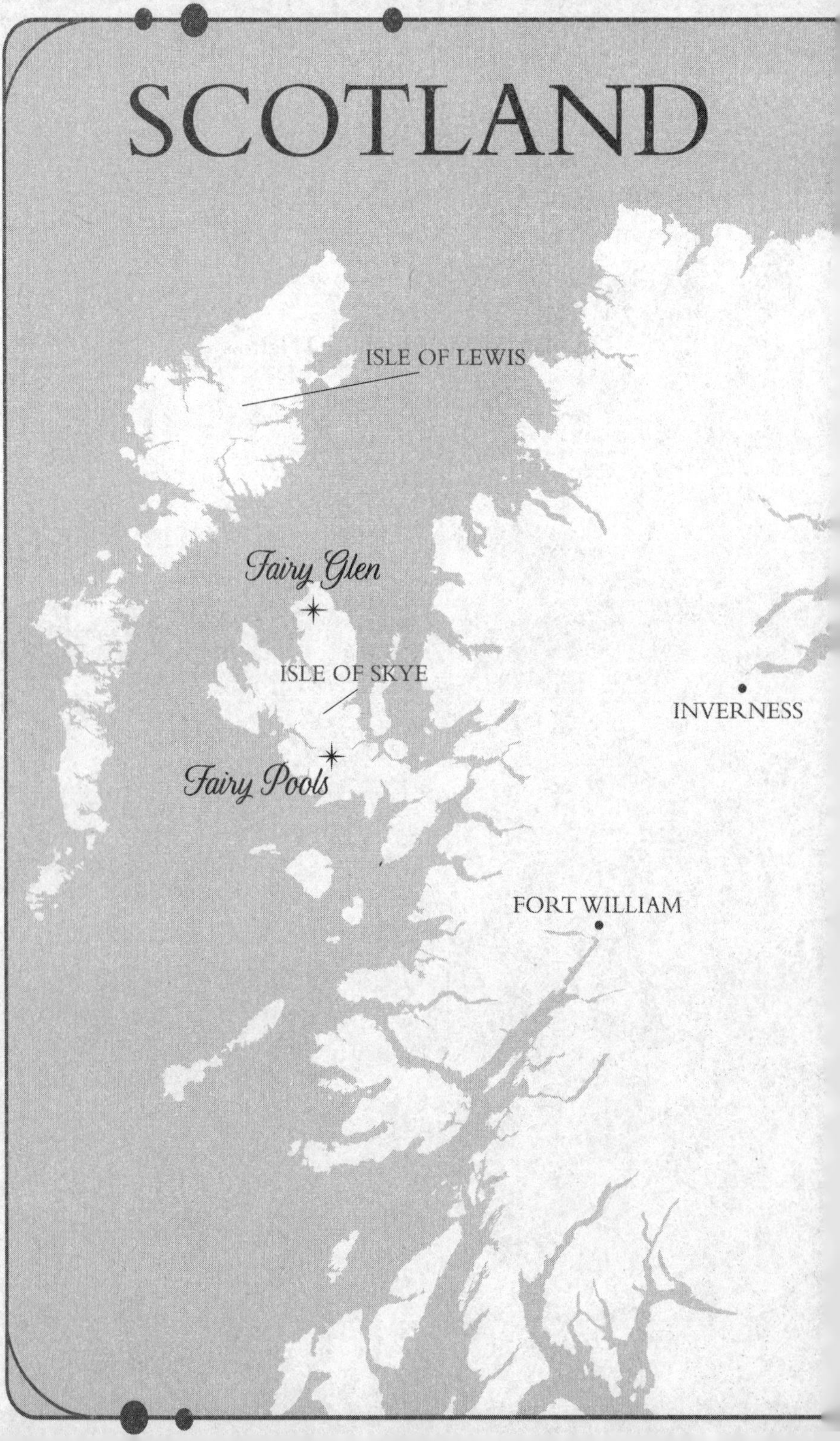

SCOTLAND

ISLE OF LEWIS

Fairy Glen

ISLE OF SKYE

INVERNESS

Fairy Pools

FORT WILLIAM

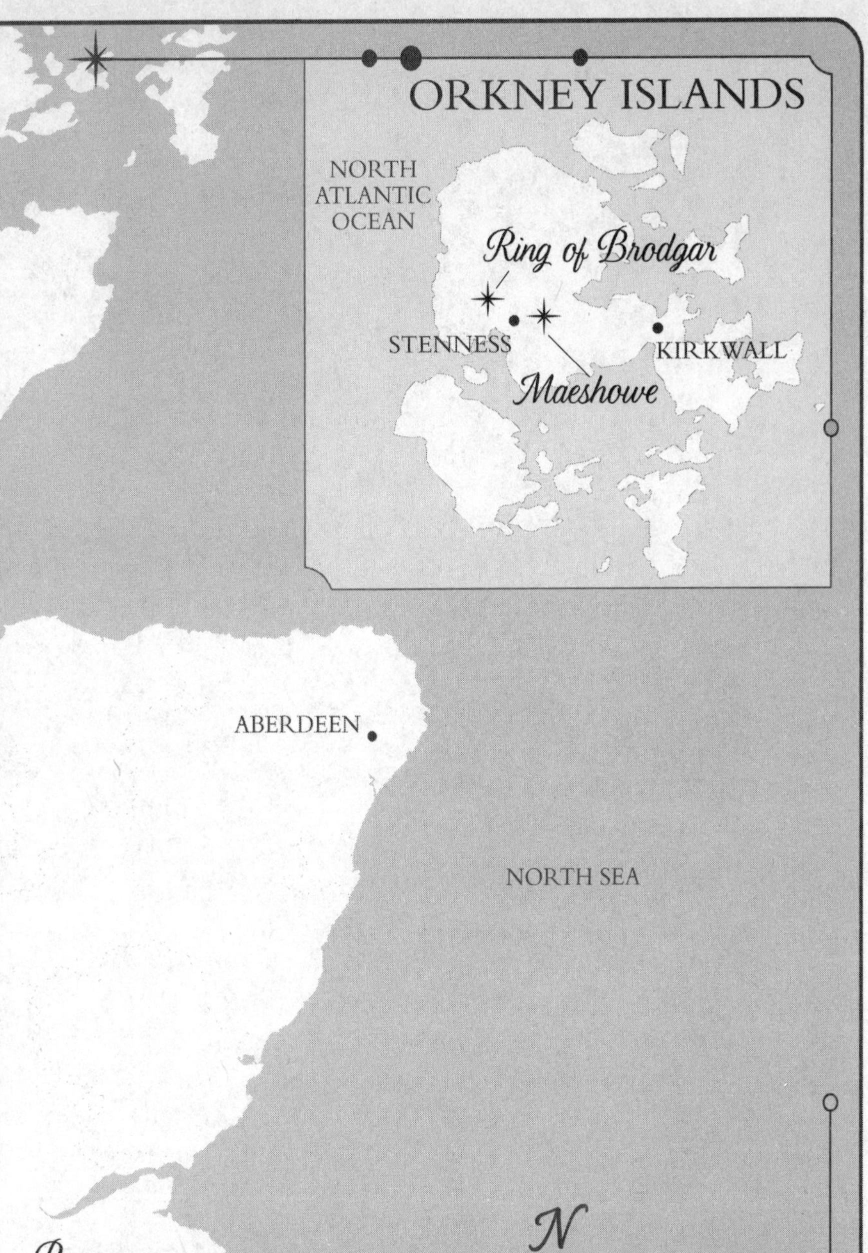
ORKNEY ISLANDS
NORTH
ATLANTIC
OCEAN
Ring of Brodgar
STENNESS
KIRKWALL
Maeshowe
ABERDEEN
NORTH SEA
N
Rosemere
EDINBURGH

CHAPTER ONE

KLARA

1568

Light searing her eyes with excruciating brilliance. Fine woolen bunched in her fist. Plummeting through time and space, tumbling head over heels, her stomach twisting violently—

Then slowing, drifting.

Klara's feet settled on the ground as if she was the queen in Dad's old chess set, placed in its square in a game-ending move. *Checkmate.*

She blinked rapidly, peering through the mist that swirled around her, crouching in the fighting stance Callum had taught her. This trick still felt like a cheat, or maybe a curse—Klara was no closer than the first time to knowing where she might end up.

The answers are always there. A whisper in the rushing winds brushed past Klara's ear; her mother's voice. Loreena Spalding always said that every antique in her precious collection offered clues to where it came from—an etched design popular in the sixteenth century, a particular alloy in use in the eighteenth. To Klara's scientific mind, Loreena's words were a reminder to distill facts from impressions.

So: One, the air was cold. Two, it carried a sharp whiff of lye soap and a faint, greasy note of coal smoke. Three, beneath the soles of her sneakers were smoothed, cobbled stones. Four, above her in the night sky, *Corona Borealis*—the "Silver Wheel"—was in its summer home north of the celestial equator, tucked between the constellations Boötes and Hercules. Five, her right hand was still wrapped around the familiar gold and iron grip of her sword, and six—"Gah!"—her other hand clenched nothing. She'd lost her grip on Llaw's cloak.

Klara's heart lurched, but the truth was that it didn't really matter where the demigod had gone, since he was dead. Llaw would haunt his precious Otherworld now—and only if the gods were feeling merciful.

"You?"

The mist fell away—not like the early-morning fog in Hudson River Park that burned off by the time Klara finished her run, but in a scattering of glinting dust. The incredulous voice belonged to a young man with a weapon in his hand, shadowed in the dim glow of a street lamp, and for a brief, breathless second Klara allowed herself to hope.

"Callum?"

Then he stepped into the light, dirk dangling from his hand, and Klara's hope was torn from her chest. His face was just as handsome, but in place of Callum's unruly dark curls and piercing, unusual gaze were fiery hair, a scattering of freckles and fine, sculpted lips. This was the boy from her vision in the tomb of Maeshowe.

"Thomas! But how—" Klara paused, wondering if she could trust her eyes. "Do you know who I am?"

It was his turn to look uncertain. He shook his head as if to clear it. "I thought I did, but—I must have mistook you for someone else."

His thick Scottish brogue was so like Callum's, but there the resemblance ended. Klara's eyes fell to his dirk, the blade dark with blood, and remembered the drawing in his notebook, how Thomas had perfectly captured her likeness. "Thomas—it *is* me. Klara Spalding. The…last Pillar?"

His face turned white. "*Crivvens*—you're alive!"

"Me? Of course. But Llaw killed *you*." Nothing was making sense. Thomas was supposed to be lying in a pool of his own blood, still as the stones beneath him. "Callum saw you…"

The sword's pommel pulsed in Klara's hand, emeralds glinting, and she remembered it being nearly ripped from her grasp. Remembered Llaw's tormented dark eyes widening as he seized the blade and plunged it into his own chest…remembered grabbing for his cloak as he began to spin.

"Callum?" Thomas repeated sharply. "What do you know of him?"

How to explain? Too much had happened in the week since Klara had nearly run over a stranger lying broken and unconscious in the middle of the road. "It's a long story," she sighed. "But when I met him, he was trying to avenge your death."

Thomas gave her a hard look, taking in her T-shirt and jeans. "You are not from here. Why would Callum..."

"Same reason I'm here now." She really didn't feel like talking about it. "A demigod who's careless about who he brings along when traveling through time. He's dead," she added, almost as an afterthought.

"Llaw." Thomas's voice was grim. "I know."

Now it was Klara's turn to stare. "He was the one who—?"

"He almost killed me. But he was careless. After he stabbed me, I fell to the ground, hit my head on a cobblestone." Thomas tugged at the rough wool of his coat. "Knocked me out, but, head wounds always bleed, and it turns out he merely nicked my ribs. When I came to, I could still see him, standing in front of a portal. So I killed him. As you say, he is gone."

"No." Klara shook her head, trying to make sense of what Thomas was telling her. Though the truth was just as strange. "I saw him take his own life. He...fell upon my blade."

Thomas was staring at her sword, at the gem-encrusted hilt. Klara gripped it a little more tightly. It was one of Grams's most precious possessions, brought out only once before the day she gave it to Klara.

"Where?" Thomas demanded. "And when?"

There was a strange light in his eyes, and Klara remembered what Callum had said about the weeks before Thomas's death, how strange his behavior had become. Disappearing for days at a time, staring without seeing, muttering of evil creatures and death.

"The Ring of Brodgar," she said flatly. "In the year 2022."

Thomas's mouth worked, whether in shock or calculation Klara couldn't tell. And then his face softened, his eyes losing their metallic glint and fading to a soft blue as he bowed from the waist. He sheathed his dirk and wiped his hands on his pants.

"So you *are* a Pillar," he said formally, "like me."

And with these words, the facts shifted in Klara's mind like the rearrangement of atoms in an intermolecular reaction. Same parts, different shape. Right now, this wasn't about losing Callum, or the place she'd left behind. It couldn't be.

"We are the last ones," she affirmed. "Llaw is dead, by your hand or his own—" she wouldn't debate the question now, though she knew what she had seen "—and so it's over. But what about his powers?" Klara looked at her hands as though the answer might lie there, but nothing felt different.

"I acted on pure instinct when he attacked me," Thomas said slowly. "Llaw arranged to meet me here tonight. I've been following him—but he was always a step ahead. When he sent for me, I realized he knew I was after him all along."

So Callum had been right about Llaw getting too close to the truth. Klara fitted this new piece into the mosaic. "He's a demigod, with a goddess mother—I guess it shouldn't be too surprising that he figured it out."

"A demigod," Thomas repeated bitterly. "With a mortal father. Who should not have the power to travel in time. Or of Sight, or of passing between worlds, or anything else. It is a sinister magic he stole."

Something clicked into place in Klara's mind. Pillars were only meant to house Arianrhod's powers, not use them. Neither she nor Thomas should have been able to travel through time either—not without that same goddess's intervention and guidance. That meant—

"Arianrhod came to you, too." She didn't mean it to come out like an accusation. "She wanted us both to kill Llaw."

Thomas assessed her, then nodded. "Telling neither of us about the other."

Klara knew she had no right to feel duped. She'd been told that the gods' actions weren't always what they seemed—Cernunnos, the god of the forest, had taught her that in his own circuitous way. The gods rarely moved along a straight path when a tangled one would do.

"It's just like a goddess to give her powers to random humans without anyone's consent," she said bitterly.

Thomas gave a rueful smile. "Aye, the gods have never made much sense to me, either.

"And…here we are."

Klara took in the cobbled street in Kelpie's Close, the shuttered doors and darkened alleys, the bleary eyes of the sleepless and the guilty behind faded curtains.

"So, to recap," she said wearily, "you killed him tonight, in the year of our lord 1568." The old way of speaking came to Klara's lips unbidden, an echo of Callum. "At the same moment he took my blade and—"

"We killed him at the same time?" Thomas was in a pose of deep concentration, one hand pinching his chin in thought. "He left me for dead and went to your time to kill you. The last Pillar. But that would mean he could straddle two times at once, which seems impossible." He looked up suddenly, examining her face.

The final piece slid into place.

"Could it have been my doing?" Why did it feel like a confession? Thomas's brows rose in surprise, a smile beginning on his lips, but Klara knew it wasn't good news. "I had to save Callum." An unwelcome memory of the beast flashed in her mind, sinking its yellowed, broken teeth into Callum's side. His blood spilling into the earth. The memory twisted Klara's heart.

"I tried to turn back time," she explained raggedly. "To save him. Only a few minutes—"

"He wasn't in two times, ye mean? You mean *you* brought him here, to me, by accident?"

She and Thomas stared at each other, Klara immobilized by the enormity of what she'd done—and of what had been averted. "The death of each Pillar infused Llaw with new power… By stabbing him at that moment…could I have… like, released all that power, and hyperjumped too far?"

Thomas leaned back, assessing her hypothesis. "Maybe. It seems we each have a story to tell. Or rather…" Thomas gazed at Klara's sword. "Half a story. But this is not the place. It isn't safe for a lady."

The "lady" thing was going to have to stop, but Klara was too exhausted to bristle. She pulled her jacket more tightly around her, tucked the sword into the bag slung across her body, and followed Thomas out of the alley toward the heart of Rosemere.

It was as unfamiliar as a new city.

The buildings looked new but, in the same glance, old as time. The stones shone brighter, but the surroundings dimmed their raw edge. It was less built-up as it was in her time… which seemed odd, since Rosemere was classified as a World Heritage Site back in the early 1970s. Now it looked as unfamiliar as a distant city to which she'd never been.

Quaint houses. Plumes of smoke billowing from chimneys. And streets that if you took a single misstep, you'd be met by it head-on.

This landscape was anything but familiar.

But for some reason, it still felt like home.

CHAPTER TWO

KLARA

"The thing I can't work out," Thomas said a while later, as they tore into the soft, warm loaf that he'd nicked from a baker's cart. "You called it *your* sword. But it's the same sword that Llaw used to steal the Pillars' power when he killed them."

"That wasn't my sword—this is its twin. I was as surprised as you when I saw it. It looks just like mine." Which Arianrhod hadn't thought to mention, come to think of it. Another pointless omission.

They were sitting on the step outside a shop displaying bolts of fabric in the window, and Klara's butt was freezing on the cold stone. The bread tasted like sawdust. She couldn't remember the last time she'd eaten and still she had to force it past her lips, past her heavy heart. "It's been in my family for ages. My grandmother gave it to me."

"But how did your ancestors come to have it?"

Klara shrugged. "My Grams might know, but she never told me." Something Thomas said earlier caught up to her. "Wait—what do you mean the sword stole the power?"

"Arianrhod didn't tell you?"

"She didn't tell me quite a bit, it turns out."

"Llaw's sword was powerful. When it killed any being with any sort of magic, it stole that ability from its victim. That's how Llaw got all his power, and why he became more powerful with each kill." Klara gazed down at her own sword, stroking the face of an amethyst, wondering. She guessed it made a lot of sense.

"May I take a look at it?"

Klara hesitated. The thought of letting it out of her hands, even for a moment, filled her with anxiety.

She reminded herself that Thomas was Callum's best friend, that they'd grown up together. Callum had taught her how to use the sword, had carried it for her, and had even defended himself with it when he was attacked by one of the beasts Llaw had summoned from between worlds. "Sure," she said, hiding her reluctance as she pulled the sword from the beaten hockey stick bag that had come to feel like a second skin.

She gripped the sword in her hands. A wash of sadness hitting her like a rogue wave.

Callum.

Her eyes began to water against her will but the sword was a sturdy comfort. Like how she felt when her mother would give her a hug after a hard day. It was strange, to feel such a deep connection to the object that couldn't easily be described. But in the absence of Callum and her mother…she was grateful for it. She handed it to Thomas, the brief feeling leaving her as she passed it to him.

When Thomas tried to examine the jewel-encrusted pommel more closely, he yelped and the heavy blade fell to the ground.

"Oh God, are you okay?" Klara gasped, her heart skipping a few beats until she saw that Thomas was unhurt.

"Yes, just—the prongs are sharper than they look," Thomas said ruefully, examining his hands. Klara lifted the sword from the ground, immediately feeling less anxious to be in contact with it, and examined the pommel. "The jewels' settings might need looking at."

Klara examined the thistle design, the purple amethysts and green emeralds embedded in finely worked gold and steel, perplexed. She'd never noticed any of the settings being loose, but the thought of losing even one of the ancient gemstones was worrisome, especially since generations of her family had kept the piece in such perfect condition. "I'll have it looked at as soon as I have the chance."

As soon as I get home, she meant; Grams undoubtedly knew someone who restored fine antiques. But that wouldn't happen until Klara figured out how to get back to the future.

Thomas was still staring at the sword intently. "Does it have the same powers as Llaw's?"

"How would I know?" Klara said, slightly annoyed. It wasn't like *she* had been going around killing Pillars. "Arianrhod told me that when Pillars died, their powers returned to the earth, so that was obviously a big old lie. But if you're asking me if I got Llaw's powers when he died, I'd think the answer would be obvious. If I could bend time and space at will, I'd be home right now."

In her *own* bed in Kingshill Manor, with Finley nestled against her back, paws twitching in dreams of chasing squirrels.

Five hundred years in the future.

Llaw had killed eight of the Pillars. Eight of the ten mortals chosen by Arianrhod to unknowingly carry her powers until their deaths, to keep them safe from her fellow gods' envy and mischief.

Had Llaw succeeded in killing Thomas and her, the last of his mother's powers would have flowed into him, and Llaw would have taken Arianrhod's place with the rest of the gods in the Otherworld. Arianrhod had warned that if this came to pass, the delicate balance between worlds—and indeed, time itself—would be destroyed. Llaw would bask in his stolen glory while time in the mortal realm collapsed, and the human world burned.

It was a difficult concept to fit into Klara's scientific outlook—but as best she could understand, she likened it to the death of a star, its planets destroyed in the red giant engulfment. A month ago, Klara would have argued there was no other reasonable way to think about the universe—but after the things she'd seen and experienced since meeting Callum and time traveling five hundred years into the past, everything she believed had been turned upside down.

Misunderstanding her silence, Thomas only made things worse. "It's Callum you're thinking of, isn't it."

Klara sighed. She supposed she ought to tell him. "He and

I...became close. Callum talked about you all the time," she added, wanting to change the subject.

Thomas let out a short laugh.

"He sure has a mouth that could talk," he said. "I just hope what he said painted me in a decent light."

His voice was light, and it pained Klara to know how that would change if she told him about Callum's fate. She could hardly bear thinking about it herself, let alone share it with the one person who probably knew Callum better than he knew himself.

"Don't worry," she said, trying to push away the pang that stabbed at her chest. "He only mentioned how loudly you snore at night...oh and how he didn't miss your smelly feet," she joked. She was surprised how easy it was to talk to Thomas, especially when having a lighthearted conversation about Callum. But talking about him with Thomas, someone Callum knew so well, felt comforting.

His eyes went wide in horror. "My feet dinnae smell!"

"I'm just playing with you," Klara clarified. "He told me about what it was like growing up. And how you were each other's only family."

Thomas let out a relieved sigh.

"Aye, we were that." A shadow fell across Thomas's expression. "You cannae choose your family but I am glad he became mine."

"Looks like he was dropped into both our lives without notice." Klara smiled softly as she spoke. "But at the perfect time."

She could relate to Thomas, foolish as it sounded. He had known Callum longer but the love she felt for Callum spanned beyond time. That was one thing she knew for sure.

Thomas's eyes were distant when he spoke next. "I was four years old when the fae merchant brought him, just a wee baby. I dinnae remember much from back then, but I do remember how nice it felt to not be alone."

Klara's head snapped up. Callum had told her it was his mother who had abandoned him to Brice MacDonald. "What do you mean, the fae brought him?"

Thomas shrugged. "Just some trader, one of the *olc síth*. The dark fae. Brice bought him because he was big and healthy and he could train him starting in childhood."

Grams had told Klara stories about the dark fae. She'd had a way of making the old tales seem real, entrancing Klara for hours at a time when she visited Edinburgh as a child. *The olc síth feed on fear and fortune. Some say they are the descendants of the fallen angels.*

"There's a faerie market," Thomas continued. "Mostly only magical creatures trade there, but if a man—or woman—can find a fae to vouch for him..." His voice trailed off, giving the impression that he had firsthand knowledge.

"They sell *children*? But I thought Callum's mother—"

"—went to the market and asked a fae for help," Thomas said, bitterness in his voice. "She probably couldn't feed herself, much less a baby. Not everyone has a house and food on the table."

Too late Klara remembered that Thomas's family, too, had sold him. No wonder the subject was a sore one.

"The *olc síth* pay in coin for strong, healthy boys," Thomas continued. "And sell them to Master Brice for twice the sum."

Callum had told Klara how he and Thomas suffered in Brice's care, goaded and starved and forced to practice until their knuckles were bloody, all the years of their too-short childhoods. But that training had molded them into the finest fighters in the taverns and pubs of Rosemere, earning Brice his fortune from those who came to bet on his boys.

Master, keeper, devil, father, Callum had called Brice. Klara had dared to hope that someday her own father might offer Callum the kindness and encouragement he'd never had, that Callum would become like a son to him. But now that day would never come.

Klara furtively wiped a tear away, but not before Thomas had noticed.

"I need to get back to my own time," she said before he could mention it.

Thomas frowned. "But what is stopping you? Even if you do not have the power of the eight other Pillars, you still have Arianrhod's gifts, do ye not? You can travel through time." A statement, not a question.

"I can't…control the powers yet," Klara said, embarrassed. "Not like you."

Thomas raised a brow. "What do you mean?"

She wasn't sure she wanted to tell him—but it hardly mattered anymore. "The first time I felt Arianrhod's powers was when Llaw tried to kill me, and I…I felt something rise up inside me, and he went flying back. I had no idea what had happened."

Llaw had appeared from a grayish mist and seized Klara's throat, choking her, and something inside her snapped, a powerful burst of energy that sparked into a bright, white light.

"What else?"

"I've…summoned a god. I dreamed of the Stag God, Cernunnos, and he appeared to me between worlds, but he spun an illusion—a misty clearing. Another time I summoned Llaw, and he didn't bother with illusions." Klara shuddered, remembering the gauzy substance that clung to her skin and clothes, what Llaw had called the "matter between worlds."

"But what about when you were awake?"

"I feel this *pull* inside me," Klara said, words inadequate to describe it. "I can't control it, but I can't stop it, either. Especially when Callum and I visited the mystic centers, the ones in your notebook. When we were in Maeshowe, I had a vision of going back in time, like I was watching all of history unfold—but I don't think I actually time traveled."

Klara remembered something else that had happened at Maeshowe, after the dizzying slide show of the past—a brief vision of a handsome boy with bright blue eyes and a shock of red hair. *Are you like me?* he'd asked wonderingly, reaching his strong, scarred hand toward her. *What power you must hold…*

Thomas was rubbing his forehead ruefully. "I forgot that I gave my notebook to Callum."

"The night you met with Llaw. Callum thought you wanted him to keep it safe, in case…" Klara trailed off. It felt rude somehow to remind Thomas how close he'd come to dying.

"In case something happened to me," Thomas said, nodding. "But I'm surprised he could make sense of my sketches. Of course, I also didn't know that anyone else was working for Arianrhod. Did anything else happen at the mystic centers?"

"Yes—Llaw found us. He brought a monster with him, and it nearly killed Callum, and I felt that pull and time stopped and went backward. Only a few minutes, but enough for Callum to get out of the way. And I put my hands together like this—" she clasped them and brought them down in a fast arc "—and the beast dissolved and disappeared."

"So you *did* time travel!"

"No, I—I mean yes, I suppose I did, but I wasn't aware I was doing it until after it happened, and it was only a few moments. The next time Llaw came after me, he brought these horrible dogs, half a dozen of them. It was hard enough to fight his monster, but we didn't have a chance against so many. Callum tried to fight them off while I was battling Llaw, but…they killed him."

Klara's voice broke, and she couldn't say the rest: that she'd failed to protect Callum, failed to destroy Llaw. She'd cut off his hand with her sword, but he'd robbed her of victory by plunging its blade into his own flesh.

Thomas froze. But his eyes were anything but still. The knowledge of a best friend's death would stop anyone in their tracks, and bring even the strongest of men to their knees. The pain, that she knew all too well, was blatantly visible in his eyes.

He blinked once. Then again. With each shutter of his lids, a haunting look appeared.

"I feared the worst when you appeared…without him." He ran his hand up through his unruly locks and across his face.

"It sounds like we have developed our powers differently. Mine aren't as defensive," Thomas said, not unkindly. Klara was grateful to him for changing the subject. "But my time travel ability started the same as yours, I just had them longer. It took me a while to figure out how to go through time, and you would have learned too, if Llaw hadn't died."

"So you think the powers left us when he died?"

Thomas shrugged. "I haven't felt anything since then—have you?"

"It's been all of, like, an hour or whatever, but…" Klara closed her eyes and tried to focus on the feeling of her blood traveling through her veins, her heart beating. "Yeah, nothing. But…can we try?" she said, brows raised. Maybe if they both tried, it could work. The power of one got her here, the power of two could take her back…*right*?

Thomas paused, looking at her with his lips drawn in a thin line against his pale flesh. He then shrugged. "I cannae see the harm in trying."

"Okay," Klara breathed, straightening her spine. "Shall we?"

Thomas nodded, stepping forward with his hands held outward. She placed her hands in his and instantly, a shock went through her as they touched. *Maybe this could work.*

"I'm kinda new at this, how do we…" She trailed off.

"Summon your power from within, clear your mind and think of where you want to go. Think of your home."

Klara nodded and shut her eyes.

Home.

She envisioned the manor, its mossy stone walls, her father, his smile, Finley running free through their land on dewy mornings. And Callum, his eyes, his lips, his voice…

Callum.

Callum.

Callum.

He was her home. Home isn't just a place, it's the people who make you feel at home. Her heart swelled with a swirling vortex of emotion, so powerful that she wanted to burst.

Longing, loss, love. So much love. A tickle began inside her, growing steadily.

She was suddenly all too aware of the cool breeze that drifted through the air, the sharp scent of burning leaves in the distance, and the warmth of Thomas's hands. A fire was lit within her, her power. Thomas's power.

Then, nothing.

The spark was snuffed out, as if a gust of wind had pulled everything out of her.

She knew, even before she opened her eyes, that it failed. What she felt was just that, her. Her love for Callum. Not her powers.

She opened her eyes and saw Thomas looking at her, a flush to his cheeks and his eyes bright, if sad. He quickly pulled his hand out of hers, and she found herself wishing he hadn't. Thinking of Callum only made her remember how she'd last seen him: broken. Dying.

"I'm sorry, Klara," Thomas said, chastened. "It must hurt. It would be so much easier if you had absorbed the other Pillars' powers." He paused, thinking. "Perhaps Arianrhod didn't lie to you, and the sword releases the powers instead of transferring them. Maybe your sword *is* different."

"That doesn't make me feel better, not if there's no way home. Why would she take our powers now?"

"It makes sense. We're no use to Arianrhod anymore, so she's forgotten all about us."

"Other than the fact that we're still Pillars," Klara said, feeling a rush of resentment. "Doesn't it piss you off that she gets to mess with our lives that way, and we don't have any say in it?"

"I guess so," Thomas said, "but if she hadn't, if we didn't step in to help, then Llaw would have killed us both—and broken the connection between worlds."

They were both silent for a while, lost in their own thoughts, until the ache of what had happened became too much to bear. Klara knew she would carry the loss of Callum with her forever, but she needed to take a break from it, if only to keep from collapsing with exhaustion. But she knew all too well that pushing loss aside wouldn't help her now and definitely not help her when it would inevitably emerge again.

"Can you help me with something, Thomas?" she asked heavily. She didn't want to think about much else right now but there were other matters she knew needed addressing. "I need clothes. If someone sees me like this—"

"I was going to say something," Thomas said with an effort at tact. "Those are a man's pants, and shoes like none I've seen, and those markings—"

He gestured at Klara's worn Pink Floyd T-shirt, her glittery pink Converse sneakers. The clothes she'd dressed in the morning before she and Callum went to the Ring of Brodgar.

"Twenty-first-century fashion." She shrugged, not bothering to explain her shirt. Callum had confided to her that Thomas had never learned to read. "Which obviously won't blend in."

"We can nick something..." Thomas mused.

"And end up in jail? No thanks." Klara and Callum had risked much worse...but that seemed like another life now.

Thomas narrowed his eyes, pointing to her ear. "The gold. Would you part with it?"

Klara touched one of the little gold horseshoe earrings that had been a graduation gift from her riding instructor. It would be a shame to part with them, but if it was the only way…

"I guess."

"Then it's time to go to the faerie market."

Thomas promised that the market wasn't far, but they walked all the way through the dark and quiet streets of town and down to the water. Rosemere sat on the northern edge of the Firth of Forth, but it might as well have been the North Sea itself, a sheet of inky black meeting offshore fog under a yellow moon.

They skirted the docks and walked to a crumbling warehouse beyond an old pier. Rosemere had disappeared over the centuries, the village that sprung up in its place much closer to Kingshill Manor, but Klara thought she recognized the contours of the shore. In her own time, all that was left of the docks was a historical marker in a little beach where young mums brought their children to splash and wade.

"That used to be the shipbuilders' warehouse," Thomas said, pointing to a large abandoned building. "No one builds ships here anymore."

Klara followed Thomas around to the far side of the building, the wall dark with mold where horsetail and bindweed grew thick enough to block the sun. It would have been easy to miss the small, weathered wooden door set into the crumbling mortar.

Thomas rapped three times. *"Lòchran dorcha,"* he said in a low voice.

The door disappeared. One moment Klara had been staring at solid, scarred oak—the next, into a vast room that seemed larger than the building itself, lit with hundreds of twinkling lights strung from walls and rafters.

Faerie lights…for a faerie market. Klara looked behind her, but where the door had been was only the rough-plastered wall.

"There's someone I know," Thomas said. "Someone I've done business with before."

He gestured for Klara to follow him into the busy aisle. Stall after stall was stacked and piled and hung with all manner of merchandise, from tins and bottles of murky liquids to bolts of colorful silk to strings of glittering beads. Even more astonishing were the creatures she saw browsing, from scrawny, sharp-nosed brownies to a small, shy, dark-haired faerie clothed in leaves to a man with thick hair covering his body and a wolfish, whiskered face to a lovely fair woman with hooves for feet. There were even a few dogs nosing about for scraps, creatures too mangy and thin to be the *cù sìth*, the hounds that Grams said ferried souls to the afterlife.

Thomas barely gave them a glance, ignoring the calls of merchants hawking wares.

"Oread tears, plucked from the depths this morning!"

"Silk for your lady, every color of the rainbow!"

"Azure tincture, azure powder, azure ointment! A little goes a long way!"

"Callum never told me about this place," Klara said, hurrying to keep up.

"He didn't know about it. Brice forbid us to talk about the fae, much less seek them out." Thomas stopped in front of a striped curtain strung in a doorway and tugged a bell cord.

He turned to look at Klara, a question in his eyes. "Arianrhod told me about the market. The password to enter."

The goddess hadn't given Klara any such information, but she was saved from saying so when the curtain was pulled aside by a pale, long-fingered hand. "Thomas Buchan," a timbrous voice intoned, "and your lovely friend."

Klara wasn't sure she liked the faintly mocking tone. Beyond the curtain stood a tall, slender, straight-backed man around her father's age, but there the similarities ended. His silvery hair brushed the collar of his embroidered waistcoat, and his features were narrow and sharp, with delicate ears and thin, pale eyebrows and a slightly upturned nose. Most arresting were his eyes, an opaque milky violet with pinprick pupils.

The room was small, the size of the old root cellar in Kingshill Manor, and lit with half a dozen candle stubs dripping wax on several low tables. The walls were lined in gold silk and green and scarlet cushions were piled on thick carpets on the floor.

The man walked around a table piled with a riot of objects ranging from books to wooden boxes inlaid with mother of pearl to jeweled hairpins to a small, delicate bird skull. A half-eaten apple lay browning and forgotten next to an empty inkwell. Only the space in the center, lit by an amber glass lamp, had been cleared.

"You forget your manners, Thomas," the man chided. "Please introduce us."

"My name is Klara Spalding," she said, annoyed at being talked over. "I'm in need of—"

Thomas brought his foot down on her instep hard enough to hurt, cutting her off midsentence.

"The lady requires a dress," he said. "Something worthy of her station."

"It is my pleasure to make your acquaintance, my lady," the man said, bowing deeply and ignoring Thomas. "Malabron Traille, at your service."

"I am prepared to pay," Thomas said, "if you can offer something fine enough."

Malabron laughed. "I see. Please make yourselves comfortable."

He pushed past another curtain at the rear of the room. Thomas flopped down on a pile of cushions, legs sprawled.

"I can speak for myself, you know," Klara said.

"You could," Thomas said blandly. "But the *olc síth* are easily offended. There is a particular way to speak to them."

"I suppose Arianrhod told you that, too." Klara was as bewildered as she was annoyed by all the goddess had withheld from her. Why task them both with killing Llaw, but introduce only Thomas to the fae who might have helped?

Though to be fair, Arianrhod had only appeared to Klara after Thomas had been trying—and failing—to find Llaw for months. As Thomas had hinted, maybe the goddess would have shared the same information in time.

Malabron returned with an armload of gowns which he hung from hooks in the wall. "This organ-pleated overskirt is suitable for day," he said, pointing to the first. "This is ermine," he said, fingering the fur cuffs of the second, "with a carcinet of gold filigree, and—"

"If that's gold, I'll eat my trousers," Thomas cut in. "And that fur came from a rabbit. Don't insult me with your fakeries, Malabron. She'll take that one."

Malabron grinned, showing small, even white teeth. "One has to try. Someone will pay a pretty penny for those."

Klara reached for the pale green satin gown, giving the low-cut embroidered bodice and a tall ruffled collar a doubtful look. "Where can I try it on?"

Malabron stopped her with a hand on her arm. His touch was cold but far from inert; it sent a prickling sensation through Klara's arm, and she jerked her hand back. "First, let us agree on a price."

She looked at Malabron, expecting him to be watching her but he wasn't. Instead, his gaze was fixed inside her bag… at the sword. The glint of it reflected in his eyes. His brow lifted as she snapped her bag shut. Thomas dug in his pocket for Klara's earrings and dropped them into Malabron's outstretched hand. The fae took a seat behind the table and examined them under the lamp, turning them this way and that. Occasionally his gaze strayed from the earrings and to her bag. An uneasy feeling spread through her with each glance.

Finally he looked up and Klara was surprised when he spoke. "I'm more interested in the lady's necklace."

It was the last thing she expected him to say, given that his eyes looked curiously at the bag and the sword within.

Klara's hand went to her collar without thinking. She wore her mother's necklace—a red crystal suspended from a thin gold chain—beneath her shirt, the stone warm against her skin. How had he known it was there? "I can't trade that."

"A pity," Malabron said, standing. "I'm sorry we couldn't reach—"

"But you can have this." She pulled off her bracelet, rows

of colorful crystals knotted with elastic that she'd picked up cheap from an Edinburgh street vendor.

Malabron barely looked at it, tossing it on the desk next to the earrings. "You drive as hard a bargain as Thomas. But since this is your first visit—"

"Where can she dress, Malabron?" Thomas interrupted. "It's not getting any earlier."

CHAPTER THREE

CALLUM

PRESENT DAY

Pain.

It was the first word to return to his mind after the impact seemed to empty it of everything—speech, memories, dreams, desires. Every part of his body hurt—bones broken, flesh savaged and torn, lungs desperate for the breath that seared like fire.

Somehow he knew that he was no stranger to pain…that it been his companion for his entire life. But never like this. He wondered if he was dying…he wondered who he was and what had happened to him.

Klara.

Rich coppery red hair cascading down her back, eyes the color of the first tender shoots to push through the snow in spring. Hands warm and soft in his and lips that tasted so sweet.

His senses awakened like a lit torch as thoughts of Klara pushed the pain aside just enough for the rest of him to return.

Callum groaned and tried to sit up, but the attempt brought on an inferno of agony. His arms and legs didn't work. Blood ran into his eyes. All he could do was turn his head slightly, his vision tilting, a rushing blur of gray and green and white that slowly sorted itself into a familiar landscape.

A barren slate sky reaching for the earth, the damp chill of the sodden earth pocked here and there with moss and bent grass. Tall, looming stones—thrice the height of a man—arranged around him in a vast circle, like silent judges. But none of that interested Callum. His eyes scanned desperately for—

There—two figures, one in a black cloak that swirled around his legs. A flash of brilliant copper hair; the glint of metal; a grunt, a scream—a burst of scarlet.

"Klara..." The last bit of life and energy left in his poor broken body bought Callum only a whisper as the mist swirled ravenously around the two figures locked in a terrible embrace.

He could do nothing as the mist devoured them, spinning in a gleeful fury, only to retract in a tight whorl that narrowed to the width of a loaf of bread, a fountain pen—and vanished.

Leaving behind only a smear of red on the muddy ground.

CHAPTER FOUR

KLARA

Ten minutes later Klara stood outside the darkened warehouse feeling like an actor in a play. The dress fit uncomfortably tightly around her ribs and smashed her breasts against the scratchy lining, but at least the hem covered her sneakers and the skirt was wide enough that she could walk easily.

"I'd say it suits you—"

"Don't bother," Klara said. "I'm not a fan of yours, either."

Thomas looked down at the too-large gold and gray striped waistcoat that hung down over his grimy, worn knee-breeches. "I forgave a debt for this!" he said with mock outrage.

Somehow she and Thomas had fallen into a comfortable ease despite knowing each other mere hours, but it was laced with something darker, something she didn't want to look at too closely. Thomas was just as Callum had described him: quick-witted, clever, and observant. But he was also undeniably charismatic. Understated-sexy, as her friend Brittany used to say: not the best-looking guy in the room, but the one you can't stop looking at.

Still, it was hard to imagine Thomas brooding and distant, as Callum said he became in the weeks before his death. His smile was ready and genuine, and—like Callum—his manners were far better than she would have expected from someone raised in the streets, probably because Brice trained his boys to be able to move among the wealthiest patrons. Though he was a head taller than Klara, Thomas was more slender than she would have expected the best fighter in Rosemere to be. But Callum told her that Thomas fought like a weasel, fierce and relentless and always with a trick up his sleeve.

That's how he wins, Callum said. *He waits for his opponent to reveal his weakness, then destroys him before he knows what hit him.*

"So," Thomas said. "Where to now?"

Klara wished she had an answer. In the tiny room where she'd changed into the gown, leaving her own clothes behind, she'd tried to summon her powers to send herself to 2022, but while she could feel…*something*, surging inside her like an ember glowing in a sudden draft, it remained as ungovernable as ever.

The feeling reminded her of the first time her mother had taken her for a driving lesson, in a big empty parking lot in an industrial park in the Bronx. Klara had stared at the instrument panel, the digital displays as mysterious as if they'd been Cyrillic. Even after Loreena had patiently explained every instrument and gone through the steps over and over, it had taken several evenings before Klara felt confident enough to take to the street. But once she did…everything fell into place, and she passed the driving test on the first try.

In the past week, Klara's most basic beliefs had been tested and turned upside down. She'd accidentally summoned both a demigod and a god in the form of his animal familiar. And she'd killed a beast from between worlds with a sword that might well be bewitched.

But until Klara understood how she had done it, until she had that slotting-into-place feeling as when she finally felt confident enough to drive on city streets, her own powers remained as mysterious to Klara as driving had the first time Loreena took her for a lesson.

"I'm tired," she admitted. "I can't think straight until I get some sleep. I don't suppose you've got an extra room somewhere…?"

Thomas snorted. "I doubt either one of us is welcome at Brice's house after his two best fighters went missing."

Klara sighed, searching the roofs of town for the manor's familiar pair of tourelles with their conical slate roofs. "Believe it or not, I live at Kingshill Manor in my time," she admitted. "It's been in my mother's family for centuries, ever since it was first built."

Thomas gaped. "You're joking."

"I'm not. Unfortunately, whoever answers the door probably won't believe I'm the great-great-great-whatever-granddaughter of the current laird."

Klara and her father had only moved to Scotland six months ago, leaving Manhattan a year after her mother died and Klara had graduated from high school.

The plan had been for her to attend the University of Edinburgh in the fall while her father took over the renovation and running of the manor, which had been turned into an inn several decades ago.

But the thought of even more change, after losing her mother and leaving behind the only home she'd ever known, left Klara feeling scoured from within. So she had given up her spot at the university—but hadn't found a way to tell her father what she'd done by the day she nearly ran over a handsome stranger from five centuries in the past.

"If that's true, then the manor is your birthright," Thomas pointed out.

"It doesn't really work that way anymore," Klara sighed. Grams had moved to America in the 1980s, only a couple of decades after Scottish inheritance laws changed. Grams technically owned the manor now, but a distant cousin—Klara's Aunt Sorcha—had been running it while Grams and her wife lived in a quirky, ancient Edinburgh apartment. Aunt Sorcha was planning to retire as soon as Klara's father finished the renovations. "But that does give me an idea. Have they built Ardmillan Road yet?"

Thomas frowned. "There's a footpath at the edge of the Ardmillan manor grounds by the dairy."

"Footpath" was a far cry from the busy street leading from the center of town to the southern entrance of Kingshill Manor. But if they got lost, they could always navigate by the towers rising above the town.

By the time they reached the edge of the sprawling grounds, Klara had decided that the Ardmillan Road was a vast improvement over the muddy cow path. Her shoes were streaked with dirt and the hem of her skirt was stained a dark brown. If she was going to pass for a highborn lady, she'd have to get cleaned up first, at the very least. As of this very moment, she looked as if she had crawled out of a mud pit and into a dumpster fire.

All of which wasn't completely inaccurate.

They stared up at the three-story manor in silence. It looked even bigger without the aged pines that lined the driveway that was now no more than a dirt trail. Other than that, little had changed. In place of the discreet lighting that showcased the manor's architectural features in the twenty-first century were torches that cast a warm glow. The mortar between the stones had been replaced in places, and ivy covered the arched windows that had since been modernized, but otherwise it looked as it did on any mild evening.

They walked forward.

"That's my room," Klara said, pointing at a darkened window at the corner of the second floor. "In the future, anyway."

Thomas seemed slightly intimidated, something Klara suspected was rare. "I thought you said they'd turn us away."

"We're not going to try to get in. There's a shed—well, it's only a foundation in my time, but Jockie told me it had been a supply shed when the manor was built. He's our caretaker," she added at Thomas's look of puzzlement. "He literally keeps the place running."

Jockie Kennerty, a weathered old Scot who drove an ancient pickup and could fix anything, had worked at the manor since Grams was a little girl. Klara's father had promoted Jockie to the title of "building engineer," given him a raise, and offered to buy him a new truck—which Jockie politely refused.

He and Klara had become fast friends when he pulled the twisted remains of her bicycle from the ditch where she'd landed after blowing out a tire, then tinkered with it in his shop that afternoon and returned it good as new. Klara never tired of Jockie's stories—especially since she'd never met any of her Westwood relatives except Aunt Sorcha.

Grams was a talker, except when it came to the subject of her family. And all Loreena could tell Klara was that Grams's father had been furious when she became pregnant at the age of seventeen—so furious that Grams moved to New York and didn't return to Scotland until after both her parents were dead.

"Is this it?" Thomas had walked ahead of Klara, and she joined him on the gentle rise where the rose garden now stood. There it was, just as she'd imagined it—a square little stone building with a single window and an iron-handled door.

Unfortunately, there was also a lock. As Klara tugged fruitlessly, Thomas shimmied up onto the window ledge and felt around the edge. Seconds later, he'd managed to open the window far enough to squeeze through. Klara heard the soft thud of his feet landing, then the flash of his grin in the darkness when the door creaked open.

"Bit crowded, but it'll do," he said cheerfully.

Klara closed the door behind her and sneezed at the dust she'd stirred up. The moonlight through the open window revealed shelves groaning with linens and foodstuffs and tools and salves and seemingly everything else a busy household required.

"Losh!" Thomas said, picking up jars and setting them down. "There's enough here to feed an army."

"Or the staff," Klara said, yawning as she shook out a blanket and spread it out between shelves to make a little pallet for sleeping. "Jockie says it used to take a lot of people to keep the place running, especially before…never mind." She was going to say, "before electricity and running water," but she'd already experienced the challenge of explaining modern life to one sixteenth-century Scotsman and didn't have the energy to do it again just now. For some reason, she pulled the sword out of the ragged hockey bag, and put it on the pallet next to her. She rubbed an amethyst fondly, and instantly was flooded with a feeling of warmth: a memory of her mother prattling on about an antique trinket, the emotion of cupping one of Grams's custom teas in a mug in front of the fire. And more. All she could think of, touching the sword, was the women in her family who had come before her, all marching back hundreds of years to the lady of the house whose portrait still hung in Kingshill Manor, a stone at her throat just like the one her father had gifted her mere days—or five hundred years—before.

Thomas didn't notice. "No, lass, this is more than even Edinburgh Castle could go through in a week. Someone on the staff is stealing this stuff and selling it, I'd wager—it's a wonder no one's noticed yet."

Sleep beckoned to her but her mind was racing. "We need a plan," she said, trying to turn the conversation toward something, anything, to get her back to where she needed to be: home.

Thomas nodded, crossing his arms comfortably over his chest. "Aye. What do you suggest?"

"Okay, so let's assume you're right, and the power of the eight other Pillars returned to Arianrhod. I'm not ready to give up on our powers, though."

Thomas raised his eyebrows, but she pressed on.

"Obviously our bodies are tired. Whatever power we have needs time to reset, probably, recharge." She was grasping at straws here trying to find any type of reasoning as to why she couldn't just blip herself back to 2022. "Then we can find somewhere safe and try again."

Saying this out loud made it sound unreasonably impractical. Then again, anything she said, as she sat here in the 1500s, sounded beyond ridiculous. She was a fish out of water, not just out of her time but out of her element.

She wanted nothing more than to have Callum by her side right now. His calm demeanor, his sturdy frame, his warm lips…his kind heart.

His heart would never beat again, not with blood nor kindness.

No. You can't think like this, Klara, she thought to herself. Right now she needed to put forth any impractical plan, because she would do anything she could, *anything* to get back home. *Maybe I can even get back before he dies, really.*

"It could be," Thomas said, his voice low and thoughtful. "To be honest, I haven't felt a wisp of my powers, or any others since you've arrived." Her heart sank. Anything she had felt must've just been hope. "So, Klara, what if the powers really are gone, now that Llaw has been vanquished?"

She was hoping he wouldn't ask that, because she truly didn't know. Find the fae? Try and contact Cernunnos? Worst came to worst, she knew the *bean-nighe* had granted Callum a wish. Maybe she could do the same? But did *any* of those beings have the power she sought? "I don't know. But at least we've decided where to start."

"Maybe the sword you have there—" he motioned to her bag "—might help us."

Klara touched the cold of the blade, her eyelids fluttering shut.

With the thought of her feeble plan in mind, she let herself drift off. It was something, and something was enough for her right now when she had nothing.

She dreamed of patterns scratched into black earth under a red sky: giant knots that pulsed and shifted as a dry wind blew. The design was the same as the raised marks carved into the skin of Llaw's neck...scribbled in Thomas's notebook...printed in an ancient book in the bowels of the Edinburgh library.

The mark of the silver wheel...Arianrhod's mark.

Her perspective shifted and she saw that jagged mountains rose above the plain at its edge. Almost hidden by scrubby dead weeds was a hole in which something stirred. A persistent sound pierced her ears…a piteous bleat like that of a dying animal.

A boot on Klara's back prodded her awake.

"Thomas?" she whispered, heart pounding—just before a rough hand slammed over her mouth and muffled her screams.

CHAPTER FIVE

MALABRON

Malabron emerged from the portal with his foul mood intact. Sometimes, the moments inside its brilliant vortex acted as a tonic, softening the edges of the anger that had been driving him ever since childhood...but today the two-minute journey that carried him a distance it would have taken a day's travel by carriage was as tedious as listening to the bickering of fishwives.

The portal opened into an earthen-floored root cellar, though it had not served that purpose for many years, not since Malabron had claimed the place for his own. Now the cooks worked under enchanted lights rather than the small windows set into the massive stone walls, chopping the onions and potatoes that arrived fresh each week. No one dug in the gardens here; there was more lucrative work to be done.

When the Lord happened upon it, the old peel tower was little more than a crumbling squarish edifice of dirty yellow stone, vines trailing through the windows and wild boars bearing litters in the hall. The village it had once served sentry to had long since been overtaken by the dense woods that spread many miles in every direction, making it perfect for his purposes. He put his ragtag corps of former blackguards and thieves and rievers to work restoring the place and clearing the road that hadn't been used in centuries.

It took them nearly a year to finish the work, including furnishing the tower itself more sumptuously than it had ever been, as the Lord planned to make it his quarters when he visited. The rest of the place was shored up but unadorned, as his men did not appreciate the finer things in life, and their future guests didn't merit them. His fae subjects could have performed the work better and more quickly, but the key to Malabron's rise had always been his ability to read people, and it was an odd truth that the loyalty of a certain kind of human could be won only by maintaining an atmosphere of distrust in their ranks and then pushing them to outdo each other in a bid for the approval that would never come.

That would never work with fae—not his own kind and especially not the gentle, weak-willed *daoine síth* who riddled the land around Rosemere like gophers. Was it any wonder they'd lost so much ground to the human race? It made Malabron ashamed to carry the same blood.

The Lord moved silently, his fine boots making little sound as he ascended the steps to the dining room. Though it had likely never served the better classes, probably feeding only the town's watchmen and occasional prisoners, now it had devolved into a sort of clubhouse for his men. As usual, the room was filled with smoke and the stink of stale spirits and the raised voices of the perpetually semi-drunk, the state in which his men seemed to spend all their idle hours. But that was all right: Malabron hadn't chosen them for their character, but rather for their readiness, fealty, and savagery when the occasion called for it.

"Good evening."

Instantly, boots were pulled from the table, chair legs slammed on the floor, and jokes died midsentence. Five rough, burly men got to their feet with their hats in their hands, but none lifted their eyes to meet his.

"There has been a development." Malabron wasted no time on preamble; his men required only the simplest terms: how soon, how many dead, what they would be paid. He did not need to specify the cost of failure, having let his actions speak loudly in the past. "I have seen something that I want and you need to get it for me."

Fingal, the de facto leader of the group, scratched his bald head. "You mean, right now? Because I thought you said—"

"What I said in the past is of no consequence," Malabron said impatiently, "when circumstances change. I need the boy. You have the likeness I gave you?"

The men exchanged troubled glances, shuffling their feet, but none contradicted him. "Yes, I know I said he would be dead by morning. That did not happen." Because he had miscalculated, to his great annoyance. It had not happened in eons. "Post men at every road out of town. Search every street and alley, every ship in the harbor. Do not harm him—I need him alive, and you shan't touch his things. He has something I need."

There was a long silence. Finally the smallest of the men, a red-faced block of a lad called Donny, spoke up. "But 'e's the best fighter in all of Rosemere, sir."

The air around Malabron crackled with his rage, white sparks flying. "He is one man, a head shorter than even you, Donny. Perhaps I should replace the lot of you with an order of nuns—at least they wouldn't stand about whinging all day."

"It'll be done, my lord," Fingal assured him, cuffing Donny on the ear.

"He has a girl with him."

The men had brightened up fast. "We'll throw 'er in the cellar, will we?" Fingal said.

"Certainly *not*." The Lord had come to expect their appalling loutishness, but he took a certain pleasure in his own disgust. "You will treat her as a lady of the highest value, since that is what she is."

"Aye, then," Fingal agreed, as heads bobbed all around. "We'll put 'er in the tower."

"Good. Once that is done, I need you to find her family and assure we get a ransom fitting for such a treasure. She is surely fleeing a family, one that will pay handsomely to have their wayward daughter returned."

His business concluded, Malabron turned to go, his cloak of palest lambskin swirling pleasantly around his legs—but he paused when his gaze fell on the jugs of ale lined up on the sideboard.

He murmured a few words under his breath. When the

lads went back for more, they'd soon discover that they were drinking elderflower water laced with donkey piss.

There were tasks for which liquid courage was worth the cost in precision. This was not one of them.

CHAPTER SIX

CALLUM

As a child living under Master Brice's roof, Callum had been tormented by nightmares. His second-earliest memory was of waking in a clammy tangle of rough woolen blankets on the pallet that he shared with two other boys, dry squawking sounds the closest he could come to screams.

The older boys slept on the hard beds stacked like shelves and nailed into one wall of the old servants' quarters that served as their home until they were old enough to fight in the taverns and bars of Rosemere, Brice always at ringside taking bets. Until then—until they could earn him coin—the boys were expected to stay in their rooms when they weren't training, eating thin porridge in the gloom of the filthy kitchen windows and washing their clothes in the sink after the housemaid had gone home. At bedtime they were so exhausted from Brice's training regimen that they fell like stones into sleep—and yet somehow Thomas always knew when nightmares gripped Callum, and came silently off the wall, moving with the grace of a cat to sit at the edge of the pallet, grabbing one of Callum's thrashing feet as if to tether him to the earth.

And Thomas would talk. In a quiet voice he told stories he'd heard from the older boys, stories he remembered from his first few years in a family crammed into a single room, stories he pulled from thin air or remembered from his own, more peaceful dreams. Already it was clear that he would not grow up to be a large man but he was clever enough to make up for it, studying his young opponents and learning their weaknesses before they became aware of them themselves.

Thomas's stories were as wild and frenetic as his fighting style, taking turn upon unexpected turn and ending in scenes of spectacular destruction. Most nights, though, the words blurred together and it was only Thomas's voice that Callum clung to, letting it weave a blanket over him, lulling him into dreamless, deep sleep. In the mornings he would sometimes find that Thomas had talked himself to sleep on the cold dirt floor, arms flung out, his face in sleep the only time it was at rest.

Now, Callum did very little other than sleep. He had been awakened—days ago? months?—in a dim, cramped room by a small woman who busied herself around his pallet, changing dressings and applying foul-smelling poultices to his wounds. She didn't speak to him, but from time to time held a spoon to his mouth and muttered words he didn't understand, gripping his chin with thin sharp fingers to force him to take the broth.

Time passed, day and night undifferentiated, and whenever the pain overwhelmed Callum he pretended that Thomas was there telling his stories, carrying him back down into the nothingness again.

Sometimes Callum forgot he'd imagined Thomas and tried to talk to him. It was just as well that his cracked lips barely moved, that his shattered ribs seemed to stab him from within, because Callum had nothing to say. He couldn't say where he was, his blankets of a strange cloth that seemed woven of thin green stalks and dandelion fluff, glinting baubles suspended above him from the thinnest thread, bits of glass and snips of ribbon. He didn't know who the woman with the spoon was, or the others—indistinguishable with their graceful, slender limbs and silver-flecked hair—who came to rub salves into his wounds and, after a time, move his limbs with their clever, gentle hands, awakening his muscles and reminding them of their purpose.

Then Callum would drift into the state between sleep and death again and drift, listening for Thomas's soothing voice.

A man came with scissors shaped like a tiny silver bird and washed and cut Callum's hair and anointed him with fragrant oils. When he was gone, Callum noticed that the pain had faded. And was he spending less time in the lulling darkness now?

Callum couldn't say exactly when Thomas vanished, or the dream of him anyway, but one day he woke to find that his pallet had been moved to a corner of a large room with a long, low table around which people were eating and talking and drinking from shimmering cups. Fae—that's what they were, and Callum wondered why he hadn't put the clues together until now.

The curved earthen walls, lined with smooth-rubbed roots and studded with pretty veined rocks. The graceful folk who talked in quiet, lilting voices as they shelled peas and carved the peel from fragrant lemons and sewed garments from bolts of diaphanous fabrics…these were the *daoine síth*, the Fair Folk of the burrows deep in the earth.

Callum tried to speak the next time one of them came to lay a cool cloth on his forehead and rub his wounds with healing oils. The dressings were gone, and Callum could see that his bruises had faded to a greenish yellow and his wounds had closed, shiny scar tissue skimming over his torn flesh. On one leg was a splint made from green saplings, the ankle immobilized with a series of carved sticks like a birdcage, and the pain from his broken ribs had faded, leaving only a slight tenderness.

"Where am I?"

The words came out as a pitiful croak, rasping painfully in his throat. His fae tender, a young woman with blue beads woven into her fair hair, placed cool fingers on his neck, and when Callum tried to speak again, he was astonished to discover that her touch loosened his tongue.

"Where am I?" he tried again.

The fae considered him. "Some know this place as Crug Baile Mòr," she said. "We are in the Elder Forest. Cernunnos brought you to us a few days ago."

Callum relaxed slightly.

"Why?"

The fae looked surprised. "To heal you, of course."

Not exactly the answer he sought, but he found that he trusted the young woman nonetheless. "My name is Callum Drummond," he said, lifting himself a few inches so he could address her better, exhausted by the effort.

The fae smiled. "I'm Efa. You're very lucky, you know. Without your faerie blood, you'd be dead."

"But I dinnae..." Callum mumbled, stopping short. A brief thought flashed through his muddled mind. His eyes. Always the subject of speculation and ridicule, one blue, one hazel. Some joked it meant he was a fae bastard.

"Tell me, have you the Sight?"

"Sometimes, maybe," he admitted grudgingly.

Blue and green flashed behind his lids, just as he slipped under again.

The next time Efa came, he asked her how soon he would be well enough to leave.

"Depends how much fae blood you have," Efa told him. "Tell me of your ancestors."

Callum felt a pain that did not come from his injuries and hung his head. "My mother sold me to Brice MacDonald when I was small. I know not who my father was."

Efa hesitated before speaking. "Malabron keeps records, but I cannot advise you to seek them."

"Who is Malabron?"

Efa frowned, her face troubled. "He was born here long ago. His parents were Fair Folk. But Malabron was *heddwch*."

"What does that mean?"

"It's...hard to explain. It means 'tranquil,' and it's not uncommon—maybe one in twenty. The *heddwch* tend to be dreamy and prefer their own company, and they often have wonderful ideas and can help settle disputes and unite those who've become estranged. The *Cennad*—the fae who serves as a messenger to the humans—is *heddwch*."

"And this Malabron is the *Cennad*?"

Efa shook her head. "More like the opposite. Some *heddwch*, instead of being born to help and to dream, they are born with the *newyn*—'the hunger'—and they care only for things. Treasure, power. Their solitude means they care not for others, their ideas are instead the source of creative ego, and the ability of the *heddwch* to unite, in those with the *newyn*, only serves their ability to manipulate. They never stay; they always find their way to the *olc síth*. They say Malabron left when he was a child, but it was long before my time. He has become the most powerful *olc síth* in the land, with treasure from all over the world, but there is no end to his greed.

"He's the one who buys and sells children," she added. "Your Master Brice would have gone to him."

Callum didn't like the fear in Efa's voice any more than he enjoyed talking about his childhood. "Please, can you summon Cernunnos?" he said, changing the subject. "I have to find out what has become of Klara."

Efa's expression softened. "Klara is your beloved?"

Efa promised to do what she could, but Cernunnos did not come that day. Callum brooded over his failure to protect Klara and Thomas, unable to banish his last image of Klara in the terrible dance with Llaw in his swirling cloak.

Without her, healing seemed pointless. Callum's heart was a broken vessel now from which his dreams for the future leaked and dissolved. If he could not save Klara, if he had failed his best friend, then there was no purpose for him, and he sank into the heavy sludge of his despair.

"There is more for you to do."

A pale face emerged from the darkness. Klara.

His breath hitched. His heart stopped. Everything within him came to a standstill but the world did not. Materializing around her was a small room filled with supplies. Next to her, a sleeping form… A man.

He peered closer.

Now, his heart truly stopped.

Thomas.

As fast as the vision appeared, it vanished.

Callum's eyes shot open and he rolled up on his elbow. He felt some new vigor flow through him. And with it the recollection of his conversation with Efa. What he had seen was beyond a dream, or a hallucination. It was something he couldn't describe but knew deep down, what it was. The Sight.

For the first time he could see the details of his surroundings clearly…including Cernunnos, relaxing on a cushion.

"You finally came," Callum said, and found that he was suddenly angry, though shock thrummed in his veins from what he had just seen. "I didnae ask for this. I didn't ask to be healed."

Cernunnos tilted his head. "No, you were not the one who asked for you to be healed."

Callum felt himself being dragged back into his mortal existence and knew it would be pointless to fight it. "Save your riddles. What about Klara?"

"Yes, she was the one who asked."

"Where is she? When can I see her?"

Cernunnos clasped his hands behind his head and let his eyelids drift down, apparently content to wait him out.

It didn't take long. "And what's this about me having fae blood?" Callum blurted. "If I did, I would have been able to save Thomas."

Cernunnos opened his eyes. "You know little about the fae, I see."

"No—you're the one who knows less than you think. There is a reason I was able to survive the beast's attack, and it is from a trade I made on my own."

Cernunnos's face darkened. "That was unwise. You were warned about the bean-nighe by Aion; she may have given you what you asked for, but it is not what you wanted."

Callum knew that it was pointless to argue. The spirit had granted him the strength of ten men, but in a way Cernunnos was right: he'd only wanted the strength to keep Klara safe, and he hadn't even been able to do that. "If you won't tell me of Klara's fate, at least tell me if Llaw is dead."

The Stag God's nostrils flared and he gave a dismissive shake of his head. "My patience is not without limits. Stop fighting your nature. Ask the right question, and you will have your answer."

It came to Callum with sudden clarity, like the sound of a distant bell on a frozen, still morning. A jolt of energy rocketed through his bloodstream, shaking the cobwebs from his senses.

Klara was alive. That vision, of her with Thomas…it was real.

He staggered to his feet, holding tightly to a root protruding from overhead as his legs shook violently. His purpose hadn't left him, after all.

"I need to get to Klara," he choked out. "Take me back to the Ring of Brodgar."

Cernunnos lifted an eyebrow. "What makes you think she is still there?"

"I know she isn't, but..." Fear gripped Callum. "Then tell me where she is. Send me there. Edinburgh? Her other home, Man Hat Tan?"

"She is beyond this time—" Cernunnos started regretfully.

"What does that mean?" Callum interrupted urgently. "She is *alive*, isn't she? She must be, she must."

"—and that is not in my power to control." Cernunnos continued without pause. "There is someone who can help, but..."

"I will pass through the veil of death to be with her if I must." Callum ran out of patience. "Damn the cost, I will do anything. You must know I've little to lose."

"Your death is not required, Callum," Cernunnos sighed. "The only way to get to Klara is through a creature in Arianrhod's service. But the trade she will demand of you will be tainted by sinister magic."

"Which creature would that be?"

"There are several. You've already dealt with one."

"Ah, the bean-nighe. I caught her by surprise last time. I cannae afford to name my price this time, can I? No matter. At least let me choose for myself. Whatever she asks of me, if it is in my power to give, it will be worth it."

Cernunnos rose from the floor, unfolding his limbs gracefully. "Good," he said, with a satisfied nod. "You're nearly ready to live again."

By the time Callum came up with a retort, Cernunnos had vanished, the shimmer in the air the only evidence he'd been there at all. Behind where the god had been sitting, a sword leaned against the wall—exquisitely made, sharp and beautiful, with a hilt and pommel made of twisting thistles, studded with amethysts and emeralds.

CHAPTER SEVEN

KLARA

The hand covering her mouth was rough and smelled of onion. Klara fought like Callum had taught her, as though her life hung in the balance. For all she knew, it did. The harder she tried to scream, the more firmly the hand pressed down, thick greasy fingers cutting off the air to her nose and mouth.

She heard a thud and glass breaking as the contents of the shelves crashed and shattered on the floor. Thomas cursed while in another corner, someone lit a match that was abruptly snuffed out.

Klara felt the familiar tug, the unspooling and tightening inside her that signaled the awakening of her powers. *Now,* she thought, kicking and clawing at the man holding her down.

Now would be a really good time for her powers to kick in, before her vision started to fade and she passed out.

From the sounds of grunts and breaking crockery and splintering wood, Klara deduced that Thomas was putting up a hell of a fight. Abruptly, the man suddenly released her and went flying into the wall with the sickening crunch of breaking bone.

Klara crawled blindly behind the only shelf still standing and gasped for air on her hands and knees while the fighting continued.

A crash. A moan. Silence.

Klara flattened herself against the cold stone as another match was lit and the shed filled with the sickly yellow light of an oil lamp. Thomas lay a few feet away at an odd angle, blood trickling from a gash on his cheek. Two men stood panting above him, while a third rolled on the floor moaning and clutching his face, blood streaming from his broken nose. A fourth man lay motionless under the ruined shelves, dusted with flour from a ripped sack.

"Ye think ye can just take what you want, eh?" one of the men muttered, unruly gray whiskers spiking above missing teeth as he prodded Thomas's unmoving body with his boot.

The other man wiped at his brow with a soiled hankie. "*Look*. It's a *lass*, what broke in here with this one."

"We won't hurt you," Whiskers said, switching to a wheedling, oily tone. "Come on out, now, lassie. He put you up to this? You work in the manor?"

"Tie him up," the moaning man managed to get out, shrinking from Thomas's body. "Before he wakes up."

"Didja piss yourself, Mungo?" Whiskers jeered.

"That's the fella from the taverns," Hanky said with surprise. "The one what wins all the fights."

Whiskers snorted. "Guess we pulled it off then, eh—took down the champ!"

Mungo shot him a disgusted look as he struggled to his feet. "Took three of us, di'nnit? Four if you count Archie."

"Arch didn't do a damn thing but get clocked," Hanky said in a voice of outrage. "What's Brice's boys doing cutting in on us?"

Klara figured now was as good a time as any to play her only card. With Thomas out cold, she had to take the chance.

"Excuse me," she said with as much dignity as she could muster. "I live at the manor. When my father finds out that you've been robbing him, you'll wish you never woke up this morning."

The men gaped at her. "I ken Laird Westwood's daughters," Whiskers growled, "and ye aren't one of 'em."

"She's pretty for a thief, sure," Mungo allowed. "Too bad her fella left the fighting to her."

"I'll keep watch on her, boys, while you deal with that one," Mungo said, casting Thomas a wary look.

"Oh righ', sure we'll leave the lass to you while we do the dirty work!"

As the men argued, Klara looked frantically around her for anything she could use for a weapon. Her sword was lying just out of reach, tucked under the edge of the blanket. If she could just—

"Oh no ye don't," Mungo said, stepping in front of her.

"I say we do 'im here." Hanky, too, was keeping his distance.

"We can't kill 'im!" Whickers scolded, whacking Hanky in the face with a glove. "What's Brice to think? You want his faerie friends to come lookin' for us?"

There was a sudden flash of movement and Thomas seemed to fly up onto his feet. Klara didn't see the punch that sent one man staggering backward, but she watched Thomas spin and deliver a roundhouse kick to the other's gut.

"Run!" Thomas yelled. "I'm right behind you!"

Klara didn't have to be told twice. As Mungo ripped a splintered board from the ruined shelves, she reached through his legs and grabbed the sword. Mungo managed to grab a fistful of her hair and Klara yelled in pain as she struggled to get a grip, all while bodies crashed around them.

A howl unfurled from somewhere deep inside Klara, rocketing through her body, electrifying her before breaking free.

Mungo shrieked and released her, holding up his hand in agony as if it was on fire. At last she knew: her powers weren't completely depleted. Klara ran for the door and hurled it open, the cold night air hitting her face.

"Meet me at the stables!" she shouted over her shoulder, praying Thomas's reputation for scrappy fighting and always winning wasn't exaggerated.

She zigzagged through the gardens, hampered by the unfamiliarity of the grounds, the onerous task of carrying her skirts and petticoats slung over one elbow, and the sharp pain in her side when she breathed too deeply. A boxwood hedge blocked the shortcut past the reflecting pool, and she had to circumvent a smelly hog pen where the loaner bicycles would have been parked in her time.

When finally Klara reached the stables, though, nothing

had changed. The row of stalls was occupied by six startled horses that stamped and snorted their displeasure at being awakened in the middle of the night. Klara chose a sleek chestnut mare with a broad white blaze along her head and stroked her silken snout as she slipped the bit in place.

"I'm sorry about this," she said, "but I really need a lift, and I'll find a way to make it up to you. Any chance you know the way to a nice Hyatt?"

She kept up the chatter as she led a second horse, a sturdy buckskin stallion with black socks, for Thomas—when it occurred to her that she had no idea if he could ride. There wasn't much to be done about it now if he didn't, since—

A figure came streaking across the lawn toward her. Thomas, his coat flying—and a few paces behind him came two of the thugs, Mungo and Whiskers from the looks of it, one of Mungo's arms hanging at an unnatural angle. *Shit*—these guys were tougher than she thought. "Here!" Klara threw the reins at Thomas's outstretched hand and mounted the pretty mare. She was still struggling with her skirts when Thomas vaulted into the saddle.

Apparently he *did* know how to ride.

"You lead!" Klara shouted, though she would have much preferred the opposite. But she didn't trust herself in the ancient streets, wary of reaching a dead end where she wasn't expecting one.

Thomas whooped and, galloping past her, reached over and slapped the mare's flank—and the animal exploded forward. Klara hadn't quite got her feet in the stirrups and she nearly slid off, saved only by holding to the pommel with all her might until she could right herself.

It was what she got for choosing the finest horse, the one who was obviously the favorite of the laird or his wife, given the ribbon woven into its mane. Somewhere in the manor Klara would bet there were shiny ribbons won in competitions.

I don't know how you do it, her riding instructor used to marvel. There were over seventy-five horses at the Riverdale Stables in the Bronx—yet Klara always managed to choose the finest and best tempered. She'd never been thrown; her horse never resisted or fidgeted when she took it through its paces.

"Come on, Bonnet," she urged, because with her large cream-colored patch on her forehead, the mare reminded Klara of one of her favorites. "Run like you mean it!"

The horse whinnied in response as though she understood and soon they were closing on Thomas. He slouched forward in the saddle and waved his arms wildly, but somehow still had full command of the horse, leaning forward and—

...*singing*? Klara caught a few words of what she thought might be Welsh and despite the precariousness of their situation, couldn't help but smile. This seemed just like the Thomas Callum had described, fearless and full of life, singing a bawdy ditty as he rode for his life.

The buff-colored horse, however, was struggling. Foam clung to his snout as his gait grew more and more irregular and Klara realized her mistake—the horse had already been taken through his paces that day. It needed rest, not to be pushed to its limits a second time.

As Klara pulled abreast of Thomas, she risked a glance over her shoulder. "They're gaining on us!" she screamed.

If Thomas was worried he didn't show it, giving Klara a

jaunty salute and a wink, as if they were making a friendly wager rather than a desperate getaway. Klara had an image of a younger Thomas and Callum, battered and bruised after a grueling night of fighting, slapping each other's backs and laughing despite their blackened eyes and split lips.

Callum. The ache hit Klara hard and fast and dangerously, because in the breathless seconds it took to push back her grief, she nearly let Bonnet veer off the road into the field. At the last second she pulled hard on her reins and Bonnet swerved back in line.

But in those precious seconds she'd lost sight of Thomas. Klara craned her neck to look behind her and gasped at what she saw: Thomas, lying sprawled on the ground as two of the thugs dismounted next to him. Thomas's horse was trotting back toward the manor.

The third man was galloping straight for her, a murderous gleam in his eye. It was too late to outrun him now. As Klara cast about desperately for some way out, she sensed something very wrong: the field in front of her seemed to roil like a bubbling kettle, dirt rising up in a cloud that obscured the moon. From within it a blur dissolved into the individual forms of riders—seven, eight, nine of them—coming straight toward her.

Klara was trapped. Unlike the ragtag band of ne'er-do-wells from the shed, these men were outfitted in fine riding clothes, their horses strong and fast, the gleam of blades signaling they were well armed. But most terrifying of all were their masks—opaque black fabric that hid everything but their eyes.

Two were coming straight at her while the others fanned

out, surrounding her. In the back of her mind Klara wondered why she and Thomas merited this kind of army when all they'd done was break into a shed and steal a few provisions. But it was pointless to keep running, and Klara slowed to a trot, steeling herself.

But then something unexpected happened. The masked riders streaked past her and attacked the thieves instead. The air was filled with grunts and curses as the thieves were badly outmatched. One was thrown from his horse immediately and the other quickly subdued when his scattershot punches were met with the disciplined blows of a trained fighter. In what seemed like seconds, the two thugs were knocked unconscious and their limp bodies dragged into the woods. It had happened so fast that Klara didn't have time to react. Too late, she realized she'd missed her chance at escape—but maybe the masked men *were* her escape. She racked her brain, trying to figure out who might have sent help, and why.

But Klara still didn't know why Arianrhod—the goddess of time—had chosen her to serve as a Pillar. Or why the Stag God bothered to appear to her when he never seemed to offer any real help. The two of them showed up when they felt like it, on their own terms and without warning…but for once could they come when she truly needed them?

Klara's hopes were dashed in the next instant when she saw Thomas engaged in a brawl with two of the masked men while others overpowered the rest of the thieves.

Whoever the masked men were, they were not here to help.

One of them circled back at a gallop and whipped past her, missing by inches, while another raised a heavy club high in the air as he approached, hunched low on his horse.

The club was meant for her. Klara had the horrifying realization that the breath caught in her throat in terror might well be her last—and then a voice whispered in her mind.

It's not your time, my darling.

Klara's eyes went wide. It was her mother's voice, as real as the ground beneath her and yet already curling into mist and floating away. Bonnet snuffled and stamped the ground.

The club arced through the air.

CHAPTER EIGHT

CALLUM

Callum's strength returned fast after that, and he started training again. At first, he couldn't even lift the long wooden bread basket above his head or pace the length of the room without tiring, but in very little time—and consuming as much of the food and drink he was offered as he could—he was feeling nearly himself again. It felt like mere hours, but it must have been days; the healing power of the fae, Callum supposed.

The scar on his chest had faded to a shiny spot the size of a baby's fist, and there were a few faint, silvered lines from the deepest gashes, but his leg had healed straight and strong. The next time he woke, Callum washed and put on the robe that had been hung near his pallet. The loose, supple fabric was cool against his skin. Before he left, he took the sword

Cernunnos had left behind; Llaw's, he hoped. He dreaded to think that it was its twin, the one that belonged to Klara, for she would never want to be parted from it. He followed the sound of music down a narrow twisting passage lit with dozens of tiny lights that danced above him, and heard laughter and singing as the passage grew wider and opened onto a large, sunken room in which dozens of faeries feasted and danced.

No one seemed surprised to see him, pirouetting around him in an invitation to dance.

"What is this celebration?" Callum asked, shouting to be heard.

"It's *Mabon*!"

The word was vaguely familiar from his childhood, the autumn day when daylight and darkness were equal, rumored to be a faerie feast day. As Callum gazed around the room, his eyes fell upon a familiar face.

It was Grams. She looked at him with a soft warm smile. She strode across the room, her shawl billowing behind her in vibrant colors.

"My dear boy!" She greeted him with open arms and he fell into them without a moment's hesitation. Even though they had only a few moments together in the past, she was an extension of Klara, and she was a welcome presence in this increasingly unfamiliar world.

She patted his back before they separated. Grams looked at him, truly looked at him. Her eyes drifted over his body and she smiled sadly when her gaze met his again.

"It's so good to see you," he said to her, placing a hand on her shoulder.

"How are you?" She brought her wrinkled hand up to his and gave it a squeeze. "You have been through what most could never fathom experiencing."

She spoke in a way that seemed as if she knew of everything that had happened. Sadness, worry, and a mingling of other somber emotions danced across her face.

"I am alive."

Her cheeks flushed a joyous red as she nodded. "That you are," she said warmly.

"But Klara—" he started but she cut him off.

"I know. That is why I'm here. I have something for you, to help you get our girl back." She dropped her hand that held his and reached into the satchel that rested on her hip. From it she pulled out her phone.

"I have a message for you."

His heart leapt. "From Klara?"

"Sadly not. But it will help you in finding her."

She turned the phone to him and a familiar, angular face appeared. It was Aion, the faerie from Finn & Fianna, the one who'd chased him and Klara to the tavern, who'd laughed when they fought in the street and spoke boldly in riddles before disappearing. He looked terrible, thinner than before, his skin waxy and gray and his hair lank.

"Come." Grams beckoned, taking his arm. "Let us go somewhere quiet. It's important you hear what he says."

Grams led Callum through the crowd, greeting some by name, and into another narrow passage. Callum tried to mark its position so that he could find his way back but the passage was one of a dozen that branched in every direction.

"How do you know of this place?" he asked as they turned a corner.

"There are many places I know of in this city. My wife and I dabble in circles which introduced us to this world beyond most mundane eyes."

Callum had many questions but just as he was going to speak, Grams stopped and opened a door. It swung open revealing a library, topped with a glass dome that let sunlight stream in and dance on the spines of thousands of books and scrolls that lined the walls. Grams led him to a long table made from the ringed cross section of an ancient tree, burnished until it glowed.

A looming mantel carved from a rich, deep mahogany made up the fireplace. He admired the carvings in the frieze, depicting a battle. The figures on the left dominating those on the right, swords out and bodies splayed out. It branched upward toward twisted bodies in war transforming into delicate engravings of thistles and thorns, a harsh contrast to the gruesome battle below. It was an exquisite piece, only made better by the fire roaring within the hearth.

As he sat, he laid the sword upon the table, and Grams looked at it with surprise. "I didn't know there were two."

"How do you know it's not yours?"

She smiled. "It's been a family responsibility for a long, long time. I would know if this was ours."

"Then this is Llaw's." Callum looked at it, thinking of the terrible things the demigod had done with it. "And that means Klara's mission is over."

"A woman's work is never done, they say." She looked sad then, and handed her phone to him. "The end of her mission has catapulted her beyond our grasp in this world, but this might help. Aion had left a message for you. It is a video message." He must've given a questioning look because she clarified, "A moving picture. I told him I'd get it to you."

Callum nodded, confused, not by this moving picture but as to what the fae would want to tell him that would help him in any way…especially after the way he treated Callum when they last saw one another.

"This will be the last time you see me."

He remembered Aion's words, which was why this furthered his confusion.

"He filmed this video for you shortly after you last saw him."

So maybe the fae did stand by his words.

"I will leave you here to watch it. Just press the triangle for it to play." She pointed to the white symbol on the screen. "I'll just be outside."

She stood and left him alone with Aion, in the small box, on the screen. How did he manage to get in there?

Callum pressed the triangle and the image of Aion came to life.

"Hello, Callum." His voice held a weak cadence. "I need to tell you a story, *my* story. I need you to listen carefully. I know our last interaction doesn't credit me much but this is important for you to hear and it is a kindness that I'm willing to share."

Callum huffed at his words. Kindness wouldn't be a word he would associate with Aion, who locked him in basements, stole his property, and followed him and Klara. Nevertheless, he listened. At this point, he didn't have much to lose, and if Grams said it might bring Klara back, then he must take heed. "I am old. Older than many lives of your kind. Long ago, I studied to be a metalsmith; I wanted to make the most beautiful cups and bowls that anyone had ever seen. I had finished my apprenticeship and was setting up my trade when I was asked to help retrieve a young one who'd fallen into the hands of a dark fae who meant to sell him as a curiosity. A living doll to dance for the wealthy in a castle."

He spat the words with such vitriol that Callum shrank back involuntarily from the phone. "Malabron had long dabbled in this trade, but rarely had he tried to make so evil a deal. Of course I went along," Aion continued. "There were five of us, friends from childhood, pretending to be braver than we felt. Because we all knew about Malabron's keep where his men take kidnapped children. We'd heard that the entire place was charmed, that poison spilled from the top and spears shot from the walls.

"But as it turned out, Malabron met us outside. He didn't seem surprised to see us and when we asked his price to bring the child home, he asked to see what we'd brought to trade. We emptied our pockets—the elders had given us crystals to trade—and he called for sweet wine while someone fetched the boy and readied him for the journey home. But then a servant girl came out to..."

Aion's voice trailed off and his eyes lost their focus as he retreated to his memories, then abruptly cleared his throat. "Anne, people called her. She'd been taken from her home so young that she couldn't remember her family. The keep was all she knew, cleaning and cooking and caring for the stolen children until they were ransomed by their families or sold into service. But when we met, I knew—and she knew, too—that we were meant to be together.

"We had to meet in secret. I made up excuses to return to the keep, and when I couldn't find a reason I snuck out anyway. We passed many pleasant hours in the scullery and the dairy and when I asked her to wear my mark, she said only if we wed. A human wedding means nothing to a fae, but—well, what Anne wanted meant everything to me. And so I knew that I would have to buy out her bond.

"The price was high, but it didn't matter. Once she was mine, I didn't care where we lived, and we planned to find a little house where we could raise a family."

Callum raised his brows, surprised by Aion's desire for normalcy. It seemed so at odds with the man he had met. Aion gave a bitter laugh. "You might be surprised at this," he said as if he were looking at Callum's reaction right now. "The ignorance you humans have toward those who live amongst you. I doubt you have any idea how many of us live among you."

Callum had a sudden urge to apologize but it wasn't as if Aion could hear him, nor did he deserve any apology from him. Especially since Aion had treated him so rudely in their prior encounters.

"Anyway," Aion said, "I approached a Seer of my people for a blessing, but was told dark news indeed. She told me that Anne would be dead before I would see her again. I was…I lost my reason, I will tell you, Callum. I nearly tore out my own heart but then I thought of a way out. I sought out the bean-nighe—yes, the same creature you were foolish enough to deal with."

Callum remembered the conversation they'd had, and how Aion had warned him against dealing with the hag.

"I gave up years of my life, hundreds of them, to be with my beloved again. And the bean-nighe kept her word, in a fashion."

Callum tried to ignore the chill that ran through his veins. "She gave me the money in a wooden trunk, promised me that Anne would be alive when I saw her, and I hired a carriage and went immediately to the tower, arriving as night fell. Anne came running out to meet me, and knowing she was alive still sent a thrill of relief through me." Aion's voice broke and he took a moment to steady himself. He looked around the dark room he was in before focusing his gaze back toward the phone. "It was not to last. A storm had come up but she didn't even seem to notice the rain. She looked so beautiful, calling my name, and I didn't wait for the carriage to stop, I was so happy, I jumped down to the ground, and—and her foot hit a slippery patch, and suddenly she was falling, down into the lake, disappearing under the water.

"I ran and jumped in after her. Because I knew I was meant to save her, you see. I was almost giddy with it, knowing that it was drowning I would save her from…I swam under and my fingers found her skirts and I pulled her to me and swam for shore. I carried her up onto the bank and pulled her into my arms, and she was so cold, not moving, not even breathing—but I held her against me and pounded at her back until she coughed, and water ran from her mouth. I was overjoyed because I knew that I had saved her. She looked into my eyes and I knew it had all been worth it, to see the way she looked at me."

The light faded from Aion's eyes and when he spoke again, his voice sounded bleak. "But I did not know that she had struck her head on the rock. Her skull was broken...blood was pouring down her back and I didn't know, I thought it was the water. As I looked into her eyes I could tell something was wrong, she was fading away, she was leaving me, and I kissed her lips and they were cold. I cried out because somehow I knew. The bean-nighe kept her promise, and Anne lived to see me again, but only for mere moments. I had lost everything. My life was Anne, I'd sold my entire future to buy out her bond, but without her, that was no life at all. A sentence to live eternally without the one you love is worse than death."

A pang of sadness shot through Callum. The thought of losing Klara was unimaginable. Unlike Aion, he had the chance to save her and he'd do anything in his power to make it happen.

"And by the time I came to my senses, I'd thought of something I wanted more than death."

The fae paused and the flashes of grief had vanished, leaving something hard and dangerous in his gaze. "I'm sure you can guess, if you are half the man I think you are. I want revenge."

Callum thought of Thomas's blood on the cobblestones. "Revenge," he muttered. He knew the feeling well.

Aion continued, "With your help, the bean-nighe's bones will break beneath my boot and I will laugh while I do it."

Callum pressed the triangle and the image of Aion froze. Unlike Aion, Callum still had hope. He couldn't think of anything else until he found Klara. And Callum trusted that bright, sudden clarity he'd felt, that Klara lived.

"I am also leaving this message for you because I want to help you. Call me soft, but love wins. Love always wins and I would never wish my fate upon anyone…besides a select few. The bean-nighe deserves death, but before that can happen, I believe she can help you get to your girl.

"Klara's grandmother will help everything align but this is probably your only chance to get to Klara and I'm giving it to you. You have a role to play, Callum Drummond, and if I am to get my revenge, you must embrace this fate." Callum rocked back on his heels, remembering the last time he'd seen Aion, full of riddles and evasions. It made him uneasy. The gods, the fae: none of them could ever be fully truthful. It seemed almost foolish for Callum to listen to Aion but somehow, he was willing. He said it once and he'd say it again. He'd do anything to get Klara back.

"I need you to go down to the river in Dean Village and call for the bean-nighe. I don't know if she will appear but if she is as I think she is, she will be keen; she's probably mad with fury that you tricked her the first time, and eager to keep tabs on you. You may be wondering why I can't simply do this."

Aion quirked a brow. "The bean-nighe knows what I'd do if I saw her wretched face again so she would never come. That is why you need to call to her and make your wish. Tell her you want to be taken to Klara. She has the power to do so. Yes, you will need to make a sacrifice but choose your words wisely. Don't end up like me, don't be as foolish as I was.

"I want you to have the chance with Klara that Anne and I never could. And yes, I do see this as the only way to get to the hag, but think of this as also a kindness, because it is. I do wish you happiness. Just don't arse it up by using the wrong words with that trickster.

"You would also have an advantage. Cernunnos told me you might have the Sight. It will allow you to see her, to call to her. Not every human can but if you have the Sight, it is almost definite she will hear your call." There had been several times, since the night Thomas died, that Callum felt… *inklings* of things that later came to pass. But were they really so different from the random coincidences that marked anyone's life?

"Good luck, my friend. Your fate is calling."

A sinister look washed across his face and then the message ended.

Now he knew what he had to do.

Find the bean-nighe.

CHAPTER NINE

KLARA

The last thing Klara saw before her vision went dark was the club exploding into a giant black flower.

And then she was catapulted into the air, blinded, arcing and twisting before landing hard on her side. She smelled dirt and blood but could see nothing, not even the gleam of the stars. She tried to crawl but soft hands restrained her. No—not hands, but yards and yards of soft, silky black fabric that insinuated itself around her arms and legs, wrapping her like a cocoon until she could barely move more than a few inches.

It hadn't been a club at all, but some sort of net that tightened around her the more she struggled.

Bracing herself for a blow that could come at any moment, Klara twisted and writhed until she managed to free her face from the fabric's folds. Her sword was pressed to her back in its scabbard, but she had no way to reach it. She lay alone on the ground, one of the riders watching her silently from his horse a few feet away. In the distance, she saw Thomas on his knees, his hands bound behind him, another of the masked riders looming over him with his arms folded.

Thomas raised his head defiantly and shouted something, but the wind carried his words away.

The rider backhanded him and Thomas's head whipped to the right.

Klara screamed…and then she abruptly stopped. She couldn't provoke these men, not now. It wouldn't help anything for both of them to get beat up.

"What do you want from us?" she demanded instead.

Her guard said nothing. He didn't move. It was as though he hadn't even heard her.

Okay, Klara thought as she struggled against her bonds, *if we're pretending you don't see me, then I guess you won't see this, either.*

Sure enough, the guard did nothing as she stopped trying to use brute force to free herself and instead began to work her way out of the lengths of fabric from within its layers, certain she could reverse the fabric knots if she worked slowly and deliberately. But time did not appear to be on Thomas's side: as Klara watched in trepidation, the masked man crouched down so he could look Thomas in his eye.

Was he cursing Thomas? Threatening him? Telling him all the ways he was going to make him suffer before he killed him?

Like a brother, Callum had called him. Callum had been

ready to die to avenge Thomas's death, and instead the quest had cost him his life. Klara couldn't bear the thought that it would end like this—two vital, courageous young lives ended with their killers going unpunished.

Rage sparked deep inside her, a tiny polished kernel that rapidly grew into a force so strong it shuttered her senses and focused all of her energy into a tight, pulsing knot. Klara stretched out her hands against the net, moving both of her own volition and not, the power inside her melding with her body, *becoming* her—and with a great ripping sound, the net shredded and flew off her. Klara was on her feet and running toward Thomas by the time she came fully back into herself, realizing with a whoop of glee that her powers weren't gone, she just had to get to Thomas, they had to get away, and then they could try again to get back to her time.

The guard cursed, the first word he'd spoken, and she felt the impact of his pounding feet through the ground as he chased her. She made it within a few feet of Thomas—close enough to see the defiance flashing in his eyes—before she felt a rough hand close around her arm and the ground went out from under her.

From her knees, she watched the man crouching over Thomas strike him with his fist.

This time, Thomas did not lift his head again. The last thing she saw was the man throwing Thomas's limp body over his shoulder and walking away.

The hands that removed the scabbard from Klara's back and pulled a coarse sack over her head and bound her wrists and ankles were neither kind nor brutal. The men spoke quietly among themselves, and though Klara strained to hear, there were few clues to what was happening. After a brief discussion Klara's horse was released to return to the manor; when the stable hand came in the morning, he would find both of the horses Klara had stolen waiting outside for their oats.

There was no mention of Thomas, and when Klara was unceremoniously tied like a rolled-up rug and lifted onto the back of one of the horses, she could only pray that they were being taken to the same place.

It was far from the most comfortable ride of her life, every bump and jounce being absorbed by her ribs and belly while her bound limbs dangled on either side of the horse's haunches. It seemed to take forever, but Klara guessed they rode less than an hour before she heard a shout and the horse slowed to a walk. There were other sounds, too: the clanging of metal and the sound of footsteps; the creak of a gate and a woman's irritated rebuke. Faint light cut through the sack covering her head, the flickering light of candles or oil lamps, and her ankles were untied and she was pulled roughly from the horse.

When Klara was set on her feet, they buckled beneath her. She threw her hands in front of her by instinct, not as though she could catch herself, tied as she was. Someone grabbed her elbow, clucking.

"Look at the sight of her!" A woman's voice, older by the sound of it, and annoyed. "He'll have your heads for this."

"Shut up, old woman, it's just a few scrapes. They'll be just as glad to have her back."

"Enough with you," the woman snapped. "Leave 'er to me now. Janneth, get her a wash, then up to her room."

"In the tower, missus?" A younger voice, a girl her own age or a little older, Klara guessed.

"Where else? You want to put her down with the dogs tonight?"

"No, missus."

Other hands took hers and placed them on what felt like someone's forearm, their touch soft and cool. Klara tried to resist the feeling of gratitude that rushed through her. As the evening had proved again and again, there was no telling who was on her side and who was not—and so far, nearly everyone was in the latter category.

She resisted the gentle tug. "Where is Thomas?" she demanded, hearing the exhaustion in her own voice. "The man I was with. Where is he?"

There was a murmur of surprise from the women. "Talks odd, don't she?" A new voice broke in, the rasp of an old man.

"That's enough." A man's peeved voice, one of the riders. "Take her from us, Janneth. Mrs. Fitchet, we'll have our supper now."

"Supper's done. You'll wait for your breakfast, just like the rest of us," the older woman snapped.

This time when the gentle hands tugged, Klara gave in and let herself be led. She couldn't think of any reason to fight for the right to stay here and listen to these people bickering. Especially since Thomas wasn't among them.

How did she know? Klara wasn't sure…but it was back, the swirling energy inside her, and the relief at it was just about the only thing keeping her upright. She wondered if it had been unleashed by the same force that had recalled her powers…such as they were. In the past she'd been overtaken by this force she couldn't name in times of great danger. Of great *anger*, Klara corrected herself, because hadn't she been in danger from the moment she tumbled backward in time?

"Too tired," she mumbled. She hadn't meant to speak out loud, but if she didn't lie down soon she was going to fall asleep on her feet, despite—or maybe because of—the adrenaline that had coursed through her this night, and the dangers that lay ahead.

"What's that, missus?"

Klara shook her head, too tired to explain. "I'm Klara," was all she managed, because the thought of being called "missus" again was even worse.

She was being led slowly over smooth stone, their echoing footsteps suggesting a narrow passage of some kind.

"There's steps now, missus," the young woman said, and then she lifted Klara's hands and placed one on an iron rail. "There, see? Move your foot until you feel the stair or you'll trip on it."

Klara did as she was told. "Thank you," she mumbled, starting up the stone steps, going slowly and holding to the rail while the girl—Janneth—held her other elbow.

There were a lot more stairs than she'd expected. The rail curved in a spiral, bolted every few feet into a wall of polished blocks of stone. Marble, maybe, given the cool slick surface. Klara was breathing hard by the time the girl stopped her with a hand on her shoulder.

"I've just to unlock it, missus."

Klara heard the sound of a key sliding into a heavy lock. Then another…and another. The keys clanked as the girl returned them to her pocket and Klara briefly wished she'd tried harder to free her hands on the ascent.

But what then? Even if she managed to rip off her hood and overpower the girl—who didn't seem to mind the climb and was probably as strong as an ox—the best she could do would be to lock her inside wherever she'd been taken…and then she'd still have to face the men at the bottom of the stairs. And she couldn't leave, not without knowing what they'd done with Thomas.

Klara opened her eyes wide behind her hood. Would she really risk her own life, given the chance, just to save his?

Callum wouldn't expect it of her, Klara knew that. Justice, no matter the cost, had been *his* quest. Besides, in her shoes, Callum would probably trust Thomas to fight his way out of whatever scrape he'd gotten himself into…just as he'd somehow eluded death on the streets of Kelpie's Close.

If someone had told Klara that she would fall deeply in love in the space of a week, she would have laughed. But there was something about traveling through time, spending her days suspended in the space of centuries, that had sharpened every experience, every emotion she felt. A day with Callum deepened their relationship in a way that should have taken months or even years. And Klara had given in to the feeling because it felt so right, as if it had always been meant to be.

But now, even though such intimacy was usually achieved in a lifetime, in the space of a single night, she'd come to care deeply for another person. For Callum's best friend. It wasn't love—Klara's mind recoiled from the idea even as she remembered Thomas's blue eyes searing into her—but it was something real, something she couldn't turn her back on. They were connected in a way that meant she couldn't leave now even if a passage back to her own time opened up in front of her—not without knowing that Thomas was safe.

I have to. The words came to her with certainty, as much for herself as for Callum. Even if Callum was truly dead and gone, she must still do this. It was nothing more than that: *I have to.* Unlike every step with Callum in the last week, Klara didn't think that saving Thomas would help restore order to worlds roiled by discord between humans and gods and fae. One life, one scrappy fighter without a coin to his name, would make no difference at all.

Except that it would. Because somewhere in the course of traveling through time and battling sinister forces and monsters pulled from nightmares, Klara had come to understand that the smallest decisions, the choices made in moments of indecision, were at the core of everything.

Helping a stranger. Taking a chance. Trusting. Believing.

And so she would do her best to save Thomas. Partly because no one could say how he might change the world if he was allowed those moments and decisions of his own… and partly because his life was now entwined with her own in ways she didn't understand and wasn't sure she wanted to.

"The man I was with," she croaked.

"Hush now," Janneth said, taking her hand once again and leading her forward. "I'll draw you a bath."

She guided Klara to a soft, cushioned surface, a seat or bench of some kind.

"I was with a man," Klara tried again as she sank gratefully down. "Did they bring him here?"

A moment's hesitation, and when the girl spoke again, there was both regret and something darker in her voice.

"There was no man," she murmured. "You came here alone, missus."

CHAPTER TEN

CALLUM

Once the video from Aion had ended, Grams had swiftly taken Callum away from the glow of celebrations and into the dark Edinburgh night.

"I would like to admit, I did watch the video," Grams said, giving him a wry smile. "I am a nosy person, I can admit that, but I also trust Aion."

If Callum was asked if he trusted the fae before the message, he would have laughed. But afterward, seeing the raw emotion on his face, knowing what he lost…he had to agree. It wasn't only revenge that drove him forward, but love. When those two feelings compete, as he would well know, love is the stronger of the two but they needn't have to pick one over the other. Aion would get his revenge and Callum would get back to his love. To know he had given Callum a chance at getting Klara back, but also still managing to get his revenge for Anne, it was almost perfect.

But he knew that there was still a way for them to go before either of them would get what they wanted. First, Callum would have to manage to summon the bean-nighe, get what he wanted while also managing not to be tricked by the trickster itself.

"Me, too," Callum responded as they rounded a corner into Dean Village. It was a quaint bundle of buildings just outside the metropolitan landscape of Edinburgh. Peaceful, even. The river flowed between the houses here, rushing past them and out of sight as the river rounded the buildings to their right and left. Ahead of them was an old bridge that connected the two sides of this area of the city. It was made of stone and had a roadway for cars down the middle, though he saw none.

"This way." Grams ushered him down a set of winding stairs to the canal's edge. He was grateful for the old woman's presence, though he knew they would have to separate soon. He couldn't bear the thought of something happening to her because of his plan with Aion.

"You would also have an advantage," Grams said to him as they walked. "Cernunnos told me you might have the Sight. It will allow you to see her, to call to her. Not every human can but if you have the Sight, it is almost definite she will hear your call."

They stopped and he turned to her. "I am grateful for your help and hope that beyond this moment, the Sight can help guide me as well as you have."

"Oh, hun, it is my pleasure. But to be frank, I'm not just

doing this for you. My little girl needs your help. I know she is out there…wherever *there* is, and I'd be damned if I couldn't help in some part of it. Go get our girl. So, the pleasure is mine. Good luck, my boy."

She swept him into a bone-crushing hug, surprisingly strong for her age.

"I will get her back. I promise you that." And he meant it, truly. He would die trying.

A moment later they separated, and she disappeared into the night.

The dim glow from a street lantern was his only companion.

Not for long. He thought. He hoped.

"Bean-nighe, I summon you." He almost felt foolish, calling out into the night for the bean-nighe like this. Talking to nothing but shadow. The wind rustled through the trees that surrounded the canal. Leaves drifted down from their branches. Autumn was here but the bean-nighe had yet to show.

He waited a minute. Scanning his surroundings, but the only presence he could sense was a squirrel darting up the bark of a tree and disappearing into the night.

"Bean-nighe, I summon you," he repeated. He did this another two times before huffing out a breath. She wasn't showing herself. He thought back to the trick he'd used—was it only a few days ago?—of leaving a blood-soaked piece of clothing in the river to call her, but that had taken days to work, and Callum wasn't sure that he, or Klara, had that time to spare.

Anger flooded through him. That witch deserved whatever she had coming for her. The trickery, the deceit…

"Bean-nighe, I summon you," he growled.

The light flickered. The wind roused. And suddenly, the fallen leaves started spinning as if captured in a vortex. He shielded his eyes with his hand.

A splash.

He turned to his right, looking toward the canal's edge where a hunched figure sat.

The bean-nighe.

Her worn, muddied cloak was half in the water. He couldn't see her face but he saw her hands. They were twiddling something within them.

She turned, almost expectantly, and dropped what he now saw was a small bone into the canal and stood.

The hag spoke, flashing those rotten teeth of hers. "Last time you caught me by surprise, but this time I get to exact a price." Her brow dropped menacingly and a rancid smile, if he could even call it that, tainted her already horrible face. "She's alive."

I knew it. Heart pounding, he responded. "Klara?"

"Yes yes yes. But she is being held captive captive captive." The hag's low, shaky voice held a glint of glee.

"Where is she? Another land? In the Otherworld?"

"In the year 1568."

Callum froze. He'd felt in his heart that she was alive, he knew he would get to her, but he'd never imagined *this*. No wonder Cernunnos had been so evasive.

Still. He would get to her.

He just needed to bargain with the devil.

"I want you to get me to her."

The hag smirked. "For a price price price." She said it as

a statement. "I can do this, yes…yes I can. But the price… will be grand grand grand." She tisked at the end of each repeated word.

"What is the price?" Callum demanded.

She turned fully toward him. The lamppost dimmed further. "I will allow you to travel back to your time where she is, but for you, this will be a one-way trip. And I require ten years off your life."

A chill shuddered through his body. "My life?" What if he was destined to die in ten years' time…that would mean… no, he would not think of this now. But the one-way ticket meant that in the end, Klara would return to 2022 and he would have to stay in 1568.

"Are you denying my bargain?" the hag said, brow crooked upward.

He shook his head. "No. I accept. I accept your terms."

"Enjoy your fate." She snapped her fingers and suddenly the world around him went black.

It was just like the first time Callum had spanned the centuries: the air thickening with a swirling, glittering mist that spun faster and faster until he was lifted into its midst, then a breathless suspension in an opaque white tunnel before he abruptly landed with a spine-jarring thud.

Callum lost his balance and sat down hard in a sticky, foul-smelling puddle on cobblestones. Blinking away the brightness of the tunnel, he spotted a white owl perched atop a stone wall. The same white owl he saw the night Thomas died…

He was in the Kelpie's Close of his own time, almost exactly where Thomas had been attacked. The street was empty now, the shuttered buildings hunkered down in a gray dawn. At the far end of the street an old woman coughed in a doorway, but there was no one else about.

Thomas lived. Callum felt it even more strongly now, as if Thomas's heartbeat echoed in his own. Whatever had happened to him, it had to have been undone by magic.

Callum started to get to his feet—then froze in horror. His hand came away smeared with the dark red of blood. It was everywhere—pooling on the cobblestones, splattered on the side of the building, seeping into his clothes.

Panicked, Callum staggered in a circle, trying to understand what he was seeing. No man could survive a scene like this.

"Klara! Thomas!" he bellowed.

A clatter of boots, a shout. Callum whirled around to find two policemen running toward him. One of them was slinging a club.

CHAPTER ELEVEN

KLARA

The air was sweet and humid with the fragrance of the essential oils. Klara could hear the girl moving around the room, her feet almost silent on the tiled floor. She started when Janneth spoke from behind her.

"I'm going to take the blindfold off now, missus."

"Please. Call me Klara."

"Klara," Janneth repeated softly.

Her fingers made short work of the knot in the drawstring, and then she was lifting the sack over Klara's head, her fingertips brushing against her neck. Klara blinked in the light of at least a dozen candles arrayed around a room nearly the size of her bedroom back in the manor. At its center was a tub big enough to bathe a cow, or at least a healthy calf. The walls were painted a pale sky blue that gave way to cottony white painted clouds near the ceiling, and the blue-and-white tiles on the floor were echoed on the basin.

"This doesn't look much like a prison cell," Klara observed, unsure if she could trust anything Janneth told her.

To Klara's surprise, Janneth laughed, then covered her mouth with her hand. "You're lucky. Most of 'em have to stay downstairs."

"Most of who?"

Janneth blushed and didn't answer, instead opening the bath's second door, opposite the first, that led into a large square bedroom punctuated with small windows, its dark, heavy, drapes drawn. A huge, heavy canopy bed rested on beautiful woven carpets and the gleaming brass sconces mounted between the windows cast a soft glow as Janneth set about building a fire in the tiled hearth.

Klara followed her to the doorway. "But then why…I mean, I'm not exactly a guest, am I? Unless the master greets all of his guests with the point of a knife."

Janneth's smile faded and she bowed her head slightly. "No, miss—I mean, Klara. 'Mon now, get in the bath before the water gets cold."

Klara felt a little odd stripping off her filthy gown in front of a stranger, but she hadn't had a shower in ages and was desperate to wash off the mud and filth and the smell of horse. Only after she had submerged her body in the blissful warmth of the water did Janneth pick up the discarded gown and begin to fold it.

"So why am I getting the deluxe treatment?" Klara asked

as she used the folded flannel and lavender-flecked ball of soap Janneth had set out to scrub her skin.

"Look at you!" Janneth exclaimed in surprise. "Can't 'ave the likes of you in wi' t'others."

"Why not?" Klara didn't mention that she'd been sleeping in a supply shed earlier in the night.

Janneth gave her an uncertain smile, as if wondering if she was being teased. "Well, now, the babies stay in the nursery until they're sold, of course. The boys and girls from the village, they don't stay long, do they? Not if they're strong and healthy, and the master won't take any other sort, so they bunk up downstairs, girls in one room and boys in another. It's only the noble ladies who stay in the tower."

Babies and children…being sold. Klara's stomach twisted at the realization that their fate would be the same as Thomas and Callum's. Though if these men were also kidnapping rich women, it wouldn't be to put them to work, which left only one possibility: ransom. And while Klara was sure her father wouldn't hesitate to pay it, she knew no one in this time with any money.

Which meant she was going to have to escape. Klara gazed around the square room with views in every direction. Why would they make the windows so small?

A memory came to her, an illustration in one of her mother's books about Scotland's ancient buildings. Large, fortified keeps with towers such as this—"peel towers"—were built to serve as lookouts for advancing armies. Small windows would protect soldiers while allowing them to fire onto those below.

Which would make this a pretty good headquarters for a criminal enterprise.

From the windows, sprawling lush land stretched far in rolling, shallow hills. The grass in Scotland, whether in this time or hers, was different from the States. It was thicker, richer, as if each blade held a glimmer of magic.

She longed to be outside with her feet planted firmly on the ground, looking up at the tower instead of being trapped within. "So I'm being held for ransom," she sighed.

"Yes." Janneth glanced at the door they'd come through, as if to make sure no one was listening. "If the rich families are to pay the master's price, see, they expect their daughters and wives to be well taken care of."

"But I'm—"

Klara stopped herself. She'd been about to protest that she was no lady, that no wealthy father would be coming with a full purse to claim her. *Way to go, genius*, she mentally scolded herself.

"You have a family, don't you, Klara?" Janneth said, a bit anxiously. "A husband? Someone to come for you?"

"My family is…far from here," Klara hedged. By distance, the Manor was only a matter of miles away, but she figured five hundred years ought to count as far. "But that might not be the reason I was taken, actually. The man I was traveling with—" She tried to figure out how to explain the situation. "He's in danger. Someone tried to kill him."

Janneth's sharp intake of breath, the stricken look in her eyes, convinced Klara that she had no part in their kidnapping. *I have to trust* someone, she thought. Grams always said she could tell within minutes of meeting someone if they were friend or foe—if they were the type to cheat at bingo at the senior center or could be counted on in a pinch.

I just pay attention here, Grams would say, tapping her heart.

In the last month Klara had discovered she possessed shocking powers, at least some of the time, but clairvoyance was not among them. Nevertheless, she got a good vibe from Janneth, who surely had better things to do than hang out with a prisoner, folding her dirty laundry.

"Actually," Klara said quietly, "they tried to kill me too, and they killed my…fiancé." She'd been going to say "boyfriend," but the word didn't seem to fit the sixteenth century. The word had the intended effect, however, Janneth's shock deepening into sorrow.

"But that's terrible! Oh, Klara, you have been very unlucky."

A laugh bubbled out of Klara's mouth despite herself. "I never used to think so, but in the last few years…"

She went silent then, because as hard as it was to imagine sharing the unbelievable details of the week since she'd met Callum, it was even harder to talk about what had come before that. Two years ago she'd been a happy, relatively carefree high school student in New York City, applying to the University of Edinburgh—her dream school—to study astronomy and prepare for a career in science.

And then her mother had gotten sick, and everything changed. Six terrible months later Loreena Spalding was gone, and Klara and her father moved to Scotland to take over the manor and be closer to Grams and her wife. There was so much to love about her new life; just as it had been her mother's dream to live there someday, Klara felt at home in the little town of Culross in a way that she never had back in the States.

Janneth was watching her, exhaustion mingled with concern in her pale gray eyes, and for the first time Klara noticed the chapped skin of the maid's hands, the much-mended skirt of her uniform.

"I'm so sorry," she blurted. "I'm sure you'd like to get to bed after a long day. Please don't let me keep you." Her gaze fell to the neatly folded gown in Janneth's hands. "And I can wash my dress in the tub and hang it to dry."

Janneth seemed scandalized by the suggestion. "Mrs. Fitchet would have my head. I'll clean it myself and bring it back tomorrow. Meanwhile there are some things in the armoire that should fit." Her gaze wandered to the sparkly pink Converse sneakers Klara had pushed under the tub in an unsuccessful effort to hide them. "Your…shoes, Klara. They are quite…"

Klara kicked herself for not taking Malabron up on his offer of more appropriate footwear. Then she had an idea: Callum had explained to her that while the wealthy important townspeople refused to acknowledge the existence of faeries and looked down on anyone who believed the old stories, the fae were still very much alive in the imaginations and beliefs of the lower classes.

"My friend brought them back from the faerie market," she said, ducking her chin as though embarrassed. "I usually keep them hidden in my room at the manor. I only wore them tonight because my skirt hid them."

Janneth's eyes went wide. "You've been to the faerie market? In Rosemere?"

"That's the one."

Janneth's plain face broke into a grin that made her much prettier. "My fiancé brought me this from the market!"

She lifted her hand to show a narrow silver band on her little finger. At its center a small, cloudy blue stone seemed to glow faintly.

"Very pretty," Klara said. "How did your fiancé get into the market?"

Janneth's smile faded and she jammed her hand into her pocket, backing toward the door. "I misspoke, missus. He bought it from a friend who said it came from the market, but who knows if he was telling the truth? It's just a little trinket. Good night."

Klara barely had time to say good-night in return before Janneth slipped out the door. The sound of the heavy locks sliding into place echoed through the room, and then there was silence.

Klara stayed in the tub a little longer, watching the candles flicker. The water that had felt so warm and soothing had cooled, and an ache had settled into her bones.

She was safe, for now, in much better accommodations than she had any right to hope for—but out there somewhere was Thomas, the man she'd vowed to help since Callum could not, the man who'd risked his life to help her.

"I'll find you," she whispered, a promise that she had no idea if she would be able to keep.

CHAPTER TWELVE

CALLUM

It was not the first time Callum had been to the local jail. Twice, Master Brice had sent him to collect Thomas when he'd gotten dragged into fights with bar patrons who suspected a match was rigged after Thomas beat much larger opponents.

Brice left Thomas in the jail for a few days each time, hoping to teach him a lesson before bailing him out, but when Callum came to fetch Thomas he always found him in good spirits, joking that he'd eaten and slept better than he did under Brice's roof.

Now, though, there was nothing to laugh about. This time, he was the one being led into the cell, and he felt no closer to finding Klara than before. Still, he held his head high as he walked into the small antechamber, where a guard was carving a donkey from a stubby block of wood, shavings falling to the floor.

"Found the robber, did ye?"

"That and more. Standing in a puddle of blood, he was. Soon's we find the body he'll be a murderer, too."

"That much blood?" the guard said. "Then how'd 'is victim get away?"

Having no answer, the policeman gave Thomas a rough shove toward the open cell. In the other, the sounds of snoring barreled through the small barred window, the smell of liquor wafting out. The guard heaved himself up from his desk with a sigh and locked the cell with a large iron key. "Luck is with you, boy. Laird's not comin' until Friday so you get to enjoy our hospitality until then."

"Which laird?"

"What does it matter to you? Thinkin' you might know him?" Both men laughed at the absurdity of Callum moving in polite society. "Laird Johnstone, since you ask. He decides all the local matters. Unless it's murder you've done, and then they'll take you to the high court in Kirkcaldy."

Callum felt like punching a wall—and from the look of it, he wouldn't be the first. The stains on the stone walls might have been blood or vomit or their supper, and probably all of that and more.

Friday was two days away. Even if Callum somehow managed to convince the laird he was innocent, those were two days he couldn't spend searching for Klara.

Callum had heard the name Johnstone, but couldn't distinguish among the few local lairds who'd come to bet on fights. Wealthy men seemed to care little for the fates of the lower classes, judging from their treatment of the barmaids and publicans, not to mention the fighters.

"Busy day, eh?" the policeman joked, tilting his head at the other cell. "Aul' Rob been entertaining ye?"

The guard chuckled. "Only other thing that happened so far this week was a break-in at Kingshill Manor. One of the grooms woke up in the middle of the night to find thieves makin' off with some of the horses. No sign of 'em since."

"Some nerve!"

"Sure, but don't you know, an hour later here comes those horses. Walked right up to the trough."

"No!"

"And that's not even the worst of it," the guard said, obviously enjoying telling the story. "In the morning, the laird was in the garden and sees one of his storage shed doors open, goes in and there's manner of goods lying on the floor. Dried meat, flour, soap, sheets, yard goods—and two of the staff were gone and haven't shown their faces since. Sure enough, it's all missing from the house. Now, there's a mystery for you."

"You mean if the staff were stealing from him, why'd they leave it behind and the door open?"

"What do we always say? Thieves get caught because they're stupid. I think the lad was in on it—maybe he got caught trying to cross the others."

"The lad?"

"That's the oddest part. The other thief was a lass. Red hair loose over her shoulders. Pretty face."

Callum's head snapped up. A redheaded lass bold enough to steal horses from right under the nose of the stable boys at

Kingshill Manor…could it be anyone other than Klara? She'd told him that she knew how to ride, and if she wanted to go somewhere, she'd need a horse. But where would she go?

And who was the man with her? He prayed it was Thomas. That his Sight was correct. At least Thomas would know how to protect her in this land.

The guard was still talking about the girl, making an hourglass gesture with his hands. "Chebs like ripe peaches, according to what I heard."

"Nice one," the policeman leered. "That would brighten up the place."

"You've no chance. The lasses are too fast for you, old man."

As the men finished talking and the policeman took his leave, Callum seethed at the coarse words, wishing he could teach them all a lesson—and end up like Thomas, locked up for fighting. The thought of other men touching or even at looking at Klara made him so angry that he considered finding out if the strength of ten men would be enough to tear the bars from the floor and use them to strangle his captors.

But he couldn't risk getting deeper into trouble if he was to have any chance of winning his freedom so he could go after Klara.

At night, as Aul' Rob gibbered in his sleep, Callum was occupied by thoughts of Klara. The stone floor was cold, and he had nothing to cover himself but a thin blanket, so he spent the time imagining holding Klara in his arms in front of a fire, or buying her a warm woolen coat in a proper shop. Taking her away from Rosemere, where too many knew him, where he'd known such sorrow, to a place where there was honest work for a man with a strong back and willing hands. He could build Klara a sturdy little house, and at night they could look up at the stars and she could teach him all the things she had learned in school.

The fantasy left Callum feeling empty and despairing. Even if he found Klara, he could not ask her to stay here with him. He had no money to his name, and she was a lady who belonged in a manor. His face burned with shame when he remembered the guards' laughter at the mere thought of him in the company of the rich, important townspeople.

And if Callum could somehow get past all that, he couldn't ask Klara to leave everything she cared about—her family, the manor, all of her nice things—to be with a man who had no family, no friends, no future, who had traded away years of his life.

And yet the images and memories continued to drift through his mind. Waking to Klara's lovely face after she'd found him unconscious in the road. Her lively joy when they danced together at The Black Hart. Klara at the window of a tower, gazing out in horror at something on the ground. Her hand at her mouth in shock, crying out—

Callum sat up with a start, sweat soaking his body. A dream, only a dream…but it had seemed so real.

Tell me, have you the Sight? the fae had asked him.

Callum remembered that moment, lying in his sickbed in the faerie mound, when he was suddenly certain that both Klara and Thomas lived.

Now he put his hand over his heart in the darkness of his jail cell, feeling its strong beat, the blood moving through his veins.

Fae blood.

"If I am to have the Sight," Callum whispered, "then show me what to do."

There was only silence. If he truly had that power, it answered not to him.

The two days dragged in agonizing slowness. Callum would have preferred to be back in the mound, drifting in and out of consciousness. No amount of pain could be worse than knowing Klara was out there somewhere, especially once Aul' Rob recovered from his bender and started yelling and cursing and throwing his food, earning himself a dousing with a bucket of cold water when the guard got fed up.

At last it was Friday, and after Callum had eaten the hard bread and bowl of broth that served as breakfast, he heard a carriage pull up outside. The guard and policeman, who'd arrived moments earlier, stood up straighter and stopped joking around.

Earlier that morning, the guard's wife had come to dust and sweep and place a chair before the cells. Now Callum rose and gripped the bars to watch the laird and his men enter.

Laird Johnstone was a tall man of no remarkable features: graying brown hair thinning at the top, slightly rheumy brown eyes, a nose that was perhaps a bit too large and a chin a bit too small. His clothing was resplendent: a ballooning linen shirt over fine woolen trews, atop which a plaid of richly dyed wool was belted. He carried a sealskin *sporran* trimmed with ermine tails too small to serve any practical purpose. Judging from the fine tailoring and materials of his manservant's clothing, they were no ordinary attendants but men of some importance.

"What have we today?" the laird asked without preamble, taking a seat in the chair provided for him while his men stood slightly behind.

The policeman cleared his throat and nodded at the other cage. "Well, milord, you can see for yourself Aul' Rob is at it again."

The laird narrowed his eyes. "Three lashes and a day in the stocks," he decreed. "Who does he work for?"

The guard's snicker died on his lips when he realized the laird was serious. "Er, 'e's down at the docks when he's able."

The laird nodded. "Tell the dockmaster to send his wages to his account at the store. Nothing for him until it's paid off."

The guard was scribbling in his ledger. "Yes, milord."

"Now this other one's a different story," the policeman said. "Name's Callum Drummond, age nineteen. We picked him up Wednesday morning in Kelpie's Close."

"Did he confess?"

"No, milord," the policeman said, shuffling his feet. "He, er, insists he witnessed a murder."

"A murder!" the laird echoed, looking interested. "Had one been reported?"

"No, Lord Johnstone. And I've had my men out asking around, but Kelpie's Close—"

"A despicable place," the laird interjected. "I'm sure they've been stealing from each other. Liars and wastrels, all of them."

The policeman and guard exchanged a glance, but it was obvious neither dared to comment.

Laird Johnstone studied his fingernails as he addressed Callum. "What have you to say, young man?"

Callum was prepared for this moment. He'd had plenty of time to plan what to say, even if he would have liked Klara's help in choosing his words. Unlike Thomas, whose quick wit and clever tongue had got them out of many a scrape, Callum was most comfortable speaking only the truth—or as much of it as he was able.

"I am innocent, milord. Tuesday night, I found myself in the alley—"

"Says he's one of Brice MacDonald's fighters," the policeman said. "Wanted us to believe his friend—also one of Brice's boys—was stabbed right there before him, and he did nothing to stop it. We did find blood on the ground, sure, but I say it's more likely he's the one what did the stabbing…milord?"

His voice trailed off in confusion as, after finally deigning to look at Callum, the laird had gotten up from his chair to approach the bars, staring at him with an expression of shock.

Callum took a step back, so unsettling was the intensity of the laird's gaze, laced with not just astonishment but a dark sort of hope, as if this moment was one he'd long awaited.

"Your eyes," he said hoarsely. "One blue, one hazel."

"Aye, we saw that too," the guard piped up. "Me gran says that's a sign of witchery."

The policeman shot him a warning look. "Laird Johnstone isn't here to listen to your tales and faerie nonsense."

"Who is your family?" the laird said, ignoring them.

"I dinnae know my da," Callum said, refusing to bow his head despite this shameful fact. "They say me mam was a washerwoman."

"Where were you born? Who raised you?"

Callum studied the laird, confused by the rapid-fire questions. "Milord, should we nae be trying to find the man who spilled Thomas Buchan's blood? For he is not a man at all, I say, but a mortal desperate to walk among the gods."

He'd spent quite a lot of time composing that sentence the night before, knowing that a claim of a murdering demigod would likely be met with disbelief. But the laird barely seemed to have heard.

"I asked you who raised you. I care not about the fate of this man you speak of."

Callum glanced at the policeman, who was frowning and shaking his head. "I…guess that would be Master Brice. I dinnae remember my mam."

"I know who Brice MacDonald is." The laird addressed the other men. "But I do not frequent the sort of establishments where fighting takes place. Tell me: Is it true what they say—that MacDonald has dealings with the fae?"

Now it was the others' turn to look shocked that a man of the laird's importance would admit to believing in the old tales.

"It is said, my lord," the policeman said carefully when it was clear no one else would speak. "Though I cannot confirm…that he buys the biggest and strongest wee lads from a merchant in the faerie market. Not sure where else he gets his boys."

"He steals them in the night!" the guard blurted. "Me gran says he leaves a changeling, one of their own weird babes. It happened to her neighbor, and once that changeling learned to walk it started killing chickens in the night."

"Enough, fool," one of the laird's men said angrily, cuffing the guard.

"I'll take the prisoner with me," the laird announced. "I will question him further at the castle. Bind only his hands, Raibert, and take him to my library. Stay with him until I return."

"But my lord—" the man called Raibert—a man with very little neck and thighs as thick as trunks of oak—said, obviously alarmed. "He is a dangerous criminal."

"We do not know that," the laird said coldly. "Determining his guilt or innocence is the purpose of my inquisition, is it not? I am simply choosing to conduct it in my library."

"But the blood on the ground—" the other man ventured.

"You are obviously not the man for the job, Dougal," the laird snapped. "Your lack of enthusiasm is noted. Raibert, are you also incapable of this simple task?"

"N-no, your grace. Guard, the keys!"

As the guard scrambled to open the heavy lock, the laird gave Callum one last look. "I shall continue the questioning this evening."

He turned and took his leave without further comment, Dougal racing to open the door.

That's the glory of power, Callum thought with disgust. *Abuse those of lower station. And plans that benefit no one but yourself.*

For he was certain that the laird had plans for him. And Callum could not say whether they would lead to freedom… or pull him further into the evil schemes of others.

CHAPTER THIRTEEN

MALABRON

Malabron was pleased when his men came to him deep in the night with the scrappy fighter unconscious and slung over Fingal's back.

"Don't tell me he got himself killed, too?"

The men looked at each other uncomfortably. Fingal deposited the young man on the floor with exaggerated care, as though he were a basket of eggs. "'e's not dead, just knocked out."

Malabron rolled his eyes and took a small blue bottle from a shelf and uncorked it. He shook out a bit of fine powder and tossed it in the unconscious man's direction. Immediately Thomas started coughing and crawled onto his knees, and when he saw Malabron, his face transformed into a look of surprise.

"Malabron. What is the meaning of this?"

"Most humans," Malabron said calmly, "would feel afraid to find themselves before one such as I. At the very least one would think they'd remember their manners."

"To the devil with *manners*," the lad scoffed. "You just *kidnapped me*!"

A smile teased the corner of Malabron's lips. In different circumstances, he would have hired Thomas on the spot. "Well, I'm not the one who murdered a demigod for his own benefit."

Thomas looked around the room, inventorying the windows and doors, calculating his next move. Malabron wondered if he suspected the truth—that he'd be dead in seconds if he tried to run. "I don't know what you're talking about. I agreed to help Arianrhod stop an evil force from destroying our worlds."

"Perhaps," Malabron allowed. "But that isn't why you killed him."

Thomas's gaze snapped back in outrage. "It is! And how dare you—"

"Ordinary mortals are not strong enough to resist that call—and Arianrhod knew that. But she was willing to sacrifice you, knowing that each time you came close to Llaw, you absorbed a little more of his energy. Your humanity could not defend against it." He coughed delicately. "It's why you're looking a bit the worse for wear, I'm afraid. But never mind that. While your humanity crumbles, Llaw's will grows within you. You begin to think as he thinks. Want what he wants."

Thomas said nothing, thoughts racing behind his ocean blue eyes.

"You killed him to save yourself," Malabron went on. "And you thought—and I cannot blame you, given Arianrhod's callous treatment—why should I not have what he sought? Why should he, who had everything, be entitled to even more while you, an orphan spurned by his own *mother*—"

"It's true." Thomas finally chose honesty, standing a little straighter. "But Arianrhod underestimated me. She thought the powers of the other Pillars—the eight Llaw had already killed—would revert to her when he died. She never even stopped to think that I could get them instead."

Malabron raised an eyebrow. "Indeed? Is that what happened?"

"I can feel them in me." Thomas smiled. "And I didn't even need his sword to do it."

Malabron turned away and busied himself with pouring a brandy to hide how pleased he was. This conversation was going better than he could have hoped.

"Where is the sword, Thomas?" Malabron asked.

"It's no use," Thomas demanded. "It turned to fire in my hand. It will not allow me to use it."

"That's inconvenient," Malabron said modestly. "But I can help you break the protection spell on the sword."

Thomas said, "So what do you want? In payment for lifting this enchantment?"

"Only your promise to speak on my behalf when you assume your place with the gods. To put it plainly, I have grown impatient. It has taken me hundreds of years to amass the power that I have. I will not wait as long again to rule the entire realm. Take your place among the gods, deliver the sword to me, and I will rule this realm."

"But Arianrhod said the world would break if all the Pillars died—what will you rule?"

"She is prone to exaggeration. There are certain gods who would be pleased to see the human race destroyed. Who would like to see the fae have dominion over all the realms. I ask only that you advocate for me to lead that charge."

Thomas considered for a moment. "How do you know that I would keep my word? Why should I, once I leave this realm forever?"

This time Malabron's smile was cautionary. "It is a mistake to think that because the gods are immortal, they are also invulnerable. Ask yourself this: Why do you suppose Arianrhod distributed her powers among you Pillars in the first place?"

"So other gods wouldn't…" Doubt clouded Thomas's eyes. "She said they were jealous."

"And you believed her." Malabron slipped in just the right note of pity. "The truth, my friend, is that she was being punished."

"Why?"

"I think that's enough questions for now." The meeting had gone on long enough; he'd said what he needed to. "You'll come to know, in time. Suffice it to say that you shan't be invulnerable, and you'll want allies in the other worlds—unless, that is, you wish to spend eternity in the dunce's corner."

CHAPTER FOURTEEN

KLARA

The wardrobe at one end of the room was a massive thing, taking up most of the wall. One half was filled with men's garments sewn from sumptuous, colorful fabrics, some adorned with intricate embroidered knot-like designs. Grams had given Klara a primer on the basic knots—the trinity, shield, four-cornered, and so on—but these were far more complex, some mazelike, others curved and ornamental. The clothes were neatly pressed and in perfect repair, and below them several pairs of clean, tidy shoes and slippers were lined up.

The other side of the wardrobe was another story. Dresses and shoes were piled on the floor in random heaps and petticoats and kirtles hung from hooks in tangles. Though they had obviously been worn by wealthy women, sewn from intricately fitted silks and brocades and satins, many were wrinkled and dirty and even torn.

Klara shuddered to think about how the gowns' owners had arrived here. Coming from the future gave her advantages, chief among them what her dad liked to call her "spirited nature" but which her teachers had described as "stubborn" or "headstrong"...and what Klara herself liked to think of as an "act first, apologize later" policy.

By contrast, Janneth—who was only a few years older than Klara's eighteen, if that—was timid and shy, obviously accustomed to following orders. The noblewomen brought to this tower might have put up a fuss, but the girls stolen from lower-class families wouldn't have dared.

Klara didn't know a lot about period fashions—that had always been more her mother's interest than her own—but she found a long linen smock that she figured would make a decent nightgown and pulled it on, then blew out the lamps ringing the room.

Klara hesitated before blowing out the last and tugged one of the drapes open, and was rewarded with the faint starglow of a moonless night. She cranked open the window and leaned out as far as she could through the narrow opening, drinking in the bracing night air.

The keep was situated at the shore of a small lake and surrounded by dense forest that went on as far as she could see. The sky was a breathtaking carpet of glittering stars. Growing up in one of the busiest cities on earth, Klara's first experience of the true night sky came at an upstate sleepaway camp when she was eight years old, and she'd been so entranced that she decided on the spot to study the stars when she grew up.

Klara searched the sky for the Silver Wheel. "Arianrhod," she whispered, and maybe it was her imagination, but she thought she heard the hooting of an owl way down in the trees.

Klara had always been charmed by the whimsical names given to the constellations, even as she dismissed earlier civilizations' attempts to understand the heavens through their myths. Now she knew that gods and goddesses were real and resided in the Otherworld, where they reigned over the dead. Klara had visited once, summoned by Arianrhod herself, and seen her mother briefly. Though Klara knew that the Otherworld was in a dimension all its own, that even if she could see millions of miles to the farthest stars she would never find it, she felt closest to her mother when gazing at the celestial realm.

And closest to her true self. Klara sighed and closed the window nearly all the way, shivering in her thin nightdress. She pulled back the counterpane and crawled into bed, sinking into its softness, and felt the tension begin to seep from her body as if she'd been poked full of holes.

It seemed impossible that the day had begun in 2022 at the Ring of Brodgar…that Callum had still been alive. So much had happened since then that Klara could barely hold it all in her mind.

But now, it seemed all she had was time.

Just after her mom died, Klara remembered the numbness that encased her in the beginning. The days after her death felt like they were the longest of Klara's life. The numbness, her constant companion, simmering deep in the center of her chest where her broken heart still beat. It felt like a piece of her died when her mother took her last breath.

The numbness was pain, grief, she realized. The immense emptiness that filled her heart was only broken in the mornings with debilitating sadness when she woke up, knowing she'd have to face a world without her mother in it.

Grief was a fickle thing, one that evolved from each death she experienced. She remembered, shortly after her mom died, googling: *Does everyone experience the five stages of grief?*

It wasn't because she hadn't experienced denial, anger, bargaining, depression, and acceptance…she just didn't know how they would manifest in a world without her mom. The final stage, acceptance, came eventually. It wasn't that she didn't think of her mother daily, but she came to terms that no matter how hard she wanted her mother to be alive, something like death couldn't be reversed.

With Callum, it was different. More than different, it felt wrong. Not that her mother's death didn't feel wrong, but this was different. The world she lived in when her mother died was not the same as it was when Callum took his last breath.

Yes, it kept spinning, people kept living, she was still here but she also wasn't. The world she once knew was so much more than she, even now, could fathom. This magical world, one that she discovered and fought through with Callum, was a landscape which she found almost impossible to walk through alone.

Now she was alone. In another time, without Callum and deep down, she knew what she was feeling was more than just denial or numbness. It was anger. She was mad. Mad that Callum died and she lived. Mad that even though Llaw died too…that it would never be enough to fill the gaping wound Callum's death had left on her heart—her soul.

She was good at pushing her emotions away, yes, but now she felt it. She understood it.

It bubbled to the surface like bile and she finally allowed the grief to be released. Not with tears but with a scream.

She didn't care who heard.

She only wished Callum could hear her. To know she grieved him. That she loved him. Klara released it not to accept his death but to allow this godforsaken grief to be heard. She screamed until her throat was sore and her eyes were drained of tears.

Nobody came to her room to see if she was okay. She wasn't surprised, nor would it be welcomed. The only person she wished for right now was Callum but that wish would go unanswered. She was alone now, but she would make loneliness her companion.

She lay down on the bed; her cheeks felt hardened by her tears.

Dawn couldn't be far away now.

One thing she wouldn't allow her grief to do was allow her to give up. She couldn't, if not for herself, then for Callum.

She thought now of herself. If they came to demand the names of her family, she had nothing to tell them.

What would happen when they figured out she couldn't be traded for a fortune? Kicked downstairs with the other girls whose value was measured by strong backs and callused hands, to be sold to the highest bidder?

Klara let out a groan and shifted under the feather tick, too tired to worry about what would come in the morning. Her breathing evened out; she felt the blanket of sleep beginning to settle on her. Far off in the distance, she thought she heard the owl again…and then she sensed a shift—in the air, in the darkness past her eyelids, in the rhythm of her heartbeat.

"You called me, Klara," a familiar, sonorous voice crooned.

Klara sat up fast, throwing off the covers. Sure enough, Arianrhod stood in the middle of the room, shimmering in a field of silver, almost too bright at the center to look at. Her long hair floated around her, studded with tiny sparkling flecks; her ageless face wore an inscrutable expression.

"I did *not,*" Klara said. "Just because I said your name when I was looking out the window doesn't mean I have anything to say to you."

"Touchy, touchy," the goddess murmured. Only now did Klara notice that her appearance was less distinct than in prior visits; it was almost like old film that had degraded before being converted to digital, blurred and cracked and blinking intermittently. Also, they weren't in the tower room anymore, but in the same sort of misty glen where Cernunnos had appeared in the past. "But that has nothing to do with it. I'm here because you need my help. You do seem to have a talent for attracting trouble."

"Fine." Klara was too tired for this. "If you want to help me, how about starting with getting me out of this place. If your magic eight ball's working you already know I'm not exactly auditioning for Rapunzel."

The brilliant halo around Arianrhod flared, silver flames shooting skyward. "This is *serious*, Klara. The threat to our worlds is not over."

"Don't you think I know that?" Klara shot back. "Callum is *dead*—"

Her voice broke and she shook her head, unwilling to cry in front of Arianrhod. "Listen," Klara tried again. "Llaw is dead, just like you wanted. I get that the worlds are a lot more messed up than anyone knew, but that's your job now, you and the other gods. All I want is to get back home and never hear from you again."

"Llaw is dead," Arianrhod echoed in a voice as jagged as gravel. "And his powers—the ones he took from the other Pillars, the ones that could upset the balance of the worlds and lead to their destruction—they're missing, Klara. What do you know of that?"

Klara caught her breath. "Missing? You said that when those carrying the power died, the magic *returned to the earth.* Is that another thing you lied to me about?"

The goddess's face remained impassive, taut. "I owe you *nothing*, mortal. You are *nothing* next to me."

"Yeah?" Klara's temper flared. "If I'm such a peon, why are you here? *You still need me.*"

The goddess raised one eyebrow, her expression thick with disdain. "After I split my powers among the ten Pillars, I was meant to reclaim them bit by bit as the Pillars lived out their natural lives, never knowing what they carried inside them… and at the moment of their deaths the inert powers would return to me until, upon the final Pillar's death, they would be fully restored. I did not tell you, because your outsized, overdeveloped, *swollen* sense of human justice and fairness would have muddied your understanding of the direness of the situation."

"Fine. And what's that got to do with me now?"

"The powers never returned to me when Llaw died. Which means, as I said, *they are missing.*"

Klara softened. "I don't know. I'm just a stupid human, remember? I did what you asked. Llaw is dead. The rest wasn't up to me."

"Did *you* kill Llaw?"

"All I know," Klara said slowly, her mind spinning furiously, "is that after the beast killed Callum, I watched Llaw die…and then I somehow time traveled back to Kelpie's Close and Thomas was there.

"Speaking of whom," Klara continued. "You don't think it would have been convenient for me to know that there was another Pillar on the job of tracking down Llaw? There's an awful lot you've just *neglected* to tell me. Like the fact that Llaw's sword is my sword's twin."

The goddess raised an eyebrow. "Twin?" She turned her full attention to Klara now, eyeing her greedily. "You hold the mortal sword of Kingshill?"

"I thought you knew, like, everything. Had the Sight, or whatever."

The expression on Arianrhod's face turned bitter. "There are barriers presented even to goddesses, and knowledge of the two power cleavers is one of them. But, no matter: Did you kill Llaw with the sword?"

Weirded out by Arianrhod's sudden greedy intensity, Klara hedged without outright lying. "No…he killed himself. Or Thomas stabbed him. I'm not sure which."

And then, to forestall any further questioning, she added,

"And while you're getting me out of this meddling, you need to make sure Thomas is all right. You owe us both that."

The light surrounding Arianrhod flared. "There are things about Thomas you don't know."

Klara rolled her eyes. "Okay, Captain Obvious. Neither one of us knew you'd decided to turn us into human Tupperware so you could keep your powers fresh and tasty, and thanks a lot for that, by the way. I don't know what you think Thomas did or didn't do, but he risked his life today trying to help me after losing his best friend and getting attacked, and not to be all 'what have you done for me lately' or whatever but if I have to pick sides..."

Arianrhod gave her a crafty look. "And yet *I'm* the one who came to see you. Why isn't Thomas here if he's so worried about you?"

"Um, because he's *unconscious*? Or were you getting a beer from the fridge during that part?"

Arianrhod tossed her hair impatiently. "Thomas is blocked from me," she said irritably.

"What does that mean?"

"Some...force, another god or a fae, has put a blocking spell on him. There's no way for me to communicate with him or know where he is."

"I didn't know that was a thing," Klara said. "Where can I get that? Because once I get home, I really don't think I'm going to feel like chatting with you ever again."

"Not even the creatures in my service know where he is."

"Wait. You have *cronies*? Like some sort of supervillain." Why hadn't she noticed how *crafty* the goddess was before?

"Of course. I may not meddle in the lives of mortals, but it doesn't mean I can't have others do it for me." She sniffed.

"Yeah? Well, who are they? So I can make sure not to cross paths with them, like, *ever.*"

A small smile crossed Arianrhod's face, like a human recounting the names of her kittens. "I have some relationships with the powries, nuggles, and of course, all the banshees and bean-nighe are mine."

"Naturally. The banshees. Just, great."

"Klara," Arianrhod said, her voice taking on the quality of fingernails scraping across a chalkboard. "You're really quite tiresome, aren't you? I'll leave it at this: you must find out anything you can about Thomas. Where he is, obviously, and what he's been doing. Who he's been talking to. I think he's fallen in with malevolent forces, and if *he* is in possession of my missing powers, they will ruin him, they will change him. Once you help me find them—with Thomas or no—I will help you return home. You're in no real danger here, so use this time to learn what you can, about who is blocking Thomas, about my powers."

"No *danger*?" Klara snorted. "Did you somehow miss those guys with the masks and the big knives?"

Arianrhod waved her hand impatiently. "The dark fae won't hurt you."

Klara was confused. "Those guys were *fae*?"

The goddess gave a humorless laugh. "Of course not. They're men willing to do anything for coin. But they *work* for the dark fae. Come now, darling, you didn't really think men who grew up poor as dirt, men like Thomas and your precious *Callum*—" her lip curled with distaste "—could furnish and defend your pretty little tower, did you?"

"What—what are you saying?"

The air surrounding Arianrhod was starting to become opaque, shimmering more brightly, and Klara knew her departure was at hand.

"You humans suffer such a failure of imagination," the goddess huffed. "Enchantment is all around you, but you see only with your eyes. But, like I said, they won't hurt you. They can't—at least not until they figure out how to take your powers."

"I don't suppose you've told all of the dark fae about your fun little power cleaver sword that you neglected to disclose to me?"

Arianrhod scoffed. "If you want to live, if you ever want to get back home, you'll do as I ask. But remember this, Klara: you may not trust me now, but you'd be a fool to trust anyone else. Not other gods, not the fae, not Thomas."

With one last flare of light and a whoosh of air that pushed Klara backward, she was gone—and Klara was back in her tower that might or might not even be real.

CHAPTER FIFTEEN

CALLUM

After the laird was gone, Raibert made no secret of his displeasure at being charged with Callum's transport, binding his wrists unnecessarily tightly with rope borrowed from the guard, tucking Llaw's sword and the faerie scabbard under his arm. He gave the rope a hard yank and led Callum like a donkey toward the door.

"If I may," the policeman said nervously, "when will Laird Johnstone return his judgment?"

"What makes you think I know?" Raibert said impatiently. "In due time, I suspect. Meanwhile, I've better things to do than mind your prisoner, so I suggest you say nothing of this to anyone unless you wish to inconvenience me further."

Once they were outside, Callum stood blinking in the sun

while Raibert woke his driver, who'd fallen asleep under a shady tree, with a string of curses that would have made Thomas proud.

Thomas. His head thrown back with laughter, blue eyes alight with mischief above the scattering of freckles that covered his cheeks. Callum's throat tightened at the memory and he was glad of Raibert's stony silence as the carriage carried them through the streets of Rosemere, across a field at the edge of town to blockish, unremarkable Udne Castle whose jutting towers seemed designed by a child playing with his blocks. As lads they'd dubbed it Ugly Castle and planned imaginary battles involving catapulting themselves across a brackish pond or ambushing guards by a stunted yew where they went to piss.

Callum had never wondered who lived in the castle, certain he'd never set foot in it. Instead his idle imagining tended toward tables groaning with roasted meats and jugs of mead, grand marble halls he could get lost in, and the soft, plump arms of willing maids.

Now, as he prepared to enter, the laird's strange behavior filled him with worry. Why had he been so transfixed by Callum's eyes? They were an embarrassment, sure, and a cause for whispering among the maids with their endless appetite for gossip.

"The boy has halfling eyes," one maid said to the other.

"Cursed eyes, I'd say," she replied.

But they had long since stopped attracting notice in the streets.

And yet…the business about him having fae blood made the strangeness of his eyes take on new significance. Eyes like his were supposedly the sign of a halfling, one born to a human and a faerie parent.

As the carriage pulled up to the front entrance, Raibert gestured to the rope that bound Callum's wrists. "Ye won't be making trouble, now, will ye?" He still gripped the end of the rope, but it was lax in his hands, and they both knew that one hard jerk was all it would take for Callum to rip it out of his hands.

"No," he replied, because Raibert didn't know the half of it, Callum thought grimly. With his unnatural strength, he could have taken the reins and kicked Raibert from his seat—but then what? He wouldn't make it far before the police caught up with him, and then he'd be back in jail with an additional mark against him. Callum didn't know what the laird was planning, but he'd take his chances rather than be imprisoned again.

And so he allowed himself to be led like a goat into the entrance hall.

Unlike the castle's exterior, the interior held its own against the dazzling Kingshill Manor, with its gleaming brass fittings and fine, thick carpets. In Klara's time, the furniture was like none Callum had ever seen: plump cushions as soft as duckling down; tables of thick, smooth glass; beautiful lamps that lit with the turn of a switch; curtains patterned in fantastical designs. Udne Castle's furnishings were just as sumptuous but much less strange, from the intricate carved chests that lined the walls to leather carpets trimmed with gold to ornate tapestries bearing the Johnstone crest that hung from the walls. Cups of gold and silver were filled with roses and placed at intervals along the tables.

"You there," Raibert called to the only person in sight, a footman stacking wood in the massive fireplace. "Leave off and fetch Mr. Wedderburn at once. Then go to the cellar and put water on for a bath."

The footman eyed Callum and took his time getting to his feet. "Surely it would be more proper for the lad to bathe in the pond," he said pointedly.

"If I wanted him in the pond, I would have taken him there," Raibert snapped.

"But is the bath for him?" The footman eyed Callum, seeming more confused than impudent. "Because cook comes in and out in the afternoons and she won't thank ye to find that lot in the tub."

Callum, too, was alarmed at the prospect of bathing in the staff quarters, fearful that his scars from the Ring of Brodgar would attract more questions. But Raibert was determined to win the argument.

"That's none of your concern," he said impatiently. "Off with you, and once you fetch the steward, go lay a fire in the library."

This time the footman hesitated before objecting, his hands tugging nervously at his sleeves. "There's no one in the library, and the laird is not expected back until evening."

"*I'll* be in the library, you idiot!"

Finally, the steward seemed to think better of any further objections and hastened away, taking the stone stairs two at a time. Moments later a sturdy woman in a starched smock and bonnet came hurrying down carrying a pitcher that sloshed water.

"What's this business, Mr. Raibert? We've got plenty to do without you ordering the staff about."

Raibert ignored that. "Never you mind, Mistress Drever. The laird expects to speak to this prisoner when he returns. I'm taking him to bathe, and then I'll stay with him in the library until the laird arrives. He'll need some clean clothes, and I could do with a bit of kip. I told Wedderburn to see to a fire, so you can send a tray in with him."

The maid snorted. "You'll not interrupt the floral arrangements just so I can wait on you. You'll wait for supper like everyone else. What's 'e done, anyway?" she demanded, jerking her chin at Callum. "And what does Laird Johnstone want with him?"

"Killed a man, so they say. Or stabbed him, at least."

That got the maid's attention. She gave Callum a good look, her eyes going wide at the sight of the soiled clothes he'd acquired in Klara's time...but when her gaze reached his face, her expression changed to one of shock.

She dropped the pitcher, and it shattered against the hard stone.

It was only an old copper tub in the basement of the castle, but it was still the most luxurious bath Callum had ever experienced, not counting the waterfall that came from the ceiling in Klara's time. The water was warm and there was a lump of lye soap and a clean cloth to dry himself as Johnstone turned his back and stared at the wall, still holding Llaw's sword like a broom instead of a world-ending instrument of power.

Dressed in the much-mended, patched uniform of a stable attendant, Callum followed Raibert to the library. In lieu of tying him again, Raibert carried a sharpened dirk, one he'd sent the steward to fetch. He seemed strangely unwilling to draw the thistled hilt of the power transfer sword.

"Stand there," Raibert told him, bidding him wait in the corner of the room where the light barely reached. Despite her protests, the maid had left a platter of cold roasted chicken and potatoes, and Callum's stomach growled as he watched Raibert eat.

It seemed weeks since he'd had a meal that filled his belly, even though it'd been mere days since staying at that inn with Klara. Callum passed the time imagining crusty bread from the oven, creamy milk, savory sausages—and Klara to share it with, her laugh lighting up his heart, and her copper hair catching the light like magic. Before Raibert could finish his meal, however, the library doors opened and the laird walked in, pulling off his coat and making no attempt to hide the fact that he was staring at Callum.

"Leave us."

Startled, Raibert looked from the laird to Callum and back. "Are you sure?"

The laird gave him a hard look. "Do you wish to join Dougal in mucking out the stables?"

Raibert's face darkened, and he gestured with the fork he was still holding. "I was only concerned, milord, with your safety."

"I'm perfectly fine." The laird waited for Raibert to get up from the table and back out of the room, casting a resentful look at Callum. "Leave the sword, Raibert." Reluctantly, he propped the sword up on the wall next to the door before shutting it behind him. Once he was gone, the laird gestured to a chair. "Please excuse the rudeness of my staff. I shall have them whipped."

The bright sheen to the laird's eyes suggested he was being facetious. Callum lowered himself onto the edge of the shiny cushion of the chair.

"I see they offered you a bath. I hope the facilities were…" the laird steepled his fingers, searching for the right word "…to your liking? We've just installed the most modern piping in all of Rosemere. The fittings came all the way from London."

Callum found the question bewildering. What was the laird playing at? He decided to launch right into a defense. "My lord," he said after taking a deep breath, "I am not a murderer. My friend was killed in Kelpie's Close. I—I believe it was his blood on the stones. I was trying to save him."

The laird nodded. "That is gallant, if true. Also very brave. But it is not why I asked you to come to my home."

Callum did not point out that no asking had been involved. "Then why?"

The laird stared at him a long moment before saying, "Because, Callum, I believe you are my son."

Callum had been expecting interrogation and perhaps flogging—but nothing could have prepared him for the laird's words. "Your…son?"

"It was the eyes, you see. Callum is a common enough name, and even the year of your birth could have been a coincidence, though you look so much like your mother that I might have been convinced even without—" The laird shook his head, as if astonished all over again. "No other child has been born in Rosemere with eyes of different colors in at least a century."

"But—but I dinnae understand. My father died before I was born. My mother could not raise me, so she..." Callum didn't trust his voice to continue. He had never been able to talk about what his mother had done without the deep ache of it overtaking him.

"Who told you that?"

"Master Brice. And Thomas, my best friend—the one who died in Kelpie's Close—he was a lad of four or five when I came to live in Master Brice's house. He says he gave me a piece of raw potato to suck on to make me stop crying."

Why had he shared that detail? Callum had always been embarrassed by Thomas's cheerful retelling, but also comforted—that even when they were small, Thomas had tried to protect him.

"That may be true, but you only have Brice's word to go on. Tell me, do you consider him a trustworthy man?"

Callum stared at the laird, his eyes losing their focus. Of course Brice was not to be trusted—he never told the truth when a lie would do—but it had never once occurred to Callum to question the story of how he came to his house.

"My son was born in June of the year 1549," the laird said gently. "My wife—your mother—did not survive. She lost so much blood, there was nothing the doctors could do to save her."

Callum's mouth fell open in shock. *Your mother.* Not the crabbed, tight-faced woman he'd always imagined, dressed in rags and eager for the coin, but...

"What was she like?"

The laird did not seem surprised by his question, nor by his raw, hoarse tone. "The most beautiful woman I ever saw. Fair, like you, with eyes the color of the sky and golden hair that reached her waist. She used to brush it in the evenings before the fire." The laird gave a sad smile. "I met her entirely by accident when she brought my medicine to the castle, you see. She worked for a merchant who sells particular tinctures and herbs, among other things, and I had heard he might have something for an old injury that plagued me sorely from time to time. Ordinarily the steward would have taken the delivery at the back door, but I was returning from a ride when I looked down to see this enchanting creature, and I spoke to her before I could stop myself. She didn't know who I was—she thought I was just a stable hand.

"She resisted my attentions at first—" the laird smiled at the memory "—even though I could tell she loved me in return. She was afraid of what her master would do if he found out. Because, you see, he was *olc síth*."

The laird studied Callum as he let his words sink in. His mother had worked for a dark fae merchant. They rarely worked with humans. Which meant his eyes—

"Your mother was a halfling. Her mother was a Flemish weaver who came to Scotland with some other girls to teach their craft to the guild in Edinburgh. When their ship pulled into the harbor it was waylaid by *olc síth* marauders who were after their cargo—but one of them saw your grandmother and stole her, too, and kept her as his wife. Their only child, a daughter they named Catherine, went to work for the richest merchant at the fae market when she was fifteen.

"You must understand, Callum, that the noble and important members of our society do not acknowledge the existence of the fae—but that doesn't mean that none of them believe. But to admit it would be scandalous, and to marry a halfling would have ruined my reputation. And so we lied. I paid the merchant a healthy sum to silence him, and told everyone that Catherine—your mother—was the impoverished daughter of Flemish royalty, and that her father had given me her hand before he died."

Callum's mind reeled. Not only had his mother been part fae, but also became a lady of wealthy society. "I cannae…" he said faintly.

"It is a lot to understand," the laird said, nodding. "Despite her rough upbringing, your mother was a quick study. I took one of my staff into confidence—a maid whose mother had served as my own mother's lady-in-waiting—and tasked her with teaching Catherine everything she would need to know. Before long she could hold her own with the wives of my peers. She enchanted them, as she enchanted everyone. When news of her pregnancy was announced, there was such joy…"

The laird's eyes took a faraway look, and Callum dropped his gaze to spare the laird his pain.

The laird…his father. Was it really possible? And if so—

"The same maid attended your birth," the laird continued after collecting himself. "Mistress Drever was about your mother's age, and they had become close. She allowed no one in the room for the birth, but after Catherine died and she saw your…unusual eyes, she wrapped you in a blanket. She told the guards that mother and child had both died, but that she was bringing my son to me so that I could look upon him before he was prepared for burial.

"Mistress Drever came to me in my quarters—imagine it, I was awaiting the news of my child's birth, and instead she had to tell me that I'd lost my wife. I did not even notice the babe—you, Callum—until you started to cry. I had barely absorbed the fact that Catherine was gone when Mistress Drever told me that I must be stronger still.

"She told me that if anyone saw the babe, they would know that Catherine had fae blood. That a babe so afflicted with bewitched eyes would die before the year was out, and bring great misfortune to the house. Mistress Drever said we must get rid of you at once. I must go to the fae market, she said—there was someone there who dealt in human children. Older ones mostly, strong ones who could be sold into service, but that if I were to bring a sum of money…"

The laird suddenly seemed exhausted by the telling. "I will never be able to explain my weakness at that moment, Callum. I have prayed for mercy for what I did. I changed my mind by the end of the week. I went back to the market with twice the sum to buy you back. But the merchant told me that you had died."

"That I *died*?" Callum echoed, his mouth dry. "But why—"

"He'd already sold you," the laird said. "It didn't occur to me at the time, but you were a fat, healthy baby who promised to grow up to be big and strong. Brice might not have paid much for you, but he calculated it would be worth it to raise you to fight."

No wonder Brice had pushed Callum so relentlessly—he meant to get his money's worth for all those years of room and board. None of the other boys had come as babies; most were at least Thomas's age and some as old as nine or ten. After that, Brice considered them too old to mold into fighters.

Callum wondered now if that was why he'd always felt different from the other boys. Thomas had saved him from neglect and abuse, but he'd felt his helplessness keenly until he grew large enough to hold his own. Maybe that was why he had learned to read, an undertaking that had required him to pinch dusty books from Brice's shelves and ask a bartender to teach him in exchange for doing odd jobs. It was worth it to him at the time just so he could have something of his own.

Now, though, he couldn't help wonder if his feeling of never fitting anywhere could have something to do with losing his mother on the day he was born. He would never have a chance to know her...but it seemed that fate was offering him a belated chance to know his father, a man completely unlike any man he'd imagined.

"If you speak the truth, my lord," Callum said slowly, "then I have never been who I thought I was."

"You are the only son and true heir of the Johnstone family name," the laird said importantly. "Whatever name Brice gave you—Drummond, was it?—it was never yours. Now at last you will take your place at my side, and eventually carry on our name through your own sons."

Callum barely heard him; he was thinking of something else entirely: his shame when he, a dirty street fighter, first looked upon Klara's beauty. He'd felt unworthy of the beautiful woman who took him home and tended to his wounds and agreed to help him in his quest to avenge Thomas. It followed him even after his purpose had changed, and he understood that forevermore he would live to protect and love Klara.

When Klara told Callum that she loved him, his heart was nearly full—save for the nagging knowledge that he could never deserve the love of a lady of Kingshill Manor. That he would always feel like he *was* a thief, stealing the love of a woman who would never have looked at him in his own time.

And now the laird—his *father*—was telling him it was never true. That Callum had been robbed of his rightful place as a man of wealth and refinement and nobility, meant for a fine education and the latest fashions and a position as important as his father's someday.

But none of that even mattered in the end. Klara had loved him for him…and that meant more to him than any title.

"I'm sorry, my lord," he mumbled. "I don't mean to be rude. It is only that I am overwhelmed."

"Father," the laird corrected him. "You must call me Father now."

CHAPTER SIXTEEN

KLARA

Sleeping in a strange bed, high in a tower that she could not leave, after being visited by a goddess—Klara wouldn't have thought her circumstances would have been particularly restful, even given her exhaustion. But when she woke in the morning, the sun was streaming through the windows, well on its way toward midday.

I will find you.

Klara sat up in bed, heart pounding, looking wildly around the room to see who had spoken...but there was no one there. Had she imagined the voice?

"I'm sorry, miss—Klara, I didn't mean to wake you."

Janneth emerged from the bathroom, carrying soiled linens. Klara sagged against the pillows. That must have been what she heard—Janneth moving around the tower. She must have been dreaming, or perhaps it was her imagination, overstimulated by the fantastical things that kept happening to her.

"You didn't wake me, Janneth." She thought back to Arianrhod's visit last night—her warning about Thomas, plea to find her powers, and insistence that she wasn't in any danger. Did that mean escape was possible? She eyed Janneth. The servant girl was wearing the same coarse, plain dress she had on yesterday, but it was clean and pressed and her cheeks were rosy, her eyes bright. It was as if a burden had been lifted from her shoulders.

"Please don't worry about—cleaning, or whatever you're doing," Klara said, embarrassed to still be in bed while the girl had obviously been hard at work. "I can take care of that."

Janneth gave her an odd look. "This is not work fit for a lady such as yourself."

Oh, right, the sixteenth-century thing. Klara wondered what Janneth would think of the fact that the current owners of Kingshill Manor cleaned the rooms and served the tea themselves.

"Your dress is ready," Janneth continued, pointing at the wall where a linen garment bag hung from a hook. "And I'll bring up your breakfast."

"Wait," Klara said. The sight of the dress in its protective cover had given her an idea. The only way escape would be possible was with her sword in her hand. And, if it wasn't, perhaps she could investigate it for signs that it stored Arianrhod's stolen powers. Plus…she just *missed* it, weirdly. Like she missed her dad, like she missed her Grams, like she missed a part of her family. She missed it more than her dog, Finley, and that was saying something. "Janneth, do you know what happened to my stuff? There was a black—" she paused, pretty certain hockey hadn't been introduced to Scotland yet "—bag holding an ornate sword with a jeweled pommel."

A fearful look passed across Janneth's face. "I didn't touch it, Klara."

"Oh, no, I didn't mean—I know you didn't. But I just wondered if you knew where it was."

"Aye, whenever the men bring someone, they put their things in the library. Don't worry, it's safe there—the master will give it back when your family comes for you."

Klara's relief was tempered by the knowledge that the sword's gold inlay and jewels might have tempted one of the men to "misplace" it, only to sell it later. "Janneth, I really need that sword. Is there any way that you could bring it to me?"

The girl's eyebrows shot up. "I'm forbidden. If Mrs. Fitchet finds out she'll have my head."

"But if there was a way to do it safely…if you were certain you wouldn't be caught, could you get into the library without anyone seeing you? I promise I'll find a way to reward you."

Janneth looked doubtful. "Mrs. Fitchet keeps it locked. The only time I'm allowed in there is to clean."

"But that's perfect. If you take a mop bucket with you…" Klara realized that she was asking the girl to risk her job and, quite likely, her safety. "Janneth, listen, I need you to trust me. I wouldn't ask for your help unless it was really important, and I'll pay you. If I told you the whole story, you wouldn't believe me, but…"

Janneth's eyes were wide with alarm. "Has there been an enchantment?"

"It was given to me by my grandmother, and it has been in my family for generations. I need to have it with me now or else I have no chance of escape. I need to leave this place. You can understand that, can't you?"

But Janneth was already shaking her head. "You mustn't. If the men even suspect that you are trying to escape, they'll put you in the chains. And if you try to fight them, they'll kill you."

"I'm not planning on any of that, I promise." Klara deliberated, wondering if she could trust Janneth with the truth of demigods and powers and a connection to her family five hundred years in the future—and whether it was fair to burden her with it. "You asked me if there had been an enchantment, and in a way, there was. But it happened long before I was born. The sword has certain...powers. It was used to kill a man who threatened great evil to our world. I can't let it fall into the wrong hands."

She held her breath, waiting for Janneth to accuse her of lying or run out of the room to fetch the guard. Klara chanced one more try. "Surely you know the men in this tower are not as honest as you. And I could pay." *Somehow.* The wariness in Janneth's eyes gave way to another, complex emotion.

"I don't want your money, Klara. Soon I'll have no use for it." Now it was Janneth who seemed to be trying to figure out how much to divulge. "There is something that not many people know about my fiancé, not even my family. He's... fae, Klara, one of the *daoine síth.*" She pushed her sleeve up to reveal a design of interlocking stars composed of a series of raised, silvery lines on her upper arm. "This is his mark."

Something clicked in Klara's mind. "Faerie lovers' marks—my grandmother told me about them." *They look a little like scars, but they're a promise that a fae will always return for his beloved. And in exchange she will live as long as he does…unless her life is cut short by an accident or poison, of course.*

"You *do* know!" Something like hope bloomed in Janneth's face. "Klara…do you believe, then?"

"In the fae?" *In love that can last a lifetime?* "Yes. I believe things I've seen with my own eyes."

Janneth looked embarrassed. "When you mentioned the fae market, I thought maybe you were testing me. That Mrs. Fitchet had put you up to it."

"Why would she do that?"

"I—I'm worried she's beginning to suspect. We're not allowed to associate with the fae. If she found out, I don't even want to think what she would do. Send me to live in the stable and muck out the stalls, at the very least." Janneth shivered. "That's why we're getting married as soon as my fiancé gets back. He had to go to Edinburgh to get the money to pay off my bond, but once he returns, he says we'll go straight to meet his family and have the ceremony right there in the mound."

There was so much joy in Janneth's face that Klara couldn't help but share in her anticipation. "When will that be?"

Janneth caught her breath and gazed at Klara shyly. "He's coming tomorrow. Maybe even today, if he was able to get the money last night."

Klara's heart fell. If Janneth was going to help her, it would have to be today, and what were the odds that she could pull that off?

The girl seemed to have been having the same thought. She laid a hand on Klara's arm, nodding firmly. "I will help you," she said.

Klara was filled with relief and hope. "I don't know how I'll ever thank you," she said. "I'm so lucky that I met you. If things were different, I think we would be friends."

Tears welled in Janneth's eyes. "I grew up in a house where there was never enough to eat or coal for the fire. Four of my brothers and sisters died before they reached one year…but I have been blessed with love. You are a lady, and you have beauty and riches, but your love was taken from you. I think that I am the lucky one."

"I will never forget this," Klara promised. "I hope you and your fiancé will be happy together."

Janneth beamed, then briskly rubbed her hands. "Right, then. How am I to do this?"

"Take the mop bucket with you. When you are sure you're alone, take the sword from the scabbard, and put it in the bucket so that the water covers the hilt. Tie the blade to the mop handle with a bit of string, and no one will notice it's there. Be careful, though—the blade is very sharp."

"If it's enchanted, it will not hurt me," Janneth said, with more confidence than Klara had. "Fae magic knows its own."

"I'm not sure it works that way," Klara hedged, remembering the look on Thomas's face when he examined the blade, as though he saw even deeper dangers there. "That sword took the head off a monster as tall as this ceiling as though it was cutting butter."

Janneth giggled. She probably thought Klara was joking. "What I meant is that a fae enchantment can't be turned against a fae or one who's been marked. Just as a dark fae's magic…" Her voice trailed off as if to suggest that the less said, the better.

Klara prayed that was true. She went to the closet and pulled a couple of gowns from the pile at random. "Take these with you," she said, removing the linen shroud from the mended gown and handing it to Janneth along with the dresses. "Tell Mrs. Fitchet—tell her that I yelled at you, that I demanded these be cleaned and pressed or I would tell my father I was mistreated. Tell her he commands a battalion of fifty men."

"Does he?"

Klara thought of her dad and smiled. The closest he came to commanding anyone was his futile effort to keep Finley off the couch. "Close enough. When you come back, put the sword among the dresses. Don't bother cleaning them, I'll just get them dirty again."

Janneth gave her a doubtful look. "If I tell Mrs. Fitchet you insisted, then I'll have to clean them or she'll be suspicious."

Klara sighed. She hated to make more work for the girl, but didn't see a way around it. "Janneth, I can't tell you how much this means to me. And be safe. If you think there's a chance that you could be caught, then don't risk it." Even saying it, her heart cried out; she needed to hold her sword again.

"Don't you worry," Janneth assured her. "I'm the beloved of a fae. He won't allow anyone to hurt me. And, Klara? All my friends call me Anne. I hope you will, too." She patted her hand as she walked to the door.

Klara wished she shared the girl's optimism.

Then again…she remembered how it had felt when she was with Callum. That as long as they were together, nothing else mattered. She'd never felt safer than when she was in his arms…and she would never get to feel that again.

That bleak thought stayed with her as she watched the girl leave through the heavy door and heard the many locks sliding into place.

CHAPTER SEVENTEEN

KLARA

Klara was sitting in the window seat several hours later, gazing out at the verdant hills in the distance, when she heard footsteps coming up the stone stairs beyond the door.

Too many footsteps for one person.

Klara leapt to her feet and was bracing herself for another unwelcome turn of events when Janneth walked into the room, carrying the cleaned gowns and a scuttle loaded with firewood, stooping from the weight of her burden. Mrs. Fitchet walked behind her holding a tray laid with sliced cold meat, brown bread, and a wedge of yellow cheese. The older woman's face was drawn into a tight scowl and she slammed the tray down carelessly so that the silver clattered. At her waist hung a switch that looked like it got a lot of use disciplining her staff with beatings.

Janneth didn't meet Klara's gaze as she laid out the gowns on the counterpane. Then she came to stand beside Mrs. Fitchet with her head down. Some of her fine, pale curls had escaped their pins; her apron was dirty and wrinkled and her hands were splotched an angry red.

Klara's mind went to the worst: that Janneth had been found out and punished, that it was all her fault. But the look on Janneth's bowed face didn't look defeated. If anything, when she peeped up at Klara through her lashes, it was conspiratorial.

Was it possible that she'd pulled it off? That she'd somehow managed to get into the library, steal the sword, and clean the gowns in such a short time?

Mrs. Fitchet poked Janneth in the ribs and the girl made a deep curtsy. "Your d-dresses, milady," she stammered.

"If you had given us more time, Lady Klara, I would have had them tailored by a proper seamstress," Mrs. Fitchet said in an oily voice that sounded nothing like the barked orders of the night before. "The girl is worthless. Please tell your father that I can have the whole lot done up and sent along if it pleases him."

It dawned on Klara that the woman was angling to get in her favor, either fearful of her fictional father's wrath or hoping to be rewarded. She lifted her chin in her best approximation of Anna Sorokin.

"Why would I wear those when my closet is full of the finest gowns in all of Scotland?" she demanded haughtily, then pointed to the tray. "And what is that? Am I supposed to eat it, or feed it to the rats that kept me up all night?"

Mrs. Fitchet took a startled step backward. Janneth winked even as she pretended to be terrified.

"I will ask Cook to prepare something more…suitable," Mrs. Fitchet said. "The girl will forfeit her own dinner for her carelessness. Come along then, Janneth."

She turned on her heel and strode toward the door. Janneth hung back and murmured a few words before following her mistress out.

Klara stared at the door, Janneth's words echoing in her mind.

"The stars will be out tonight."

The star… Janneth's fae mark. Her fiancé had made it back today, after all. It was her way of saying goodbye.

A melancholy smile tugged at Klara's lips. At least one of them would get to be with the man they loved.

Not long after Janneth and Mrs. Fitchet left, another servant brought a steaming, covered platter and left with the untouched bread and cheese. Klara waited until his footsteps faded before lifting the linen cover from the gowns on the bed. Before she could even lift the first one, she felt a faint, electric stirring inside her.

Her sword, recognizing its mistress.

Klara dug through the gowns and closed her hand around the hilt, the feeling growing into an almost-euphoric rush. The sword felt at home in her hands, humming faintly with a strange sort of energy.

The hockey bag was gone, but Klara kept the sword in

her lap as she ate her lunch, a fresh-caught fish from the lake roasted with tiny potatoes. It was delicious, and since Klara couldn't remember the last time she'd eaten, it disappeared in no time.

Klara set the plate by the door, and then used one of the belts from the wardrobe to tie up her skirts so she could move unimpeded. She gripped her sword in both hands, then began the training set that Callum had taught her.

As Klara repeated the now-familiar movements, she felt some of her hope return, the weight of her grief undiminished but receding for the moment. It felt good to move her body, to slash through the air, to parry imaginary thrusts, and Klara felt increasingly energized and confident as the hours passed and the sun began to sink in the sky. For the first time she realized that returning home might not be her highest priority, after all, at least not until she had freed Thomas and found out who had taken Callum from her. And now that she had her sword, she felt…like she could figure out how to do that.

And like she could make them pay.

She wondered if this was what Callum had felt when he swore to avenge Thomas. Only days ago Klara had told Callum that she could not take the life of another, even if they deserved death. But now there was a hunger inside her that would not go away until justice had been served.

A life for a life.

An angry bank of thunderclouds blew in as dusk descended. If Klara had understood Janneth correctly, she would soon be reuniting with her love. *Anne*, Klara reminded herself with comfort. Her second friend in this strange world. Klara smiled to think of Anne's meeting with her beloved, that there were two people who wouldn't mind the rain tonight.

Soon, though, a servant would bring her dinner, and she had to find a place to hide the sword. She'd barely managed to slide it between the tick and bed frame when the door opened and yet another servant appeared, this time a girl of no more than thirteen who nearly ran from the room after setting down a tray.

Klara's reputation as an arrogant bitch was apparently getting around.

She lifted the cover from a fragrant stew studded with tender carrots and potatoes, and took her plate to the window so she could watch the storm come in over the lake while she ate. As a child, Klara had been entranced by the idea that above the clouds, the stars still glittered against the velvety black of the cosmos.

Up the road that followed the contours of the lake, a cloud of dust signaled the arrival of a carriage. The first fat raindrops pelted it as it came into view, a sturdy coach with two tired-looking horses at the drawbar. When the coach was still a hundred yards away, someone burst out of the keep and went sprinting into the road, skirts flying behind her, gold hair streaming. Klara heard Anne's joyful shout as she ran through the rain.

The carriage slowed, and a man leapt to the ground and ran toward Anne. Klara smiled in anticipation of the moment when he would lift her into the air and spin her around while they kissed.

But then the man called Anne's name, and his voice was

laced not with joy but with something much darker: fear, as cold and deep as Klara had ever known.

Anne stumbled. Her foot slipped on the wet grass, and everything seemed to happen in slow motion, Klara watching in horror as Anne pitched forward and fell down the sharp drop-off into the lake, the black waters closing over her. The man had almost reached her, closing his fingers on her skirts only to have them ripped from his hand when she fell.

Klara's heart leapt—her believer, her coconspirator, her *friend* who also knew the truest of loves. Instinctually, one hand grasped the pommel of the sword, while the other closed around the jewel of her necklace.

There was another splash as the fae man jumped into the lake. Klara put her fist to her mouth, the ruby touching her lips, and the chain dragging down. She forgot to breathe as she searched the dark lake for Anne's head to break the surface. She reached deep, searching for her power, for that pull that said that time was working backward, and she felt her heart catch—*it was there it was there it was there*—and then slip out of her grasp.

Surely Anne could swim. She had to know how to swim. *Please, please let her know how to swim.* Klara reached again, closing her eyes—*please* let me save Anne, she sent the thought up to the stars, to Arianrhod, to her ancestors—and again she felt time catch, and then slip. She gasped, exhausted, even though her power was out of reach. *I can't do it.* Tears leapt to her eyes, even as she tried and tried again.

Time ticked by, the fae man's dark head appearing every few minutes to gasp for breath. Each time, Klara reached, and each time, her power evaded her. Klara tried not to imagine the water weeds that could wrap around an ankle, the hidden rocks that could spell disaster.

The man stayed submerged so long that Klara had the terrible thought that they might both drown—when suddenly he came up coughing and gasping with Janneth in his arms. Her heart rose—maybe she could be saved without Klara's power of time reversal?—and then plummeted. Anne's body trailed limply as he swam for shore in swift, hard strokes and carried her up onto the bank.

Please, Klara prayed as she gazed down on Anne's lovely, pale face, the fan of gold hair splayed around her shoulders. Her lips were blue, her eyes half open. The man was on his knees beside her, and though Klara couldn't hear his words she knew he was pleading with her to live.

Janneth's eyes fluttered open and she coughed. Her gaze found her lover's, and he gave a sob of relief and pulled her into his arms.

It was then that Klara saw the blood that poured from the back of Anne's head. In seconds she went limp in her lover's arms.

Then there came the howl of grief, a sound so bleak that Klara felt it reach inside her, twisting with the man's pain. She felt hollow—her friend, she could do nothing to save her friend, even after everything she'd been given. Then, he raised his stricken face to the sky, his lips moving in a curse.

And Klara froze in shock. She knew that man…their paths had crossed before—five hundred years in the future.

CHAPTER EIGHTEEN

CALLUM

After the laird excused himself to attend to other business with a promise to see him at dinner, a servant showed Callum to a suite of rooms on the second floor. The bedchamber was larger than the room in Brice's home where as many as twelve boys slept, with a bed so high it required a stepstool to ascend, and heavy velvet drapes and a desk overlooking the gardens.

Callum barely had time to take it all in before the servant led him into the bath and proudly showed him the new piping and the spigot that delivered water into the basin with a twist of the handle. After spending time in the twenty-first century, with its magical devices for the conveyance of water and waste, Callum found himself in the curious position of pretending to be astonished by advances that were, by comparison, primitive.

Still, the notion that he could bathe alone and whenever he liked was a level of luxury he could barely imagine.

"Suitable clothes will be sent up so that you can dress for dinner," the servant said, giving the stable boy's clothes a look of confusion. "The laird requests your company at half six."

After he bowed deeply and left, Callum found Llaw's sword, now wrapped in a length of linen, and hastily stowed it under the blankets of the bed, unwilling to let any servant come upon it and be called to its evil. Then, Callum could only sit at the desk in a daze. Being called "my lord"...servants bowing before him...Callum would never get used to it, and wasn't at all sure he wanted to. The castle was resplendent, and the laird generous and welcoming, but the former was not his home and the latter felt nothing like a father.

Callum thought of Klara's father, who he had met only briefly. A kind-eyed, gentle man, he seemed genuinely pleased to meet Callum. Mr. Spalding lived in Kingshill Manor, which had been the spiritual heart of Rosemere for centuries, a place of storied opulence and grand parties in Callum's time and a beautiful, pastoral inn in Klara's.

And yet Mr. Spalding had none of the haughtiness of the laird. He cooked his own meals and had not a single servant, and according to Klara was in the habit of making repairs to the manor himself.

Callum had the odd thought that if he could choose a father, he would be more like Mr. Spalding than the laird. He remembered something Klara had said in passing—*Dad's going to be thrilled to have another man in the house*—and his heart ached for that future with Klara. He'd do anything for it.

At the appointed hour, Callum tentatively entered the dining hall wearing the fine shirt, trews, and belted plaid that the servant brought him. The clothes fit him as if they'd been made for him. After nineteen years spent in ragged hand-me-downs, they felt both luxurious and almost as awkward as the clothes that Klara's grandmother had given him to wear, strange shirts and leg coverings in wild designs that she laughingly told him were preferred by people called "hippies."

A servant rushed to lead Callum to his place at the long table, at the end of which only two places had been laid. The assortment of plates and cutlery and the array of silver cups was both dazzling and intimidating, but thankfully Klara had given him a brief primer on their use when they'd eaten meals at fancy inns. Following her example, he unfolded the linen napkin and laid it in his lap.

Moments later, the laird swept in, having changed into evening clothes. Callum leapt to his feet and the laird gave him an approving look. "I should have known that fine tailoring would suit you," he said. "We'll take care of that hair tomorrow, and no one will ever guess that you didn't grow up among nobility."

Callum didn't know how to respond to the compliment. He was more accustomed to the insults hurled by his opponents and those that bet against him.

"Thank you," he settled for saying, "for all of this."

The laird waved off his words as servants appeared to serve the first course and fill the goblets with wine. He steered the conversation through four courses, each more spectacular than the last, seeming to be happy to do most of the talking—about his holdings in the town's various industries, his horses' lineage, his duties in local government, and other matters that were beyond Callum's ken.

Callum was unclear if the laird was informing him of all he would be responsible for as his heir or if he just liked to hear himself talk. Either way, the laird didn't seem to expect much in response, which more than suited Callum, who took the opportunity to eat everything set before him. But when the final course was served, a custard studded with currants and almonds accompanied by ruby red glasses of port, the laird turned the conversation to Callum.

He seemed alarmed to learn that, like all of Brice's boys, his education ended as soon as he was old enough to begin their training.

"But we learned our maths," Callum added hastily. "So that our winnings were paid in full. And I know how to read."

The laird brightened. "Excellent. Well then, I'll hire the finest teachers in Edinburgh to come and fill in the gaps of your education. Now, there is a matter of some delicacy that I would like to discuss with you."

Callum braced himself. "Yes…Father?"

"I'll just come out and say it, how's that? I'd like to know if there is a girl you have your eye on. A sweetheart."

"There…was, my lord." How to explain that he was certain she was still alive even after watching her being mauled by a beast from the Underworld? And that she had come from a time that the laird could not begin to imagine? "I mean there is, but she is not from here."

The laird seemed confused. "She is not a local girl?"

Callum had no wish to share the whole story with the laird, even if he was truly his father. It would take time to get used to his new situation, and the laird still felt like a stranger.

But he also couldn't lie completely, so he cast around for a partial truth. "She is related to a local family, but she grew up in Edinburgh with her grandmother."

"But then how did you meet?"

"That," Callum said truthfully, "is a long story. I was... lost, and Klara came to my aid. She was beautiful and smart and every minute we spent together only made me want to be with her more."

He caught himself, embarrassed by his passion, but the laird nodded encouragingly.

"I cannae tell you why, but Klara felt the same way about me. But it was complicated. She had made a promise to someone powerful, a promise she couldn't break, and because of it, we were separated." Callum swallowed and forced himself to continue. "When the police arrested me, I wasn't only trying to save Thomas. I was also searching for Klara."

"I don't understand."

Callum thought fast. "I was trying to help her with her obligation, which took us to another town. There, we were set upon by robbers. I was knocked unconscious while trying to fend off one of our attackers, and when I came to, Klara was gone. Since then I have not had word from her."

"Oh dear," the laird said, looking aghast. "But how do you know she is all right?"

Callum considered telling him that he might have the Sight, but given the laird's determination to hide any association with the fae, he opted for another lie. "A friend spotted her at the almshouse, but she was gone by the time I arrived. The robber took everything, so she has no money and nowhere to go, and now I dinnae know where she is or how to reach her."

"But that's terrible," the laird said. "I don't suppose you could contact her family...?"

"There's no one," Callum said. Not in his time, anyway. "Only these distant relations in Rosemere, but they have never met. I dinnae think they are even aware of her existence."

The laird's face fell. "That is...complicated. Would I know this family, by any chance?"

Callum was confused by the question. The only way the laird would know them would be if they were as important and wealthy as he was, which—

The pieces abruptly fell into place. Callum's father was trying to find out if his beloved was from the lower classes...and if she was, he would consider her a millstone, a complication to his plan to introduce Callum into society.

Callum felt a surge of anger on Klara's behalf—but then he realized that he could turn this to his advantage, if only to stop the laird from asking any further questions he didn't wish to answer.

"You might know them. The Westwoods of Kingshill Manor."

The laird's eyebrows shot up. "But that's splendid! I must send a letter to Laird Westwood at once. I'm sure he will be delighted by the news that his...?"

"Distant cousin," Callum supplied, thinking fast.

"Right. Ewan will be delighted to welcome her into his home, and once he discovers that the young lady's suitor is my son, returned to me after two decades, it would be most appropriate for us to celebrate together. I must arrange an introduction—perhaps a dinner. And for heaven's sake, we must find this poor girl at once."

As grateful as Callum knew he should be to his father for his help, he couldn't help resenting that his change of heart stemmed from the fact that Klara had ties to the most prominent family in Rosemere. But he had to set that aside for now.

"Then we must go at once to the Ring of Brodgar," Callum said. "It's the last place I saw her and—"

"But that is a voyage of many days!" the laird exclaimed. "How did you return so quickly?"

Callum realized the magnitude of the mistake he'd made. But the laird was bound to discover the truth eventually; maybe it was best to get it over with now. "My lo—Father," he began, the word clumsy on his tongue. "You spoke of my mother's mixed blood. It seems to have passed to me, as I was able to travel by faerie portal."

The laird recoiled, his face going pale. He picked up his wine and drained it before speaking.

"Please do not speak of that again, to anyone. Your mother, while of mixed blood, never showed any predilection for..." He searched for the right word. "Witchery. Oh, now and then she'd know who was coming down the lane, or predict an unexpected storm, but nothing that would draw undue attention to our family. That was the only reason I was able to introduce her into society. But, Callum, your eyes will already make this difficult enough without additional...distractions, so from this day forth you must promise to turn your back on all this nonsense."

The laird's disgust was obvious. Callum thought of Cernunnos, of the *daoine síth* who had nursed him back to health. He wasn't sure he wanted—or would even be able to—close off that part of him.

How different it was in Klara's time, when her grandmother—daughter of a Westwood laird—openly admired fae culture. But Callum couldn't risk alienating the laird, not if he wanted his help. "Yes, Father. I understand."

"The policeman and the guard have seen you," the laird mused, rubbing his chin. "That can't be helped, but a little gold will ensure their silence. That leaves Mistress Drever, but she remains loyal to your mother's memory, and the rest of the staff will follow her lead. I shall have her fashion a patch for you to wear over one eye, and we shall say you were injured in a duel." The laird seemed quite pleased with his solution. "After all, should you ever be called upon to prove your swordsmanship, you'll exceed their expectations!"

Callum only nodded, the conversation threatening to overtake him. The laird noticed and patted his hand.

"It has been a long day, my son. Let us continue this conversation in the morning. Should you need anything in the night…"

He paused, staring into Callum's eyes with a faint sense of unease, and Callum wondered if he was thinking of his fae blood.

"I'm sure I'll be fine," Callum said, averting his eyes. "Good night, Father."

CHAPTER NINETEEN

KLARA

As cries of anguish rent the air, Klara heard the household down below come to life. Members of the household staff streamed out the door below her window, holding torches to light their way.

Klara recognized Mrs. Fitchet from the dull gray braid that hung down her back under her sleeping cap. She was still pulling on a coat over her nightdress as she hastened down the drive toward the lake, where the driver had left the carriage and stood helplessly by.

It seemed impossible that the sweet, pretty servant girl who'd been so full of joy at the prospect of marrying her sweetheart, who'd helped Klara at such great risk to herself, could be *dead*. That she'd been saved from drowning only to die from a head wound moments later.

Anne must have struck her head on a rock when she fell. A terrible tragedy, to be certain…and one that did nothing to explain what Aion was doing there five hundred years before his time.

But how could he be here?

Unless…

With a sudden force, everything clicked. Of course, Klara remembered that fae lived much longer than humans, their lifespans reaching hundreds and sometimes thousands of years. This Aion was the same one she met in her time, but a past version of himself. Time, as she had come to understand it, was linear and this was Aion pre-events that happened in 2022. She'd met him, but his Aion had never met her, yet.

Klara never would have believed it possible to cross the dimensions of time and space—until it happened to her. She'd trusted Arianrhod at least in part because she was the goddess of not only time but of the stars, and when she'd experienced a vision of the goddess in the night sky, it only deepened her doubts about everything she'd ever believed.

Klara had once refused to believe in anything whose existence couldn't be proven. But then she'd been offered that proof in the most convincing form of all—her own senses. A goddess, a demigod, a fae—not to mention her own boyfriend who'd been born centuries in the past—Klara had seen them with her own eyes, heard them speak, listened to their stories, traveled their worlds. And as she experienced more and more of her new reality, it hadn't occurred to Klara to doubt what was in front of her.

Klara tried to remember everything she could about the fae. She had learned some of this from her mother and grandmother, whose interest in Scottish mythology Klara had always understood to be a hobby, a passion. Now she wasn't so sure. Grams seemed to know more about the sword than she let on. Her mother had left her a necklace that seemed to have powers or value that Klara did not yet understand.

As for *this* fae, Callum had gone to Aion for help interpreting the entries in the notebook Thomas had given him just before his death. Aion figured out that Thomas had been visiting the mystic centers or "thin places" he'd drawn in his notebook in pursuit of Llaw, attempting to stop him before he could destroy the balance of time that connected the worlds.

After that, Aion had come to see Callum once more, in a local pub where he and Klara had gone to hear some music. He'd been both aggressive and evasive, speaking in riddles and talking about a bad bargain he'd made with the bean-nighe—who, Klara realized with bitterness, she now knew was in Arianrhod's service—and the two men had nearly come to blows before Aion slipped away.

Now Klara had a very uneasy feeling that Anne's death was somehow the result of that bargain. Anyone who got involved with Arianrhod's schemes or sought to trade with her creatures seemed to be taking a terrible risk. First Thomas had nearly been killed after agreeing to help Arianrhod. Then Callum had lost his life to a monstrous creature Llaw had plucked from between worlds. Klara was still alive only because of her enchanted sword.

But it went even further back than that—all the way to Llaw's childhood. Arianrhod said that her son had become greedy and jealous, inflamed with resentment that he could never walk among the gods, and that was why he had tried to steal his own mother's powers even at the cost of destroying the mortal realm that had always been his home. She'd also said that she'd been forced to assign her powers to the ten Pillars to protect them from jealous gods who might steal them.

But Klara had seen no evidence of the jealousy that Arianrhod insisted she inspired in Cernunnos, the god with the closest ties to the mortal realm, the one who'd visited her and Callum.

Grams had always described the gods as unpredictable, easily bored and given to fighting with each other. "They have the temperament of children," she'd once said, "and domain over all the worlds, which is a very bad combination." Klara wished that Grams was here now; she had a thousand questions and no clear idea what was at stake.

Down in the street below, Mrs. Fitchet was attempting to coax Aion away from Anne's body so that the men could carry her inside. But Aion seemed oblivious to everything but his grief, his tears falling onto Anne's hair, his breath making ragged clouds on the frosty air.

With no warning, Mrs. Fitchet looked up at the very window Klara was sitting in. Their eyes met and Klara took an instinctive step back, her heart pounding. In the older woman's expression she saw shock, anger, and a bone-deep weariness—but also raw fear.

What was she afraid of? Some prickling sense cautioned Klara not to let Aion see her, not yet.

As a small child, Klara had once wished to be a faerie herself. Grams's tales made it sound so exciting. "Maybe you have the Sight, poppet," she teased when Klara came to visit in the summers. "You wouldn't be the first in your family, you know. One of your great-great-great-aunts was put on trial for witchcraft when she predicted that blight would kill the crop one year."

Loreena would tut and scold. "You're scaring her, Mom," she'd say. "Let's keep it to the faerie dust for now and save the rest for when she's older."

But Klara's mom had mistaken eight-year-old Klara's reaction. It wasn't fear that made her clutch Grams's hand harder, but excitement. She was old enough to know that no one got tried for witchcraft anymore, and to her young imagination, the ability to predict the future or know what other people were thinking seemed like a marvelous superpower, one she could use to get out of scrapes and into all kinds of adventures.

Later that night, when they were squeezed into the narrow bed in Grams and Alice's guest room, Loreena mentioned it again. "You know those stories are made up, honey," she said. "Grams just has a great imagination. Like you."

But the dream never really left Klara, even if it receded when she got interested in science. Since Callum's arrival in her life, she'd felt these stirrings a few times, and they'd brought nothing but dread and a feeling of terrible responsibility, reminding Klara to be more careful what she wished for.

With shaking hands, she pulled the drapes closed tightly. Then she snuffed out the candles and went to bed. It took a long time for the chill to leave her body, even under the heavy covers.

Anne had been the first ally Klara had made since falling back in time, the first who felt like a friend—other than

Thomas, of course. And now Anne been ripped from her destiny on the eve of her wedding, her dreams shattered. And the worst part…Klara had the power of time, yet it was useless in the moment she needed it most. That Anne needed her most.

As Klara tossed and turned, she hoped that the things Arianrhod had told her about mortals' afterlife were true. That even now Anne was with those she loved in the Otherworld, the beautiful realm of the gods.

Maybe Anne would someday even cross paths with her mother there. "You'll like her, Mom," Klara whispered in the darkness. "Tell her thanks for everything."

A tiny, half-formed thought intruded, like a mental hangnail. *Find out who did this*, it urged. *Get justice for Anne.*

Callum. Thomas. Anne. The longer she stayed…the more Klara's responsibilities kept multiplying. How was she going to prevail against the powerful forces that kept destroying those she cared about?

And could she live with herself if she failed?

CHAPTER TWENTY

CALLUM

Callum was roused from his nap by a knock at the door. For a moment he forgot where he was, expecting to find himself on the rough dirt floor of his jail cell, but the faint perfume of the fine bedlinens brought it all back.

He was in Castle Udne, the son of Laird Johnstone. The thought made him feel slightly queasy. "Yes?"

"A visitor, milord," came the muffled voice of a servant.

A visitor? Callum's mind raced with the possibilities. Could it be Cernunnos? But no, the Stag God would not need to go through a servant to appear.

Maybe it was the guard, come to haul him back to jail. "Let him in," Callum said, resigned to his fate.

But the man who bounded through the door, ran across

the room and threw himself onto the bed was none of these, tackling Callum before he could catch his breath.

"Callum, you old sod!"

"Thomas!" Callum drew back in shock. His vision was right—did this mean he did truly have the Sight? His friend was before him, not an apparition or a ghost. The hand that thumped him on the back was real, flesh and blood and the mischievous grin that glimmered on his lips was just the same. "Can it be—are you really—"

"It is, and I am!"

Callum studied the face of his oldest friend, then squeezed his wrist to feel his heartbeat, desperate to believe. "But I saw you die!"

"You saw me *almost* die," Thomas corrected him cheerily. "But what happens to them as bet against me?"

"They go home empty-handed," Callum recited automatically, the lines Brice hired barkers to shout outside the pubs where his fights were scheduled. Tilting his head at the servant waiting awkwardly in the door, he cleared his throat. "That is all."

Callum felt extremely awkward giving orders to the staff. Thomas had always been so much better at speaking to the wealthy patrons, learning their ways and language the better to inveigle his way into their favor—and their purse.

The servant bowed. "Yes, my lord."

"Michty me," Thomas said when the door closed. "You, the son of a laird!"

Callum felt his face heat in embarrassment. "I can't think about that now. Thomas, I cannae believe it. There is so much I must tell you. Things you will have a hard time believing."

"I may be able to save you some effort," Thomas said, sauntering over to the low table placed between two brocaded chairs near the fireplace, where the servant had left a platter of fruit. He picked up a bunch of grapes and tossed one into his mouth. "When I came to after Llaw stabbed me, he was about to deal the killing blow, but I was able to block him. I'd hit my head when I fell, but the wound in my chest was superficial." He opened his shirt—wrinkled, filthy, and smelling none too fresh, which probably explained the manservant's confusion—and sure enough, the flesh had knitted back together in a small scar. "But Llaw didn't know that. There was so much blood, he must have thought I was expiring, so he was careless. My dagger was still in my hand, and I plunged it into his body…and then something very strange happened.

"I was pulled into the sky by a twisting wind," Thomas said in a rare moment of awe. "I cannae explain it, Callum, except to say that some strange force seemed to seize me and hold me in its grasp in a terrible wind, until once again my feet found solid ground. And where Llaw had been standing, there was a girl with long red hair. She was holding a sword, its hilt set with gems, blood dripping from its blade."

"Klara," Callum said, barely able to breathe.

"Ah, you're getting ahead of me," Thomas said with a wink. "But maybe you'll figure the rest out faster than I did. Your Klara reached the truth first: she and I had both stabbed Llaw at the same time, only she had done so five hundred years in the future. And that caused her to be pitched between times and she landed here, while Llaw was sent to his death."

"I cannae believe it," Callum said, remembering the beast's horrifying roar as it tossed Callum through the air and went galloping toward Klara, fangs bared and razor-tipped tail lashing. "Llaw brought hellhounds and beasts from between worlds. I didnae think she had a chance at first."

"She is a remarkable girl," Thomas said. "Courageous and also beautiful."

Callum didn't like the enthusiasm in his best friend's voice, but he pushed that emotion aside. "So it's true. You really were working for Arianrhod all this time."

For the first time Thomas looked regretful. "I wish I could have told you, Callum. Never before was there a secret between us, but she would have had me believe that the fate of the worlds depended on my telling no one." His gaze turned bitter. "Of course, after I talked to Klara, I realized that even a goddess is not above lying and cheating to get her way."

"You talked to Klara," Callum repeated. "After you killed Llaw together. But that was days ago. Where is she now? Why isn't she with you?"

Thomas's face fell. "I failed you twice, old friend. First by not taking you into my confidence, and then by letting the mercenaries take her. But we will get her back."

"Mercenaries!" Callum cried, leaping from the other chair. "When did this happen? How did she fall into their hands?"

"Only yesterday. She can't have been taken far. I was struck in the head and lost consciousness, or I swear I would have fought them, Callum."

"I know you would have. But where were you when you were attacked?"

"About a mile from Kingshill Manor," Thomas said. "We'd been trying to find shelter for the night—it's a long story."

"Please, Thomas, go back to the beginning."

"All right. Let's see…after we realized what had happened, Klara told me that you were dead. She was devastated," he added reassuringly.

Callum's head felt as though it might burst. "This is all too much to take in. Each of us believing the other dead—"

"She saw the beast attack you, and just like you, came to the conclusion that you couldn't have survived. So you can see why, when she found herself back in our time, her only thought was to return home. But I can tell you that is easier said than done."

"But with Arianrhod's powers, it would have granted you the power to move through time, so that you could pursue Llaw." The same "gift" the goddess had bestowed on Klara, who had only begun to learn to control it, her powers too new for her to use them to defend herself against Llaw.

"Correct, but time travel isn't as easy as a snap of your fingers. It's a skill that must be learned, and that didn't come easily for me, which is why I had to use the energy of the last location time travel occurred in, Kelpie's Close, to aid me with its lingering energy, the surge of power from Llaw's death to return. And of course, jumping as far as five hundred years alone is beyond the most powerful Pillar."

Callum nodded, trying to wrap his head around yet another clause of time travel, when another thought struck him. "But this means that Klara is not the only remaining Pillar!"

"Two of ten of us, still alive," Thomas said bitterly. "I guess I should be grateful to Arianrhod for that, at least, but I never asked to be her damn vessel in the first place. And the moment Llaw was dead, she abandoned me. I haven't been able to use my time powers since."

Callum's mind was racing. If the goddess had revoked Klara's powers as well, that meant that if Callum hadn't made his second bargain with the bean-nighe, Callum never would have seen her again. The thought made his blood run cold.

And now Klara had no way to return home again, not unless she made a sinister trade with one of the gods' magical creatures. Callum thought despairingly of his own dealings with the bean-nighe, of her duplicity. There had to be another way.

"So you can see the problem we faced," Thomas was saying. "The first thing we did was to find some clothes. A girl in strange clothing draws too much attention, especially one as lovely as she."

Callum looked at Thomas sharply. This was the second time he'd commented on Klara's beauty, but then again, how could any man fail to be moved by it? "It seems you know my Klara well."

"Never fear, Callum, she speaks only of you," Thomas said with a wink. "Her heart will not be won by another. I only wish that we'd discovered you were alive before she was taken."

If wishing could make things so, Callum thought, many things would be different. "How did you know I was here? How did you find me?" Another thought struck him. "And how did you get away from the mercenaries?"

"You know me, old lad," Thomas said. "I woke tied up in a shed with a drunk guard sitting at the door. I told him I had to piss, and the moment he loosened my bonds, I rang his bells but good."

Callum could imagine the hapless guard thinking he was

dealing with some skinny, helpless gadgie. He probably had a hell of a lump on his head.

"I went to see everyone I could think of, but no one knew where Klara had been taken. But I did hear a rumor that a man fitting your description had been arrested in Kelpie's Close. And since no man has eyes like yours, well, I had to go to the jail to see if it was you. But when I got there, they told me you'd been taken to Castle Udne." He looked around the room with a broad grin. "I was expecting to find you chained up in the cellar. My plan had been to wait until dark and sneak in, but the laird has guards posted everywhere."

"I know. He's terribly afraid of thieves."

"And so I decided to make up a story and take my chances. I told the maid who answered the door that I was your best friend and that I had evidence that would prove you weren't guilty, but she didn't have any idea what I was talking about. She said the only young man in the house was the laird's long-lost son, who'd only just come home. And then I talked her into sending me upstairs—"

"What would you have done if it wasn't me?" Callum asked, astounded as always at Thomas's daring. "And for that matter, what was this 'evidence' you claimed to have?"

"How could I have evidence if I didn't even know what crime you committed?" Thomas laughed. "If anything had gone wrong, I was pretty sure I could outrun a sleepy maid and a fat old laird, and I already knew where all the guards were posted."

Callum shook his head. "Thank you, I guess—but you could have been caught and sent to the same jail."

Thomas gave a cocky smile. "I'd never let that happen."

"Thomas, you dolt, you used to let that happen all the time. How much coin have I coughed up to get you out?" Still, Callum felt oddly reassured by Thomas's familiar bravado. "But back up. Tell me everything from when you first saw Klara."

The series of events that Thomas described was nothing short of shocking: searching for shelter on the grounds of Kingshill Manor where Klara thought they would be safe, only to find themselves invading the headquarters of a ring of thieves, who pursued them past the edge of Rosemere and into the Elder Forest on horses that Klara stole from the stable. ("Though since she is descended of Westwoods, the horses were hers to take, were they not?" Thomas interrupted himself to muse.) They might have outrun the thieves who'd taken chase had not the band of mercenaries, mistaking Klara for a noblewoman due to her opulent dress, waylaid them and spirited her away.

"Still got a bit of a goose egg from when they knocked me out," Thomas said ruefully, rubbing the back of his head. "Luckily, before I gave that guard something to remember me by, I convinced him to tell me where Klara was taken. We can go at first light and get her back if you are ready to fight."

Callum could only imagine what the "convincing" had entailed. "I would fight anyone for her. I have already made a deal with a devil to get here, a fight would be a welcome change."

Thomas quirked his brow. "What do you mean by 'deal with a devil'?"

Callum winced, thinking of the bargain he had struck which in hindsight, wasn't much of a bargain at all. But he did it, not for himself, but for Klara. "I made a bargain with the bean-nighe, a trickster hag. She granted me my wish to be sent through time back to Klara. And in return…I would forfeit ten years of my lifespan and be stuck here, in 1568."

Thomas blew out a whistle. "That is something…quite extraordinary. But also stupid."

Callum shrugged. "I'd do anything for her. She's worth it." Callum shifted slightly. "How can you know she is still there?" Callum said, swaying the conversation back to something they still had within his control.

"The guard told me that they work for the *olc síth*—the dark fae," Thomas said, growing serious. "If it's true, they'll be waiting for her ransom. The *olc síth* have been kidnapping noble daughters for ages. They're probably feeding her well for now—but if no one comes for her soon, that'll change."

Callum's gut twisted with anxiety. "Where are they holding her? How many of them are there?"

"I see you haven't changed," Thomas said with a smile. "Ready to fight all the harder when we are outmatched. There is an old keep with a peel tower a few miles from the southwestern border of the forest. One of the dark fae conceals it with enchantment. He has a dozen men from the village working for him." The smile slipped. "Callum, it is the same man who Master Brice buys boys from."

His stomach twisted harder. "How will we breach it?"

"How am I to know? That's a problem for tomorrow, old friend," Thomas said. "Can we sneak out before the household is awake?"

Callum heard movement in the hall, the staff beginning their day hours before their master would emerge from his chamber. "I think we can do better than that."

Callum opened the door and found a servant carrying a load of firewood in the hall.

"When the laird is ready for his breakfast, please summon me at once," he said, trying to inject confidence into his voice. "Please ask the maid to set an extra place at the table, as my friend will be joining us. And—" Callum cleared his throat. It felt so strange to be giving orders; he could not think of another time in his life that he had done so. "And if you would be so kind, my friend is in need of clothes, as he was waylaid on his journey and robbed. Could that be arranged?"

"Of course, my lord," the servant said, bowing. "I will have them sent at once."

Waiting for breakfast while Thomas leafed through every item in the bedroom, Callum's thoughts were consumed with the return of both Klara and Thomas, the deaths they'd barely avoided, and the revelation that he was not the impoverished orphan he'd always believed himself to be. All of it seemed impossible—and yet the thick carpets he paced were real, the ornate iron sconces on the wall, the splendid clothes he'd been given to wear.

And Thomas was also real, exclaiming over his new clothes, his tousled hair falling across his fine features to make him look impish—and that made up for nearly all the suffering Callum had endured to bring him to this point.

Nearly losing Klara was a devastation from which he would never recover.

Thomas dug his elbow into Callum's side as they entered the grand dining hall. Three places had been set at the same end of the long table, where his father sat studying a ledger.

At their approach, the laird got to his feet, a stiff smile on his face. Yesterday he had made it clear that he wished to control the news of Callum's arrival, and he was obviously displeased to discover a stranger in his home. "Good morning, son. And who is this?"

"This is Thomas Buchan," Callum said, nervously delivering the lie Thomas had come up with. "His father owns many buildings in town."

"I help him manage them, my lord," Thomas said with a bow. "I met young Callum when he managed to destroy most of a tavern we own."

"Thomas exaggerates, Father," Callum said, reddening.

"Aye, well, I suppose it was the patrons who did the damage," Thomas conceded, "but it was Callum's match they were brawling over. Yet he was so earnest in his apologies, I forgave him and invited him to our estate, where he charmed my entire family. We've been best friends ever since."

The laird relaxed slightly at the mention of the fictional estate. Thomas had always done a spot-on impression of the wealthiest patrons, mimicking their mannerisms and way of speaking, and the fine clothes supplied by the staff only strengthened the impression. The long hot bath and a fresh shave didn't hurt, either.

"I hope it's all right, Father," Callum said. "I knew Thomas would be worried when I went missing, so I asked one of the staff to let him know I was all right."

"I am known for my discretion, my lord," Thomas added. "One cannot manage a portfolio the size of my father's without knowing when to hold one's tongue. And the truth is, I'm looking forward to being able to stop pretending that Callum is a distant cousin when we're in public."

The laird gaped. "Are you telling me, young man, that you've been pretending Callum was highborn all along?"

"I am guilty, my lord."

The laird laughed. "Well then, I would suggest we toast to Callum's debut if it were not a bit too early to break out the spirits."

Callum shifted uncomfortably at their banter. He would never be able to do what Thomas did, slipping in and out of identities as easily as entering a room. But judging from his father's smile, Thomas was skilled enough for both of them.

"Thomas had news for me, Father," he blurted. "He knows where Klara is. Mercenaries are holding her in a peel tower."

"Mercenaries?" The laird's smile vanished.

"Indeed, a plague upon those who would attack the highest reaches of our society," Thomas said with a perfect imitation of the contempt shown him and Callum in the streets. "It does not seem to enter their small minds that we are also the ones who keep order and provide honest work so that our people can eat."

"They took an eleven-year-old girl from the grounds of a Culross manor only last month," the laird said faintly. "They cut off her hair and sent it to her father as a threat."

Thomas shook his head in sympathetic disgust. "The good news," he said, "is that since several days have passed with no word from Klara's family, they've lowered the ransom to a paltry sum. But if someone doesn't come for her soon, she'll be sold into service along with the rest of the peasant children…or worse."

"And you say she has no family," the laird mused. "Other than the Westwoods."

"It is true," Callum lied. "She had no brothers or sisters, and the only other living relatives moved to France years ago."

He could see the calculation the laird was making—an opportunity to strengthen ties with a prominent local family at a relatively low cost, versus the danger involved.

"We will set out at once," he said decisively. "I will bring my best men. For the return of my son's beloved, no price is too high."

CHAPTER TWENTY-ONE

CALLUM

It took some time for the laird's men to make the preparations for the journey. The laird insisted on taking a carriage so that Klara could travel in comfort, though Callum suspected that his own comfort was also on his father's mind. The "friend"—Thomas wouldn't say who it was—who'd alerted him to Klara's fate had drawn a detailed map to the keep and estimated that it was half a day's ride, so they would be arriving at night—something Callum feared would work against them should they meet resistance. But he was afraid to mention it lest it dissuade his father from helping.

Besides, what Thomas had said was true—as the judge in all local criminal matters, the laird employed an abundance of guards; and the four he chose to accompany them were surefooted, strong, and well armed.

Thomas disappeared after breakfast and did not return until the horses had been saddled and brought out and the carriage readied. While he was gone, Callum found a simple scabbard for the sword, and wrapped its delicate jeweled pommel and hilt in thick, common leather. For some reason, he hadn't been able to bring himself to tell anyone about the blade, and all he knew was that he trusted no one with so powerful an enchanted weapon. He took the job of disguising it seriously and slowly, and before he knew it, hours had passed before Thomas returned.

"Where were you?" Callum asked him.

"Just needed a couple things in town," Thomas said shortly. His jovial mood seemed to have vanished, replaced with a brooding silence that reminded Callum of the weeks leading up to his near-death at Llaw's hands. During that time, Thomas had vanished for hours and even days at a time, and talked of death and strange and violent visions. He prayed that whatever had plagued Thomas then had not returned.

But before he could figure out how to ask Thomas about it, the driver took his seat and the laird got into his carriage. The lead guard signaled the two of them to ride ahead, while the remaining men took up the rear.

Callum waited until they had entered the Elder Forest to bring the subject up again.

"I cannae tell you how much joy it brings me that you and Klara are both alive," he began carefully.

"And you're a wealthy man now, don't forget."

There was a familiar edge to Thomas's voice, a sullen note

that crept in whenever he felt passed over by good fortune. Callum considered and abandoned half a dozen things to say before he concluded it would be best to simply come out with it.

"In the weeks before the night you fought Llaw, you disappeared a lot, Thomas. It was clear that something was bothering you. You were not yourself—and now I know it was because of the terrible duty Arianrhod had given you."

Thomas shot him a look, but said nothing.

"But Llaw is dead now, and you are free of the goddess. You and Klara didnae ask to be Pillars, true, but Arianrhod will not interfere again as long as you both live. And yet... Thomas, I fear it is happening again, whatever burdened your heart and mind before."

"Just because I did an errand in town?" Thomas snapped, but then he seemed to reconsider. "Callum...I'm sorry. You're right—my temper has got the best of me lately."

"But you never had a temper at all!" Callum blurted. "Until the goddess appeared to you, there was none more carefree than you. All the years you looked after me, and you a boy only a few years older, you never lost your patience with me."

A change came over Thomas. His shoulders sagged, and his expression softened, and there was a hollowness in his blue eyes at contrast with the tense anger Callum had glimpsed and also the spirited mischief that had always been there before. "But we are not boys any longer. And I am a fighter, Callum, and a killer."

Callum frowned. There had been deaths in the ring—too many, the product of cheating by lawless managers—but never at his or Thomas's hands. "You never took the life of any man."

Thomas looked at him directly and the bleakness in his eyes was like nothing Callum had ever seen. It chilled him to the bone. "You do not know what I have done."

"But—"

"I've seen things. The worlds—their balance is fragile, just like Arianrhod said. And there is no such thing as pure goodness. The gods are weak. I don't believe in good and evil anymore. Only in survival."

As he spoke, his haunted expression was replaced by one of assessment and calculation. He reached out to lay a hand on Callum's shoulder, their two horses keeping pace side by side. "But why talk of this now? We've a reunion awaiting us, happier times ahead. I'll do better in keeping my moods in check. Agreed?"

"Agreed." But as Thomas spurred his horse to catch up to the others, Callum had a bad feeling that the things his friend was keeping from him were worse than anything he could imagine.

They stopped in the afternoon in a clearing next to a stream. The driver pulled a basket from atop the carriage and distributed the simple meal packed by Mistress Drever, while the horses drank from the stream and rested. The laird was deep in conversation with two of his men, and Thomas brought his plate to sit with Callum on a fallen log.

"Soon you'll be spending your days on boring matters like deeds and escheats," he joked, tilting his head at the laird.

"And once you have a wife, she will keep you running the rest of the time."

"Klara's not like that," Callum said.

"I know," Thomas said, grinning. "I've spent two days and a night with her, remember? Not many women would agree to sleep on a dirt floor—or know how to wield a sword like hers—it was as deadly as it was well made."

Callum ignored the spike of anger he felt at Thomas's words, knowing he meant nothing by them. Moreover, he stiffened at the admiration in Thomas's voice for the sword, all too keenly aware of Llaw's sword disguised on his belt.

"That sword is a beauty, too, practically a work of art," Thomas went on. "She let me take a look—I think I could almost feel the enchantment running underneath my touch."

"I know what you mean," Callum said, trying not to touch or look at the one he carried, for fear of giving himself away, even to his best friend. "When I held it, I felt a kind of power contained in it. When I fought the beast with that sword, it was almost as if it had a mind of its own. And its connection to Klara is more powerful still—I've seen it leap from the ground into her hand."

"You fought with her sword?" Thomas said sharply. "But—how is that possible? I mean…Klara told me it was created for her ancestor, and handed down by many generations of her family since. Surely its powers favor only them…?"

Callum frowned. He'd wondered that himself, at the time. "Klara's Grams never said that it defied others. Though now that I think of it, she never came out and said it was enchanted, either."

"Maybe Klara did something to allow you to use it,"

Thomas pressed. “Some spell she uttered? Maybe when you weren’t watching?”

“I do not know, brother,” Callum said, though Klara would never have done such a thing without telling him. “All I care about is getting Klara back and putting all of this behind us. After that, she can toss the damn sword into the Firth of Forth for all I care.”

“You’d give up your power so easily?” Thomas pushed. “And Klara hers?”

“Yes.” Though when Callum thought about it, the answer wasn’t quite as clear. During his last days with Klara, the powers that Arianrhod had conferred on her were changing, becoming her own, mingling with those that had always been within her. She was more sure of herself—and of her purpose.

And so was he. Before he’d nearly died, Callum had assumed that he would spend his life protecting the woman he loved. He’d come to that conclusion after being tested by the struggle to defend both Klara and the future of the worlds.

But once the knowledge of his fae blood set in, Callum had begun to sense it moving within him, inseparable from his reason and even his heart…and now his purpose was shifting, too. Whether his Sight would continue to grow or not, he could no longer deny his fae ancestry, and he could not begin to imagine how it might affect his future.

“Then you’re a better man than most,” Thomas said, bringing him back to their discussion of abilities. “Men hunger for power—it has been so since the worlds were made.”

Before Callum could respond, the laird came striding toward them, holding the map in his hand. “I believe this clearing is roughly the halfway point,” he said. “From here it should be another two hours' ride to the keep. I will go alone to fetch Klara, but two of my men will ride behind in case there is any trouble."

Callum jumped to his feet. "But, Father—"

"I know you're anxious to see the lass again," the laird said mildly. "But since I will be posing as a member of Klara's family, it will not do for a large party to accompany me. In matters of kidnapping, I believe it is the common practice to demand that the person bringing the ransom come alone."

"He's right," Thomas said. "The important thing is to remove her from the keep. Once she is free, your reunion will be all the sweeter."

Callum saw the wisdom of their argument—but the waiting would be torment. "Could I not accompany you further? Surely, if we waited a few furlongs away—"

"But why take the chance?" The laird exchanged an indulgent look with Thomas. "Our lad appears to have caught the lovesickness," he quipped, and they both laughed.

Callum felt his face redden. In that moment Thomas and his father looked like a couple of members of the peerage sharing a joke. The sight disturbed Callum in a way he couldn't name.

"I'll keep him entertained while you're gone, milord," Thomas promised.

But as soon as the laird's carriage started down the road again, Thomas claimed to need to take a piss and disappeared into the woods, and did not return.

CHAPTER TWENTY-TWO

KLARA

Klara woke early, the faint light of dawn beginning to seep through the gaps in the drapes at the windows. Despite the hour, she felt restored—as if the deep, dreamless sleep she'd fallen into had scoured away the horror and confusion of the night before, leaving behind clarity and determination.

Klara knew what she must do. Thomas had sacrificed everything, even the comfort of confiding in his truest friend, to try to stop a demigod bent on destroying the world. Callum had lost his life while trying to protect her. Anne had taken a great risk to help her. Klara felt humbled by their courage and sacrifice.

Was *she* courageous? A month ago, Klara would probably have answered "not particularly." But she would have been wrong. Life had tested her by taking her mother much too young, by sending her to a new life across the oceans while she was still grieving the old one. As a result Klara had endured times of pain and exhaustion and, some days, despair.

But in the last few weeks she'd literally faced a demon from hell—or at least, from the Underworld—as well as fighting a demigod to the death and joining forces with Thomas against unknown evil. And despite all of that, the fate of the worlds still hung in the balance, and the goddess's powers were lost. As long as those powers were out there, they could fall into the hands of someone as dangerous as Llaw again.

Klara had to try again—especially now that Thomas's fate was on the line. An image of him came into her mind—his mischievous grin, those gorgeous blue eyes looking so deeply into hers—and she felt a stirring of that warmth again. And once again, she tried to push it away—but it wasn't easy.

How could she be attracted to another man so soon after she lost Callum? Klara felt almost disgusted with herself—but she knew the key to controlling her feelings was to understand them. And she wouldn't be the first person it ever happened to. In fact many of her favorite novels and television series featured love triangles.

There was something compelling about the contrast. She almost felt like Elena in *The Vampire Diaries*, but minus the vampires. Elena first fell in love with Stephen, the sweet brother with a dark past. Then in a turn of fate, she ends up with his dark and mysterious brother, Damon.

Callum and Thomas had nearly identical pasts—abandoned by their families, raised in terrible conditions to fight—but in every other way they were different. Callum was serious, sensitive, a deep thinker; Thomas was impulsive, bold, attracted to excitement. Callum was tall and broad, with a body like a damn marble sculpture, whereas Thomas was average height with the lithe grace and strength of a dancer. Callum had classic good looks, like a 1950s movie star. Thomas wasn't as handsome, but everything about his features was remarkable: the startling blue of his eyes, the bright russet of his hair, the sensual shape of his lips.

And danger bred strong emotions, Klara reminded herself. There was a reason why Elena ended up with Damon in the end. If it weren't for the multiple seasons' worth of character development on his part and the death-defying plots she was thrown into, they would've never fallen for each other.

There's something about danger that strangely brings people together in such a powerful way, even romantic, if the shoe fits. There's no first dates or awkward conversations… just survival. Love comes easily when you have formed the bond forged from fire. If she'd met Callum or Thomas at the gym rather than in the midst of a threat to her very existence, things would never have felt so intense or moved so fast.

Are you sure about that? Her mother's voice, along with such a clear memory of her gentle smile, the soft lines around her eyes.

No, she wasn't sure. And it didn't matter, because Klara had a lot more important things to do than sit around mooning over her love life.

She threw back the covers and got out of bed, drawing the drapes to fill the tower room with the soft light of early morning. The sky was an unblemished cerulean, scoured clean by the storm that had passed through. Klara went through the series of stretches she'd learned in a yoga class she'd taken back in New York, kneading her muscles and working out a few aches from her long workout the day before. It felt good to focus on the physical, to listen to her body's needs and answer them, the only thing that was currently in Klara's control.

When she was finished, she dressed, made up the bed, and used the time until breakfast arrived to think through the challenges facing her. Presumably the mysterious master of the keep was learning that this kidnapped "lady" had no wealthy family to bilk, indeed no past at all. And that was likely to piss him off mightily.

Klara wasn't afraid to be moved to more humble quarters. The problem was her sword—specifically, how she was going to manage to take it with her and keep it safe. She couldn't exactly use the mop trick again.

She was still thinking through this problem when Mrs. Fitchet arrived, looking as though she hadn't slept at all. The lines on her face were etched into sour resentment, and she didn't bother with a greeting as she slapped down a tray of cold meat and bread.

Klara had been standing at the window, gazing down at the spot where Aion had held his dying fiancée in his arms. After a night of lashing rain, the lake was roiled and brown, the road a slick of mud. With no visible evidence of what had taken place, Klara could almost imagine that it had all been a bad dream.

"Your maid died last night," Mrs. Fitchet said shortly, "as ye very well know since you're a little spy, aren't ye?"

Klara's eyebrows shot up. "I was not *spying*—"

"*I* wouldn't have taken his filthy money," Mrs. Fitchet plowed on. "Imagine paying off the bond of a tramp like that who doesn't know her place. The *idea* of it."

Since Klara wasn't supposed to know about Anne's secret betrothment, she kept silent, waiting for Mrs. Fitchet to run out of steam; after a few more muttered curses and jabs about masters who couldn't be bothered to keep their own house in order, she finally seemed to remember what she'd come for.

"Not that the likes of *you* would care. The laird's coming to fetch ye this morning. Better hope he brought a bucket full of coin since the master's comin' to do the deal himself."

"The…laird?" Klara asked, trying to hide her confusion.

"Laird Johnstone. Your father, eh? Your uncle? Or maybe your family sold you to the highest bidder when they couldn't come up with the coin? That's a pretty thought, innit, girlie—maybe *you'll* be the one getting married tonight to an old man wi' no teeth left in his mouth."

"Why do you hate me?" Klara blurted, genuinely curious—and impetuous as always. As usual, she regretted it immediately.

The look Mrs. Fitchet gave her could peel paint from the walls. "Fix your hair," she hissed. "You look like a little savage."

The older woman deliberately bumped the tray as she left, spilling the pot of tea.

As soon as the door closed behind her, Klara pulled the

sword from the bed, looking around wildly for a solution and finding none. But the hilt seemed to mold to her hand, the metal warm and faintly humming, and she gave in to the strange urge to follow its lead. She went through an abbreviated version of the practice routine Callum had taught her, but this time, the sword seemed to guide her, twitching in her hand to make small adjustments: a shoulder pulled back, a foot moved forward, a slightly deeper bend to the knee.

Klara had worked up a sweat when she heard footsteps coming up the stairs. She jammed the sword back in its hiding place and hastily wiped her face. Too late, she remembered her hair, which she'd gathered into a loose ponytail, and the dress that she'd chosen because it barely reached past her knees yet was large enough in the bodice to allow greater freedom of movement.

Whoever the laird was, Klara hoped he was rich enough to spring her, shortsighted enough not to notice her disheveled state…and dumb or careless enough to let her escape.

She stood with her hands clasped and her head bowed modestly, as Mrs. Fitchet led three men into the room. Klara snuck a look and decided the thin, tall man with the spotless white waistcoat must be the laird.

He looked neither stupid nor careless. His thin eyebrows were lowered over dark eyes, his mouth a flat line. The men accompanying him stood a respectful distance behind him.

"Lady Klara," he said gravely.

Klara did her best to curtsy, a move she'd never attempted before—and was pretty sure she botched it. "My lord," she mumbled.

Laird Johnstone snapped his fingers and one of his men stepped forward. He turned to Mrs. Fitchet. "Her things?"

"I can send along any of the gowns the lady wishes, after they've been cleaned, of course," she said in a tone of deference.

Klara thought fast. If the laird was expecting the spoiled, rude girl Mrs. Fitchet had surely described, she needed to stay in character. "Keep your filthy rags," she sniped.

The laird lifted an eyebrow, but seemed more intrigued than annoyed.

"I will be bringing my sword, of course." Klara tried to sound nonchalant as she reached under the tick. As soon as she touched the metal, her mind seemed to clear, her spine to straighten. "I do hope you haven't misplaced the scabbard, Mrs. Fitchet, as it was custom made and will be very expensive to replace."

The older woman's face blanched; obviously, she had no idea what Klara was talking about. Klara rolled her eyes and said to the laird, "Whatever you're paying her, be sure to deduct the cost."

The laird made a sound that could have been a snort or a laugh, and produced a small cloth bag from his jacket. He shook out some coins, holding Klara's gaze, and when she gave a faint shake of her head, slipped a couple back into the bag. He handed the rest to Mrs. Fitchet. "You'll let Malabron know he should take better care with his guests," he said imperiously.

Malabron. Klara tried not to react, but the knowledge that the "master" was one and the same as the dark fae from the faerie market added yet more confusion. She would have to wait until later to figure that out, as the laird was offering his arm.

"Then let us be off."

For the first time, Klara wished she'd taken the etiquette classes offered by her school back in New York. For all the times she'd read the phrase "she took his arm" in the historical romances left behind by past manor guests, she had no idea how it was done.

Klara crossed her fingers and slid her hand through the laird's elbow. It must have been the right move, because the others held several paces back as the laird led her down the stairs, through the galley and out to a waiting carriage. This one was much fancier than the one Aion arrived in, with ornate iron filigree and a silk-lined cabin.

The laird helped her in and took the seat opposite while one of the men stepped up into the driver's seat and the other crammed in next to the laird. The carriage began to move, and Klara peered out the window to get her first look at the tower she'd been held in. Unlike the sumptuous tower room, it was utterly plain, with unadorned battlements, patched mortar, and a scattering of small rectangular windows. The grounds were equally unremarkable, the gardens long since overgrown and choked with weeds.

"You're well shut of that place, I'm sure," the laird said.

"Thank you for rescuing me," Klara said. "May I ask… why?"

The laird studied her for a moment, considering. "If you'll grant me the indulgence…you'll know soon enough."

Well. That wasn't exactly helpful, and patience wasn't high on Klara's list of attributes. She lapsed into silence, just hoping what was to come would be a welcomed break. But maybe that was too much to hope for.

CHAPTER TWENTY-THREE

KLARA

Klara hadn't meant to fall asleep, not in a small, enclosed space with a stranger who wouldn't explain his motivations and his hulking, silent bodyguard. But the steady, rocking motion of the carriage eventually sent her drifting into a doze.

She dreamed she stood in the stark beauty of the Ring of Brodgar's concentric earthen rings and towering stones at the water's edge, where a torrential rain pelted the stones and slashed the muddy earth as though it was trying to destroy the sacred circle that had stood for centuries.

There was a sudden commotion behind her, the sounds of snarling and howling and tearing, and Klara spun to see Callum being set upon by hellhounds, too many to fend off. They snapped and snarled and attacked his flesh with their ugly yellow fangs as Callum pitched forward, too weak even to break his fall.

Klara screamed and ran into their midst, slashing with her sword. It felt as though she was moving *between* the pelting drops of angry rain as she spun and dodged with a new grace and power that seemed to come from the sword itself, hacking the beasts' legs and slicing their throats until they lay unmoving, their blood seeping into the mud.

Klara threw herself to the ground and pulled Callum's torn and bloodied body into her arms, screaming his name. His eyes flickered once and she would have sworn he tried to say her name…and then the light left his eyes.

As Klara watched in horror, Callum's limp body blurred and turned to a dense mist that drifted toward the sky, leaving her arms as empty as her heart. She wailed and beat the blood-drenched ground with her fists. And then, between the stones rising above her, she saw dark, intelligent eyes peering through the rain and fog.

A stag walked into the clearing. From his proud bearing and splendid antlers Klara knew it was Cernunnos, appearing before her in the form of his familiar.

"He's gone," she cried, and the stag lowered his head as though he, too, were grieving, and rested his chin on her shoulder. Klara touched the soft brown fur of his neck—

—and was suddenly hurtling through a white, whirling tunnel of fog. When the spinning stopped and the mist cleared, she was standing in the clearing where she had first encountered the Stag God, in the Elder Forest near the Rosemere faerie circle.

He stood before her in his human form, watching her sadly.

Klara remembered Arianrhod's warning. *Trust no one—not even Cernunnos.*

But she had no way of knowing if Arianrhod herself could be trusted. And besides, Klara knew she must be dreaming, because Callum was already dead—and because Cernunnos had appeared this way, through her dreams, once before.

She took a step backward, her body tensed, her mind whirling. Cernunnos tilted his head, his long, curly chestnut hair cascading around his shoulders. He was as fine a human specimen as a stag, but of course he was also neither.

Arianrhod had spoken of rules that governed the forms and places in which she could appear, but those rules didn't seem to apply to Cernunnos, who seemed to follow his own whims and purposes.

Klara wanted to ask him so many things—but he never answered her questions directly, speaking in riddles and contradictions and half-truths. Still, there had to be a reason he had appeared to her once again, and she had to try.

She wiped her eyes and tried to order her thoughts. "Why are you here? Am I dreaming again?"

"You called me, Klara."

So typical of Cernunnos not to answer the question. "I did *not*," Klara snapped. "You and Arianrhod always say that, but—"

"Who were you thinking about when you watched the servant girl die?"

Klara thought fast, wondering how he could have known that. But then again, the fae living beneath the earth in enchanted mounds—the *daoine síth*—were part of Cernunnos's domain.

"I have told you before that I cannot give you the answers you want," Cernunnos said gently. "But know that no god or fae is entirely good or evil. Just as humans can love deeply and act cruelly, all of us are governed by our conflicting desires and motivations."

His eyes burned into hers, the air around him shimmering. "The *olc síth*—those you know as the dark fae—they left the mounds and spurned their brethren when they aspired to powers that were not meant for them."

"They want to be like the gods."

Cernunnos shook his head. "There are those more powerful even than me and my brothers and sisters. Because we were not the beginning, Klara."

Klara's temples began to ache as they always did in the face of Cernunnos's riddles. "What are you trying to tell me? *Who's* more powerful than gods?"

"And when the *olc síth* tricked and traded and stole," the Stag God continued, ignoring her question, "the powers became distorted, and the *olc síth* themselves were changed in ways that could not be undone. Their greed became voracious; nothing could satisfy their need. They could no longer live in community—they could barely stand each other's company. They took to living in ruins and abandoned buildings where they hoarded what they stole. They crave bright, shiny things—jewels, gold, silk and the like—and though they can amass huge stores of treasure, they are never sated.

"Eventually, one of the *olc síth* acquired a vast building to house his spoils, and a market was established, where magical creatures and fae could come to trade. It is usually invisible to humans—which I believe you already know."

"I went there," Klara affirmed. "I traded with Malabron for a dress. But he's the one who…"

But the coincidence that had seemed so astonishing—that Aion's fiancée would be indirectly employed by Malabron—suddenly seemed much less surprising. If what Cernunnos said was true, and Malabron routinely traded in the fae market, it would only be natural for Aion to know him. The staff of the keep had to come to town for supplies, which meant Anne could have met Aion while buying onions or rags or any number of things.

"The Earth is complicated, and astonishingly simple. I can give you this, Klara," he said. "I did as you asked—Callum lives. Furthermore, know that Callum is not wholly of your world."

Callum lives. She felt his words like a heartbeat, and all the fight and anger fell from her shoulders like feathers.

"There is much you do not know about Arianrhod, and little that I can tell you. When the worlds diverged, we gods were united as never before to preserve the balance. Only Arianrhod chose to go her separate way. When our sister strayed, we were divided on what to do, but together with our creators, decided on just consequences. Limits, you might say, designed to protect our sister from experiencing the consequences of another rash act."

"The Pillars."

Cernunnos nodded. "The Pillars, not of her design, but ours. After settling on Arianrhod's punishment, most of us considered the matter finished. The Creators weren't done, though. They gave objects of great power to the fae and humans—to thwart Arhianrhod's plans and steal a god's power, but cannot harm the descendants of the first to own them.

"You wield the mortal sword, Klara, given to the first laird of Kingshill Manor and handed down through your family. Every generation of fae king since the first has protected the sword of their race until, several months ago, it was stolen and corrupted."

"But I killed Llaw with this sword. Where did his powers go?"

Cernunnos watched her steadily, but did not reply. The cylinder of light was starting to spin around them again, faster and faster. Cernunnos's final words to her were almost lost in the rushing roar of the blinding white cyclone.

"Remember that none of us is entirely as we seem."

Klara felt the thundering rush that signaled her return to her own realm, and her body sagged against the cushions, exhausted by the expenditure of energy these episodes seemed to require. The carriage still rocked steadily, she hadn't moved from her spot, and there was no sign that Cernunnos had ever appeared.

But the laird was watching her with great interest, a calculating look in his small, sharp eyes.

CHAPTER TWENTY-FOUR

KLARA

"Just a little longer now," the laird said, "and you shall have your surprise."

Klara's head shot up with a jolt. The laird's words had unleashed a strange sensation within her, his voice becoming hollow and distorted, like a flashback in a movie. It resembled the pull she'd felt in recent moments of danger, but this time it guided her toward a blurring darkness.

Klara closed her eyes and gave in to it, and in place of her vision her mind's screen burst into a million tiny pinpoints of light that arranged themselves into the night sky, Corona Borealis—Arianrhod's constellation—at the center. Then that dissolved and the stars rearranged themselves again, creating the outline of a man.

The pull became stronger, the rushing in her blood taking on a familiar urgency, the way it always did in Callum's presence.

He's here.

She tried to open her eyes, but the invisible force had her in his grip, immobilizing her, stealing her voice. Callum was near, she was as sure of it as she was sure of anything. *Callum lives*, Cernunnos had said. But how could that be? She'd seen him gored and tossed like a rag by the beast, slammed down onto the rocky earth with the force of a freeway pileup, five hundred years in the future. Her heart told her that he'd lived, and that was miracle enough. But even if it was true, he would still be grievously injured. And what would he be doing here, in the remote reaches of the wood?

A silent scream burst forth from the very core of her. "Callum," she whimpered, and the force released her.

He's here.

Klara was already opening the carriage door, the laird shouting for her to stop. She would not stop. Callum was waiting. She stumbled in the darkness and nearly fell, and there was a shout in the distance, the light of a torch—

—and Klara was running, her footfalls barely seeming to land in the weeds and rutted earth as the pull became so strong that it was all she could feel.

"Klara!"

There he was, standing in the road and shouting her name, and if he was an apparition then she would become one too, the two of them together between worlds if that was how it must be.

But then she was lifted into the air by arms as warm and

solid and strong as any she'd ever known and swung around in a joyous circle. Callum was saying her name, over and over, and then his lips met hers and her doubts disintegrated and there was only the two of them, laughing and crying at once.

The kiss was one of joy and relief and claiming, washing away the regrets of the past and fears for the future and leaving only this one perfect moment. The pull receded, giving way to a feeling of rightness that Klara had missed with every beat of her heart since they were last together.

When they finally pulled back from the kiss, Klara's cheeks were wet with tears. Callum brushed them away gently with his thumb, his pale heterochromic eyes seeing her, all of her. "Klara," he whispered in a voice rife with emotion, "I thought I'd lost ye. Never leave me again. Never."

Klara pressed her face to his chest to feel his strong heartbeat and breathe in his scent, holding him so tightly it was a wonder he could breathe. "Don't go picking fights with beasts, then," she murmured, "and I'll do my best not to get kidnapped again."

Callum's laugh rumbled in his chest, and Klara wanted to stay there like that, wrapped in each other's arms, for all of eternity—or at least a few more minutes. But over Callum's shoulder she could see three men on horseback silhouetted against the torchlight across a grassy clearing, and the laird was standing a few paces away, clearing his throat.

Reluctantly, she slipped out of Callum's arms and turned to face the laird. "I have to hand it to you," she said. "When you showed up with my ransom, I figured I was headed from the frying pan into the fire. But this was a bit of a surprise."

The laird gave a slight bow, a pleased smile on his face.

"You and my son make a handsome couple, Lady Klara."

What?

Klara whipped around to face Callum, trying to make sense of the laird's words. "What is he talking about, Callum?"

Suddenly he looked slightly uncomfortable, holding tightly to Klara's hand and bending to speak quietly into her ear. "I'll explain everything when we get to the castle."

"The *castle*?" Klara pulled back in shock. Every new turn of events seemed even more surreal than the last—and they weren't even in the grip of a scheming goddess anymore. Supposedly. "What castle? Callum, what's going on? And what does he mean by calling you his son?"

She hadn't bothered to keep her voice down, and the laird jammed his hands in his pockets and pretended to be fascinated by the sight of a perfectly ordinary meadow as he ambled toward the other men. The fact that she hadn't pissed him off by speaking so boldly only added to her confusion.

"I couldn't believe it myself," Callum said. "So much has happened, Klara—I dinnae even know where to start. The story he tells…and I've seen Cernunnos. He took me to the mound and—but there will be time to talk about all of that. All that matters now is that we are together, and soon we will be safe at the castle where we will have a warm bed and a good meal."

"But I don't understand why you didn't just come for me yourself," Klara said. "Why bring all these men? Was it just the money?"

Callum looked pained, and Klara remembered too late that he was embarrassed by his poverty. "My father offered…"

"But he's a *stranger*," Klara protested. Something about his manner unnerved her, and she wasn't about to believe his story without proof. "Can't we go our own way now? I don't mind walking."

"But it's not just the laird," Callum said, looking toward the other men—and suddenly tensing. "Where did he..."

Then he was jogging toward them, pulling Klara along with him. She had to pick up her skirts to avoid tripping on them.

"Father, where has Thomas gone?" he asked urgently.

"Thomas?" Klara echoed, stunned yet again. And sure enough, Thomas chose that moment to emerge from the trees and sauntered toward her with a familiar gait.

Klara whipped around to face Callum, whose shoulders sagged with relief to see Thomas. "Please just tell me what he's doing here and how he fits into all of this."

"He—" Callum shrugged, as if it was all too complicated to begin to comprehend. "It's a long story, but he came to the castle to tell me where you were. He told me everything, how you both ended up in Kelpie's Close after you and he killed Llaw together. How you were set upon at Kingshill Manor and attacked by mercenaries. Klara, since the moment he came to, he's been doing everything he could to get you back."

Klara tried to let Callum's words sink in and discovered that, mixed in with her relief that Thomas was all right was another feeling, one that stirred something dark and dangerous inside her.

Thomas was coming toward them with a broad grin on his face, dressed in clothes as opulent as the laird's, his russet hair in waves around his shoulders. He looked like he belonged on the cover of one of Grams's historical romance novels.

Thomas held her gaze as he gave a mock bow. "You must introduce us properly now, Callum. I am at your service, dear lady."

There was an awkward silence, Klara glancing from Thomas to Callum and back. For his part, Callum seemed to not quite know how to respond to this version of his best friend, dressed like the wealthy men he'd spent a lifetime mocking and fleecing.

Then he seemed to collect himself and put a hand on Thomas's shoulder. "How lucky can a man be?" he said, his voice dense with emotion. "I've the friendship of a man of great courage and pure heart, and the love of the most beautiful lady in all of Scotland."

Thomas's eyes glittered an icy blue before he dragged his gaze away from Klara and his devil-may-care grin resurfaced. "A luckier bastard there never was."

"Thomas," Klara said, holding tight to Callum's hand as if it alone tethered her to the earth. "What happened after I was taken away?"

Thomas shrugged. "The short version is that after I was knocked out, I woke up in a shed with my hands and feet bound. I had to convince the man who was guarding me that I was not in need of his hospitality, and he was kind enough to tell me where you had been taken."

There was something chilling about his insouciance, especially since Klara knew what Thomas was capable of. She didn't want to think about what he'd done to extract the information from the mercenary. "But how did you find Callum?"

"My captor wasn't able to give me directions to the keep,"

he said. "My mistake, I should have asked him before he… became incapacitated. So I was forced to ask around in town to find someone who knew the way—and I heard talk of a thief with an uncanny resemblance to our Callum being held at Udne Castle."

"Udne Castle? But that's—" Klara stopped herself. In her time, the castle had been turned into a quaint museum after the last descendant donated it to the village when she moved to London to be closer to her grandchildren.

"Since you've gotten to know our Tom, you won't be surprised to know that he talked his way into the castle," Callum said fondly. "He jumped on my bed and woke me up. I thought he was a ghost at first."

There was a sharp whistle, and they turned to see the laird waving them over, holding the reins of Callum's horse.

"Lucky you," Thomas said, elbowing Callum in the ribs. "It looks like he's giving you two the carriage."

They walked over together and Thomas swung himself up into the saddle of a sleek roan mare.

"Enjoy yourselves," the laird said grandly, waving off Callum's protests. "It'll do me good to ride with the lads. Besides, soon enough you'll be the center of attention and you won't have any privacy at all."

Klara gave the laird a stiff smile, and dropped it when his back was turned. "What did he mean by that?"

"I—dinna ken," Callum said, but he wouldn't meet her eyes. "But it was kind of him to give us the carriage. We'll be home in a couple of hours."

Home? Klara thought, as he took her hand to help her up into the carriage, but then she remembered her sword.

"Can you get it down?" she asked Callum. "The laird insisted on lashing it on top, but I'd rather have it with me."

Callum retrieved the sword from the baggage hold, his own bulky old sword swinging awkwardly at his hip. As Klara closed her hand around the hilt of hers, she felt its hum of recognition, and immediately the tension began to melt away. It was as though the sword centered her in the present, reminding her that all she could control was this one point in time and how she reacted to it.

In battle, that...force? Klara didn't know how to think about the connection she shared with the centuries-old weapon, but it had saved her life several times over so far by laser-focusing all of her senses. In the moment the dance of her instincts and the sword's powers was a blur she experienced as pure exhilaration, but in each millisecond some recalculation was made, combining physics and her own will to vanquish foes that ought to have been able to overpower her.

But she was not battling now...and yet the sword still guided her, burning away everything but the purest will of her heart. As she gripped the handle with its familiar pattern of gems and gold inlay, she turned to Callum on the cramped bench and cupped his face with one hand.

The driver flicked his crop and the carriage began to move, the laird and his men falling into line ahead and behind, but inside the carriage it was only the two of them.

"I don't understand everything that has happened," Klara said. "And I know that we're probably in for more drama, and we still have to figure out this whole separated-by-centuries thing...but I *love* you, Callum."

Klara paused as a shiver ran through her. The words didn't

come easily, not since she'd lost her mother, not since loving someone started to feel like the greatest risk she could possibly take.

A part of her wanted to take it back, to make a joke or pick a fight. But if the things that had happened to her had taught her nothing else, Klara knew now how truly delicate the balance of life and death truly was, how easily she could lose what she held most precious. As recently as this morning she'd thought she would never have another chance to hold Callum, never get to tell him what was truly in her heart.

She leaned her forehead against his as she whispered the rest. "And I never want to be apart again. Callum…I want to share my life with you."

"Oh, Klara," Callum said, pulling her into his lap and surrounding her in his strong arms.

His lips met hers with such a deep passion, it set fireworks off within her heart. Klara slid her lips against his, the heat of his mouth warm against hers. Her hands bunched in his shirt, pulling him closer to her as his strong hand slid up over the crest of her neck until it met her cheek.

This kiss was a promise.

He pulled away slightly, looking her in the eyes. God, those eyes. She could read them like a book. A book where the only words that filled its pages were those of love.

"You have no idea what that means to me. I—"

Something slammed into the side of the carriage, throwing the two of them against the opposite bench. For a moment it teetered on two wheels, the horses rearing in terror, and then it crashed onto its side. Klara landed on her shoulder, pain ricocheting through her body.

"Klara!" Callum pulled her to him, his face contorted with fear, illuminated by the moonlight pouring through the window that was now above them. "Are you hurt?"

And then a host of jagged shapes seemed to rocket out of the sky as a black cloud as massive as a city bus descended upon them and blanketed them in total darkness.

CHAPTER TWENTY-FIVE

KLARA

Klara's scream was cut short by a ghastly smell of putrification that choked her airways. She felt Callum lift her and shove her through the door of the cab. She crawled along its polished wooden side until she could leap clear of the wheels, which spun lazily as chaos reigned around them.

Callum was right behind her, handing her her sword. "They're coming from the skies!" he shouted amid a blur of great flapping wings. The cloud was thinning and separating into yellow eyes and tarry feathers, and Klara gripped her sword and tensed to meet the next assault.

There were shouts and confusion ahead as the men dismounted and prepared to fight. The driver was frantically trying to calm the pair of terrified horses still hitched to the carriage as the rest, relieved of their riders, galloped into the woods.

The driver had dropped the reins and was working to free the traces when the black cyclone of wings and claws and beaks split into three beasts so ugly that they had to be an abomination against nature. Neither bird nor beast, their garbled shrieks split the air as they hopped and flapped in an attempt to fly that reminded Klara of old footage of the Wright brothers' early failed flights.

The carriage driver tried to run, but the buttons of his coat sleeve caught on the backband of one of the terrified horses. Its bucking splintered the driver's seat and tore it free of the carriage, the horse dragging both it and the driver across the rocky earth, a foamy, terrified froth at its mouth.

One of the beasts careened toward Klara, and Callum threw himself onto her, knocking her to the ground as the creature slashed at them with its long, sharp claws, its beak wide, its breath fetid.

"What *is* that?" Klara asked, rolling onto her feet, her sword at the ready.

"I've no idea," Callum yelled. "Watch its tail!"

The thing made a clumsy circle and changed direction, throwing its head back and screaming. Its great reptilian tail lashed back and forth, sharp bony ridges protruding from the top. Behind its birdlike legs a smaller, vestigial pair dangled, withered things.

It slashed at Callum, who dodged and rolled, its gnarly claws missing his neck by mere inches, but severing the belt of his own scabbard. Undeterred, he picked up a rock and lunged to smash it down on the beast's bony ridged skull.

But the blow barely slowed the thing down, and now it had Callum in its sights.

"Stay back!" Klara yelled, dodging the beast's wings, distracting it with feints and thrusts of her sword as she searched for its vulnerability. A human scream made her blood run cold, but she didn't dare look away. She prayed that Thomas was holding his own.

The beast tilted its head to stare at her with one yellow eye, and gave a powerful lash of its tail. Something hot and wet splashed against her face and when she wiped it with her sleeve, the fabric came away dark with blood.

"Callum!" she screamed—but he was still safely behind her.

"Dinnae look, Klara—"

But it was too late. A dark mass on the ground a few paces away shuddered, and then something rolled away.

The driver's head. The beast's tail had severed it from his body.

Nausea welled as Klara scrabbled backward, falling in her haste. In the distance, one of the beasts lay on its side, slowly turning to black smoke, but the other seemed to be getting the upper hand on the two men still fighting, driving them closer and closer to the edge of a steep drop-off, their swords slowing in the moonlight as they tired.

But Klara could not tire. She had to save herself. She had to save Callum.

"Get his dagger!" she shouted, but Callum was a step ahead of her, pulling the weapon from the dead man's holster. He wasted no time in leaping onto the beast's back and seizing a handful of feathers by the roots to help him hold on. He narrowly missed being sliced open by the lashing tail as he stabbed at the leathery black skin between its shoulders—but try as he might, the dagger couldn't pierce it.

Klara switched strategies, aiming for the pale skin between the beast's legs and chest, the only vulnerable patch she'd found. But it parried each thrust, snapping at her with its beak, coming closer each time.

The eyes. It wasn't so much a voice as a…feeling inside Klara, but she seized on it and focused on the veiny yellow orb staring down at her—and realized that because of the eyes' position in the sides of its skull, the beast could only see her from either side, producing a curiously coy effect as it bobbed and twisted its head.

Klara scrambled backward, watching the thing try to track her as she dipped under its field of vision. It made a lumbering turn, throwing Callum to the ground, and Klara clambered to stay out of its view.

She ducked behind a tree as it raged and bent its head this way and that. Its huge nostrils flared and Klara realized that it was trying to smell her—and it was working.

As the beast lumbered closer and closer, extending its snout to sniff at the base of the tree, Klara gave in to the feeling inside her, letting it guide her.

Wait, wait…now!

Klara shot forward like a line drive straight into center field. The beast opened its beak wide and shrieked, twin black tongues flapping, and Klara plunged the sword straight through its throat and out the other side.

The beast jerked spasmodically and made a sound like water splattering into hot grease. Black, viscous blood coursed from its throat, but as soon as it reached the ground it evaporated in a cloud of gritty black steam. Already the monster was shrinking, dissolving into a dense, dirty mist, but there was no time to watch it disappear.

"Klara!" Callum was limping toward her, a gash on his forehead dripping blood.

"I'm fine!" she yelled. "Help the others!"

Across the flattened, bloodstained grass, only one man remained to fight the final beast.

"It's Thomas!" Callum tore straight for him, slashing at the beast with his dagger, drawing its attention away from Thomas. For his part, Thomas seemed to get a second wind, fighting with renewed vigor with his old friend and sparring partner.

Klara was frozen, her heart stuttering as she watched the two men united in battle, the way they intuited each other's movements and took turns slashing and dipping. Their movements were as elegant as a ballet and as deadly as an avalanche and for the first time Klara understood that Thomas and Callum had learned to fight as one man—not to win in the ring, but to survive the horrors of their life of neglect and poverty and abuse.

"I'm sorry," she whispered, her words stolen by the wind, and she didn't know if she was apologizing to Callum or Thomas or both of them…only that until this moment she didn't understand the crushing weight of their burden.

It was Thomas who delivered the killing blow. Callum leapt in front of the beast, risking its slashing beak and claws to rain down a flurry of blows into its face. None drew blood, but they provided a distraction that allowed Thomas to dive under the beast and jam his knife into its heart, the weapon's narrow blade piercing its flesh where Callum's weapon could not.

The monster's dying wail was weaker than its brother's, half-dead already from Thomas and Callum's relentless assault. In seconds it vanished into a cloud of black dust. Callum pulled Thomas free of the putrid pool of blood and collapsed next to him, their chests heaving.

Klara rushed over and knelt between them, searching for wounds and sagging with relief when she found only cuts and gashes, none of them life-threatening. She sank back and took stock of the battle. All three beasts were dead, but the bodies of two men lay on the ground, the decapitated driver and another whose leg had been nearly torn off, his mouth a frozen rictus of horror.

Callum pulled Klara into his arms, touching her face gently as if reassuring himself.

"That's going to leave a scar," she said, attempting a smile as she carefully brushed his hair away from the long gash in his face. Callum touched the wound and seemed surprised that his fingers came away bloody.

"I didnae even feel it." He turned to Thomas, who'd crawled to a tree and sat with his back against its trunk. "What of the others? Did they flee?"

Thomas lifted his eyes and in the split second before he spoke, Klara glimpsed a flash of an emotion so dark that she recoiled—but then the rage vanished and all she saw was exhaustion.

"I saw two of the laird's men dragging him away," he said. "I don't think he was hurt, but they got him in a seat carry and took off in a hurry."

Klara didn't miss the contempt in Thomas's voice. She felt it herself—only a coward would leave a fight like that.

"And you can see what became of the others," Thomas added quietly.

All of his fury seemed to drain out of him as he sagged against the rough bark, and Klara had to resist the urge to comfort him. The strange moods that Callum described—going off alone to brood, muttering about nightmarish fantasies—they could all be explained by PTSD, though Klara had a feeling she'd never be able to convince either of them of twenty-first-century advances in the treatment of trauma.

Callum, on the other hand, seemed to have restored his strength. He had gotten to his feet and was glaring up the road, his body tense. "So they ran away and left the three of us to fight the beasts alone. While my f—while the laird left us to die."

Klara put a tentative hand on Callum's arm, feeling the tension in his rigid muscles. She shared his disgust with the other men's cowardice, but she also could see how devastated he was by the betrayal of a man who—whether or not he was truly Callum's father—had offered him that illusion.

"To be fair," she said softly, placing a hand on his tensed jaw so that he would look at her, "I'm not sure the laird's men gave him a choice. It's their duty to protect him, isn't it?"

Callum's face stayed drawn and tight as he gazed down at her…and then he relaxed and folded her into his arms. "That is so. We must hope that they were able to get to safety."

Thomas snorted. He'd recovered sufficiently to get up on his feet. "I'd like to be carried around on my bahookie, sure," he said. Catching Callum's expression, he added, "Don't worry, they'll send a search party when the laird doesn't come home. He'll be fine."

"Eh, you're right," Callum said. "Meanwhile, we can't leave the dead behind. But we've no way to transport them." He nodded at the splintered remains of the carriage. "And we've only one horse left."

Klara looked over at the pretty dappled mare. She must have possessed a remarkably serene temperament, as she was nibbling at the wild grass like she didn't have a care in the world.

"We can load the bodies on her back, can't we?" Klara said. "The three of us can walk alongside."

"We'll be walking through the night and well into tomorrow," Thomas said. "I've got a better idea."

"I pray it will hold," Callum said an hour later.

"Ah noo, it's stout," Thomas said. He was sitting atop the dappled mare with the reins loose in his hand. "Just a bit shoogly, that's all."

They'd fashioned a sled from one of the carriage's shiny lacquered panels and tied the bodies to it, then hitched the thing to the horse. A test run around the clearing left it scratched but no worse for wear.

"If it fails ye, though—"

"It will be fine," Thomas said confidently. "And if not, I'll load them like Klara suggested and walk the rest of the way. But you two deserve to spend tonight alone together."

Thomas was watching Klara as he said the last bit, her creamy skin turning a bit pink under his gaze.

"I don't know how to thank you, Thomas," she said. "This was super thoughtful."

Thomas grinned. "Consider it an early wedding present."

Then he was off, the sled sending up a cloud of dust in the last light of the day, the makeshift sled with its grisly load bumping along behind.

"I'm sorry, Klara. Thomas shouldn't talk that way," Callum blurted, embarrassed. He couldn't deny that he'd thought about Klara being his bride, but they'd never discussed it. "I'll speak to him when we get back."

"It's all right," Klara said, but she seemed troubled. "Callum…there's something I want to say. First of all, I want you to know that nothing happened between Thomas and me."

A coldness gripped Callum as he saw the anguish in her eyes. This was the fear that he'd been refusing to acknowledge, a fear that was stoked by the way that he often caught Thomas looking at Klara. "But…?"

"Nothing *would* have, either," Klara said. "But I got the sense that he was…interested. That he liked me. *That* way."

Callum's jaw hardened, anger rushing through him. He forced himself not to react, distracting himself by retrieving Llaw's disguised sword, lying alone in a pile of splinters.

"He wasn't inappropriate about it," Klara said hurriedly, "so don't get angry. It's just that we both thought you were dead, and there was some—comfort, I guess, in being able to grieve together."

"What did he do?" Callum ground out the words. How many times had Thomas called Klara beautiful to his face?

Klara rolled her eyes. "He didn't do anything! He was just—very complimentary, okay? And…gallant, I guess is the word. You know, offering me his arm when we were walking through town, taking me to get a gown and insisting on buying me the fanciest one. Saying cheesy stuff like my hair shines like gold. And I didn't like it, so don't be jealous."

Callum's heart felt heavy. He knew exactly the behavior that Klara was describing. He had seen Thomas pull the same act dozens of times with dozens of girls—right down to his comment on her hair. Though sometimes it was mahogany or opals or wine, depending on the color.

"Thomas knew you were mine," he said fiercely. "I dinnae care if I was dead, he had no right—and he'll answer for it."

Klara said nothing for a moment—and then she giggled.

"I'm sorry," she said, covering her mouth. "But did you hear what you just said? And do you really want to pick a fight with Thomas after he saved our lives?"

She moved a step closer, her smile turning wicked, and ran a finger down his face, across his lips, down his chest until it lingered below his belly button.

"And also, why are we even arguing about this when we haven't seen each other in, well, *centuries* and—"

That was as far as she got before Callum kissed her.

CHAPTER TWENTY-SIX

KLARA

Callum could light fires with his kiss.

That was Klara's only thought as she melted against him, their silly argument forgotten. Yes, she'd flirted with Thomas a little, and she'd have to be blind not to notice how hot he was—but Callum was in a whole other league.

"I can't believe my luck," Callum said, a smile tugging at the corners of his gorgeous, full lips when he pulled away. "How did I win a lass like you?"

"I'm not some prize to be won," she said, though by now she knew that Callum didn't need to be told that. No one she'd dated had ever been nearly as respectful—which somehow made him even sexier. "I'm with you because I want to be. Can we go back to the kissing part?"

Callum took a deep breath. "There's a cottage," he said, his voice rough and low. "Just over that hill. I saw it from the road this morning on our way to the castle. It looked abandoned, but it would provide shelter for the night."

Shelter, huh? Klara felt a delicious rush of anticipation as she imagined them curled up in a rustic little cabin in front of a fire, Callum taking off his shirt when it got too warm...

"What a good idea," she said. "We can make a pallet on the floor from the carriage blankets."

"Aye, I'll share a pallet with you, Klara."

From the glazed look in Callum's eyes, Klara was pretty sure they weren't talking about blankets anymore. "And there are provisions under the driver's seat," she said in a sultry voice. "In case we get hungry."

"I am not hungry, Klara."

They were suddenly so formal with each other, their words the thinnest veneer over the passions raging inside them.

"Then let's go," Klara said, grabbing his hand. "How far, did you say?"

Callum worked efficiently to gather what they needed from the remains of the carriage and stuff it into a pannier that had been torn from one of the horses. He slung it over his shoulder and took Klara's hand, and they set out.

It could have been a quarter of a mile, or four times that—time seemed to do funny things as the two of them walked hand in hand. The delicious tension between them and the silver moon rising in the sky more than made up for conversation.

Klara spotted the old cottage first, moonlight reflecting off its plastered stone exterior. In another lifetime the thought of exploring an abandoned house in the dark would have given her Freddy Krueger vibes…but with Callum next to her she wasn't afraid of anything. He'd done the impossible already to be with her, defending her against creatures plucked from hell, breaking the laws of time and space to fight at her side.

How could she ever be with anyone else after that? The boys she'd liked in high school seemed unformed and immature next to Callum. The gym-sculpted bodies she'd once admired struck her as artificial and silly when compared to the scars and calluses of a man who'd worked and fought for everything in his life.

Klara had never imagined she would be with someone like Callum—but that only convinced her more deeply that they were destined to be together. The fates—the gods, the fae, magic and spellcraft and the rest—had chosen a time of maximum imbalance in the universe to bring them together for a reason. Alone, neither Klara nor Callum could do the things they'd accomplished—but together their purpose, their *destiny* became clear.

And she wasn't going to risk losing him again. Even if she had to travel through a thousand more years, she'd do all of that and more to be with Callum.

By the time she spotted a patch of white reflecting the moonlight in the trees, Klara felt giddy, almost drunk with anticipation. "Is that it?" she asked, raising their joined hands to point.

"It'll do," Callum said brusquely. Without warning he lifted her into his arms, her skirts swirling around her, and carried her the hundred yards off the road to the old shack nestled into the trees at the base of a hill.

Paint flaked from the walls, but the glass in the windows was intact and the roof was sound. "Someone's been here recently," Callum said, running a finger along the doorframe, which was remarkably free of dust. "Hunters, probably."

He set Klara down carefully on the leaning front step and tried the door. It wasn't locked. He dug for a candle in the pannier and, once it was lit, led Klara by the hand into the tiny house.

"It's sweet!" she exclaimed. There was a scrubbed wooden table, a single chair, and shelves containing a few plates and cups. Next to the stone fireplace was stacked enough wood to burn for hours. The stains on a long counter didn't bear thinking about—after slaying yet more beasts tonight, Klara didn't want to think about game being skinned anywhere near her—but the floor was swept and there were curtains in the tiny windows.

Callum had found an old bottle and jammed the candle into it. He set it on the table, and the golden light made the humble furnishings seem almost quaint and romantic. Klara helped him spread the blankets on the floor.

When that was done, he swallowed nervously. "Are you cold, Klara? Shall I make a fire? Or if you're hungry—"

"Shut up," Klara said softly. "We've got better things to do."

Callum's eyes went wide, and he swallowed. "Aye," he murmured. "Aye, we do at that."

Klara could tell he was nervous at first. So was she. It wasn't the first time for her—that had happened on the night of her prom, with a boy she liked a lot but hadn't loved. It wasn't awful at all…but it wasn't like this.

Now was different. In all the ways she never knew it could be. This was how she deeply desired it to be.

Callum looked at her, truly looked at her. And his eyes didn't leave her gaze, even as he lifted her garments from her body. She didn't feel exposed in front of him like she did her first time. She felt cherished when his hands didn't go to her breasts but instead to either side of her face. His lips found hers with purpose. They glided against each other in sync as he slowly lowered her beneath him.

Then, suddenly, their gaze broke and he was gone.

But he didn't go far.

Callum stood, removing his shirt, exposing his torso. She had always admired his lean muscle but now, she wanted to feel it. Her eyes drifted downwards and rested on the V that tauntingly dipped below the waistline of his trousers. Klara wetted her lips, suddenly parched.

For a moment she felt an urge to look away but then Callum said, "I want you to watch. To see me. All of me."

And she did see him. All of him. It was more, much more than she could've imagined.

A fire blazed through her body. She needed him. All of him, every beautiful inch.

He descended back to her, his nakedness covering hers.

They had love in words and now, finally, perfectly, they made it.

Afterward, Klara snuggled in Callum's arms, his heart beating slow and even against her back. "That was a ten," she murmured. "Maybe an eleven."

Callum was stroking her hip, making delicious little circles with his fingers. "I dinnae ken what you mean, Klara, but I cannae imagine heaven would be any better than this."

Klara smiled, thinking that everyone ought to have the pleasure at least once of a Scottish man waxing poetic in their honor.

But something was nagging at the back of her mind, a worry she'd been carrying around with her ever since the first time she'd traveled through time. She'd put it off as long as she could, but having gone through the experience of believing Callum was lost to her, she couldn't bear to let one more day pass without bringing it up.

She twisted around in Callum's arms so that she was lying on his muscular bicep and staring up into his eyes. "Callum?"

"Mmm?"

Klara took a deep breath. "Remember earlier, when you asked me never to leave you again?"

She felt him tense and realized her mistake. "I'm not about to tell you I'm leaving," she said hastily. "It's…kind of the opposite."

"Does that mean you're staying, then?"

This was the hard part, the question that Klara feared. "What I know for sure is that I want to be together. What I don't know is whether that is in my time or yours."

"Oh, that," Callum said, his relief palpable. "Must we decide now? We've only just been reunited, and there is still the matter of Arianrhod's vanished powers. Should we not wait until that is settled and the threat is over?"

"But we have no idea how long that will take," Klara said. "Or where it will end. If someone possesses her powers now they could use them to travel to any place or time they wanted."

"I wish it was so," Callum said apprehensively. "We have to assume that they want the same thing Llaw wanted—to take all of her powers and ascend to the Otherworld. And to do that, they must still kill the final two Pillars."

Klara knew that. She and Thomas had talked about it. But it wasn't until Callum said it, his eyes full of equal measures of love and fear, that she realized what this meant for them.

"You think they will stay here in your time."

"Unless you and Thomas leave."

Something occurred to Klara, a memory of her conversation with Thomas. "Thomas told me that his powers hadn't resurfaced since we came here, that he thought they were taken or gone. But Arianrhod told *me* that the powers were already within me, that I was..."

Special. And she had believed it...but Arianrhod lied.

"That part is true," Callum said. "Think of how your sword responds only to you."

"But that's because it was enchanted when it was given to my ancestor."

"And the time you sent Llaw flying backward? That was no enchantment—that was all you."

Klara didn't know what to believe. Thomas was convinced that his control of time travel came from having practiced for a longer time. Arianrhod had used them both and would have said anything to get what she wanted.

But there were other things that could not be explained—meeting her mother in the Otherworld, for instance, and seeing Arianrhod in the stars. Neither of which Thomas had said he'd been able to do.

"Maybe you're right. Not all my powers are gone. I summoned Arainrhod," she said abruptly. "The first night I was in the tower. Unless that was just a dream."

Callum tilted her chin so that she was looking into his eyes. "I know what you're thinking, Klara, but you didn't dream it. That was real."

"How can you be so sure?"

"Because..." Callum hesitated, suddenly unsure of himself. "Oh, Klara, I didnae want to tell you like this..."

"Tell me what?" Klara rolled up into a sitting position, startled. "Seriously, Callum, if you've been holding something back—"

He sat up too, his face going pale in the flickering light of the candle. "It's just that...it's possible that I may have the Sight." He dropped his gaze, unable to look at her. "I have fae blood, Klara. The laird told me my mother was a halfling. It's why my eyes are like this."

Klara's mouth fell open in shock...and then the pieces started falling into place.

"Oh my God, Callum—but that's amazing!" She grabbed his hands and brought them to her lips. "No wonder Grams warmed up to you so fast."

"You're not...upset?" Callum said hesitantly.

"Why would I be upset? Seriously, Callum, you and I need all the help we can get. I think it's kind of awesome, actually." She drew back and considered him...and decided that nothing about his appearance gave the slightest clue.

"I'm glad. Besides, I have another surprise." He pulled his

dirty sword scabbard from where it was leaning on the wall, carefully unwrapping the top of the leather that covered the lumpy pommel. Slowly, she began to see the twinkle of bright metal, and then intricate carvings, and finally: a purple amethyst, set into the middle of a silver-hewn thistle—a perfect match for the one on Klara's ancestral sword.

Her jaw dropped. "Is that..."

"Aye, Llaw's sword. The faeries who rescued me must've thought it mine, and I've been hiding it ever since. I cannae let it fall into the wrong hands."

"Callum, Cernunnos told me that this sword was stolen from its fae guardians. We must return it."

"I'll be glad not to carry it any longer. It has an ill feeling about it."

There were so many things they had to talk about, and only hours until dawn...when they would have to return to Udne Castle, if only to rejoin Thomas. It suddenly seemed naïve that the thing that had been weighing most heavily on her was their future, when there was so much in the present to be dealt with first.

"Callum," she said sternly. "All of this is very interesting. And we definitely need to discuss it. But if I have to go to some castle tomorrow and deal with your father, there's something important that we need to do first."

She watched Callum gird himself, forcing down his uncertainty so that he could summon his determination. "Anything. What is it?"

"This," she murmured, pulling him back down onto the pallet, kissing him all the way.

CHAPTER TWENTY-SEVEN

MALABRON

The faerie market was empty now, closed from midnight until the first light of day. Malabron hadn't slept in hundreds of years, and he spent these hours in the rooms where his treasure was stored, picking baubles up and setting them down, catching sight of his reflection in the looking glasses hung from every wall.

When Malabron ruled over all the mortal realm, he would no longer have to hide his treasure away. With the backing of the gods, he could go where he liked, take what he liked, destroy what he liked. The thought made him smile...until he saw Thomas approaching in the dark abandoned street below the window.

Head down, Thomas walked with his hands in his pockets, dejected. At times, Malabron caught glimpses of the boy Thomas had been before Arianrhod had twisted his soul. It didn't worry him; the remaining traces of that boy were fading fast.

It was obvious that Thomas had failed to kill the girl Pillar and her lover, his boyhood friend, or retrieve the sword he so desperately sought. The failure would goad him into doing better, though he suspected the arrival of the friend would slow Thomas down—an unexpected twist, that, but then again, Malabron relished in the discomfort of humans.

He returned to his office and was working at his ledger when Thomas entered.

"So?"

"They killed the creatures, my lord."

Malabron scowled as Thomas told the story. He knew Laird Johnstone; they'd done business in the past. The laird was a buffoon—also a complication.

When Thomas was finished, Malabron devised a new plan. He went into one of his storerooms and returned with a small bottle and a packet of herbs.

"Here. If my creatures are no match for them, perhaps the terror inside of their own minds will do. Rest before you try again," he told Thomas as he pocketed the supplies. "Eat something. Until you kill her, your body is still as weak as any mortal's."

Thomas drew himself up to his full height, annoyed. "I'm not weak. I am the greatest fighter in all—"

Malabron slashed the air and a blast of flames licked at Thomas, who jumped back in alarm.

"If you think beating a man in a tavern is worthy of mention, then you don't deserve to walk among the gods. Leave now, before I get angry."

Something dark flashed in Thomas's eyes—and then he backed out of the room.

Good, Malabron thought as he listened to his footsteps receding.

He didn't need Thomas to respect him. Hating him was better, because hate was where the darkest deeds were born.

CHAPTER TWENTY-EIGHT

KLARA

Morning came peacefully, gradually awakening Klara with the sun filtering through the curtains. She lay in Callum's arms, her head nestled under his chin, his slow, even breathing ruffling the curls that gathered around her shoulders. The pallet of blankets was tangled now, but it had served them well throughout the night.

I could definitely get used to this, she thought. In fact the sweet little cottage would be perfect—if it were in the twenty-first century.

"What's so funny?" Callum asked sleepily, shifting her in his arms so that she was looking up at him. His hair was sticking up adorably and he had creases on his cheek from the blankets.

"I was just thinking we should bring this cottage with us once we figure out how to travel back to 2022. We'll move it to the empty lot next to my favorite donut shop—they make the most amazing mocha lattes."

Callum quirked an eyebrow at yet another twenty-first century reference he didn't understand, but let it go. They'd spent the night catching up, and Callum had told her about surprising the bean-nighe, and extracting a boon with nary a price.

"I've the strength of ten men," he reminded her. "I'll pull it from the earth and carry it on my back."

Klara laughed and basked in the warmth of his smitten grin. She wouldn't lie, she had the hots for him before, but now? Knowing that he had the strength of ten men? Frankly, this was what swooning in romance novels was all about. It was so easy to dream about their future together, but eventually they were going to have to face the difficult problem of choosing where to live. Either way, one of them was going to have to leave their loved ones behind. She jumped up, uncomfortable at the thought, and began to dress.

If only Callum's father hadn't come into his life, Klara thought—and then felt terrible about it. True, her first impression wasn't a good one, but she'd seen the way Callum had watched his father when he wasn't looking, as if he was still trying to convince himself he was real.

It wasn't fair to begrudge him that, Klara told herself sternly. She'd carry the ache of losing her mother for the rest of her life—but Callum would never know his own mother at all. She watched him fold the blankets and pack them back into the pannier, as if his mind had also gone to the sad, hollow places in his soul.

But she refused to taint this morning with talk of serious things. "Even you, Callum Drummond," she teased, "with your big, strong, manly muscles, can't carry an entire house—"

She broke off suddenly when Callum suddenly tensed, his eyes narrowing in alarm. He was staring at something over her shoulder. "By God…"

Klara sat up to see what he was looking at, and had to stifle a shriek: huge black spiders were pouring through a hole in the corner of the room near the floor. Their bodies were the size of walnuts and their legs tangled together as they crawled over each other in their zeal to enter the room.

Something hit Klara's cheek. Not hard—a tiny tap—but it stuck. She put her fingers to her cheek and brushed against a fine, sticky thread.

Another tiny tap, then another, and she was scrambling to stand up through her panic. Callum was already on his feet, slapping at his arms and cursing as the spiders zipped toward them across the floor in a horrifying column.

"They're shooting at us!" Klara yelped. "Or—*spinning* at us?"

She realized with horror that the barely-visible filaments flying from the spiders and sticking to their skin and clothing were the makings of a web, which wouldn't be so terrifying if there weren't so many of them. Hundreds, maybe thousands, with more coming every second, like black sludge seeping through the walls. Already Klara's arms and neck were covered with the sticky strands. She clawed at herself and found that the web resisted as new strands flew at it.

"Open the door!" Callum yelled as he lurched across the

room, ropes of web winding around him like tentacles, spinning faster and faster as the spiders shot more and more of the filaments in a frenzy. "Get out, Klara!"

He crouched in the corner of the room where the spiders were pouring in, tearing off his shirt, grunting with the effort of ripping away the webbing. He wadded his shirt and tried to plug the hole as the spiders oozed around the obstruction.

Klara ran to Callum and tried desperately to drag him away as webs laced around his feet, trapping him. He frantically tried to pry her hands off. "It's no use. You've got to get out!"

But Klara couldn't get out the front door now even if she tried, as it had been covered by a web so thick she couldn't see the wood underneath. The light in the room was fading fast as webs covered the windows.

Klara dragged herself across the floor where all that was visible of her sword was a bit of the hilt—but the moment she touched it, the web covering it shrank back with a sizzling sound, as if acid had been tossed on it. Klara closed her eyes as she steadied the hilt in both hands and willed it to find the connection within her…and sure enough, an electric energy flowed through her into the sword and back, a completed enchanted circuit.

Klara opened her eyes and followed the instinct wedded to her weapon. It had always been there, she understood now, from the moment she was born; the powers that flowed in the blood of her mother and grandmother and all the generations of her ancestors before them.

The sword danced, gems winking and gold and steel flashing as the blade slashed through the thick webs. Callum's eyes went wide as the blade nearly kissed his flesh and the whitish ropes fell away.

But Klara quickly saw that it wasn't enough. She'd free one of Callum's arms only to watch it be covered again when she tried to free the other, and the spiders were crawling up her legs and spinning as they went. Soon she and Callum would be knitted together in a terrible, suffocating cocoon from which there would be no escape.

Klara wrenched her body away, slashing at the web between them. She needed to focus in a way that she couldn't while staring into the eyes of the man she loved more than anything on this earth.

Do not fear. Klara wasn't sure whose voice echoed inside her, only that she trusted it completely. Fear was the enemy; fear was slowing her down and making her clumsy.

Trust your powers.

Klara went completely still, ignoring the whipping of the threads and the crawling spiders, and concentrated on listening to the voice, inviting its force to flow through her, like golden light turned liquid in her blood.

Now.

Klara brought the sword sharply toward her body, the blade slicing vertically through the web around her torso, freeing her arms. Then she spun around and struck.

The sword was like the blade of a helicopter, moving so fast in her hands that all she saw was a blur. She sliced and slashed, the air split by a bloodcurdling scream that she was only vaguely aware was her own—and soon the floor vanished beneath piles of shredded web and the bodies of dead spiders crunching beneath her feet.

"They die once they've spun their web," Callum shouted. He was half freed, one arm ripping at the webs clinging to Klara as she slashed at the other. "They've stopped coming in. We just have to outlast them!"

It was true—the stream had decreased to a trickle, as many spiders dead as alive. But even that single glance cost Klara, the webs whipping around her wrist, trying to tear her hand from the sword. It was as if the web itself possessed some terrible intelligence, some instinct for destruction.

She tried to step back and nearly fell, her legs tied together by the webbing. She was desperately stabbing at the strands binding her ankles when the door crashed open—and Thomas stood silhouetted in the sunlight.

CHAPTER TWENTY-NINE

CALLUM

Callum couldn't believe his eyes.

"Thomas!" he bellowed, tearing at the webs winding around his wrists, his torso already disappearing under the strands. "Get back!"

But Thomas ignored him, walking into the room as though he couldn't see the chaos before his eyes. For a terrible moment Callum thought perhaps he *couldn't* see the spiders, that they had somehow blinded him to lure him into their trap—but then he raised his hand as casually as if he was waving to a bartender...and the spiders seemed to shrink from him, scrabbling out of his way to create a clear path.

Thomas stood in the center of the room, his eyes heavy-lidded and distant, and murmured some strange incantation that Callum could not make sense of. Not a single filament arced from the spiders, not even the ones clinging to Thomas and Klara; they seemed almost drunk, swaying from threads and dropping to the floor.

Slowly at first, and then faster as they moved into orderly lines, the spiders began to retreat, crawling over the bodies of their dead comrades in their haste to go back through the hole. In a matter of seconds, the room was quiet save for the sound of Klara's and Callum's ragged breathing.

"What the actual *fuck*?" Klara said faintly.

"Ye could have come sooner," Callum said as he flung the remaining webs off with an expression of disgust.

Klara collapsed into the single wooden chair, exhausted. "How did you do that?"

"It's easy," Thomas said cheerfully. "Once you know the spell."

A terrible feeling started to unspool in Callum's gut, like being splashed with ice water. "What spell?"

He had been moving toward Thomas, but Klara grabbed his hand. *"Don't."*

Something was very wrong.

"Ufuddhau pry copyn..." Thomas shrugged. "I could go on, but since none of us speak Welsh, there's little point."

The hairs on the back of Callum's neck tingled at the words, his blood stirring. Some ancient instinct was coming to life within him, warning of catastrophe. "But where did you learn this?"

"That's no concern of yours," Thomas said in a voice so cold Callum took a step back. His lip curled in distaste at the sight of Callum's fine clothing, now soiled and torn and covered with webs. "I'm here to do what Llaw was too weak to do."

Klara went rigid at Callum's side, a look of terrible understanding overtaking her. "No," she said, and then, enraged, *"No!"*

Callum stepped in front of her, shielding her with his body. "Thomas, what are you saying? What has happened to you?"

Thomas laughed, a terrible, scraping sound. "I'm going to destroy you and your little hurdie," he said, sliding his eyes up and down Klara's body obscenely. "I'm going to kill the last Pillar and then I'll walk on your corpses on my way to the Otherworld. I'll see Arianrhod choke on her own regret for using me as if I was *nothing.*"

Klara was very still. "You lied to me. You said Arianrhod's powers had disappeared. But you—you had them all this time?"

"Aye, and I'd been working on it for a long, long time, it feels like. Thanks for your help on that, by the way, I couldn't have done it without you, little moppet."

Callum flinched at the bitterness in Thomas's voice, the emptiness in his blue eyes. "Ye dinnae know what you're saying. Whatever sinister magic's gripped ye—"

Metal flashed and something stung his arm. Callum looked down to see a bright, thin slash of red.

"That's your one warning," Thomas growled. "For old times' sake. Next time I won't be so soft on ye."

Klara pushed her way around Callum, furious. "When did he get to you?" she demanded. "Did he follow us out of the market?"

"He? You think I was just *turned* to evil by one stupid fae?

No!" Thomas snarled. "This is me. This has been me for a long time. All he did was give me a little leg up when I got stuck."

Callum caught Klara's hand. "I dinnae understand. Who are you talking about?"

Thomas hesitated before looking Callum in the eye. "Don't be so goddamn naïve. That's your problem, Cal—you never grew up. Not with me to look out for you. But now it's my turn."

"He sold us out," Klara said bitterly. "He's joined forces with Malabron. What did you promise him?"

The name—*Malabron*—was an assault to Callum's ears. The fae who sold children. Who'd sold *both of them*.

Callum felt dizzy with Thomas's betrayal. "You summoned those beasts," he said. "You watched those men die. My father could have been killed—"

"Your *father*!" Thomas's rage flared, spittle flying from his lips. "It all just falls into your lap, doesn't it, Callum? Would you have come for me, once you were sitting at the head of the laird's table, drinking his wine?"

"I—"

"No!" Thomas slashed again, and this time the blade cut deeper into the flesh of his arm. "You would have spit on me in the streets. But now no one will look down on me ever again."

He held out his hand, his lips moving again. Klara gasped as her sword fell from her hands, clattering on the wood floor, and Thomas picked it up.

"I…can't…" She turned to Callum, fear in her eyes, as she

swayed. Callum caught her before she could fall. "The protections. The sword's protections…" She swooned.

"Stop," he bellowed at Thomas. "Release her!"

"All in good time," Thomas said, rubbing the hilt on his sleeve, admiring the scattering of emeralds that formed leaves around the amethyst thistle on the pommel. "It wouldn't be sporting to kill her when she's like this."

He muttered something and Klara shot toward him, released from whatever hold he'd cast upon her. Callum grabbed her and pulled her back before she could land her first punch.

Thomas wasn't himself anymore…and the thing he'd become terrified him. But before he could tell Klara to run, Thomas was upon her with an unearthly shriek, sending her crashing to the ground. He easily pinned her with a knee to the chest and in seconds it was over, Klara immobilized again with the sharp point of her own family sword pressed to the skin of her neck, whatever magical protections it had shattered by Thomas's new alliance.

Callum's body felt like molten lead as he crawled toward Thomas, his muscles spasming under some malicious enchantment. He watched Klara bat weakly at Thomas's face, tears streaming from her eyes—but she wasn't crying because she was afraid.

He felt the anger rise within her as if it was his own, and with a mighty heave, she found her voice.

"Get off me."

"There, there," Thomas crooned, turning his attention to Callum. "You've always thought you were so smart. Throwing it in my face all the time, how you could read, how you could do sums. But that didn't make you a better fighter, did it? It was me—always me saving you. You'd have died a dozen times in the ring were it not for me to step in and finish your fights for you."

Callum wanted to argue, but even if Thomas's spells hadn't muted and weakened him, he couldn't deny the truth of his words—the part about Thomas saving him, at least.

Brice always billed them together, shrewdly taking advantage of the friendship that allowed them to communicate almost without speaking, saving each other from crooked bets, thrown fights, bottles poised to be smashed on their skulls.

With Thomas on the bill, Callum fought the most brutal opponents in all of Rosemere—but Thomas took the worst of it. But the rest—Callum had never held his paltry education over anyone, Thomas least of all. If anything, he'd been embarrassed by it, reading only after the other boys were asleep, scratching sums in the dirt and wiping them away with his boot. It was just a pastime he loved because it was his alone.

Klara had regained some of her vitality. "You'd be dead if Callum hadn't gone after you that night." She hurled the words at Thomas. "Llaw would have the power of all the Pillars. You'd be nothing."

"Lucky, lucky me," Thomas said sarcastically. "Here comes Callum to save the day, his pretty little lass on his arm. But you've got thorns, don't you, little rose?"

He dragged the sword's tip slowly, almost lovingly down Klara's neck, her chest, between her breasts.

Callum was nearly blinded by his rage. *"Dinnae touch her."*

"Oh my," Thomas said with feigned contrition. "I think Callum is jealous, my little rose."

Callum launched himself at Thomas and was repelled, as if he'd smashed into a solid wall.

"Don't bother fighting it," Thomas told him as Klara writhed beneath him. "You'll only hurt yourself."

"Don't you care that you'll destroy the worlds?" Klara cried.

Thomas tilted his head, considering her. "Not *all* the worlds, though." He spoke gently, like a teacher correcting a student. "Not the Underworld or, more importantly, the realm of the gods, where I'll spend eternity."

"This isn't you," Callum gritted out. "Thomas, I know you. You would never want to hurt innocent people. *Stop* this."

He caught Thomas's eye and, by some force of will, held it long enough to see a tiny flicker of uncertainty in their cold blue depths—but then it went dark.

"It's too late," Thomas smirked. "The power-transfer sword no longer answers only to one master. Or mistress, I should say. Look at it this way," he added as Klara pounded at him weakly. "The two of you will be together for eternity once I kill you. Now shut up, both of you, and let me concentrate."

Then Thomas began to chant.

CHAPTER THIRTY

KLARA

"Och cleddyf gorchymyn tywyll..."

Thomas began to utter the spell in a voice that was at once lyrical but also deeply unpleasant, as if Klara was being caressed by silk soaked in acid. Inside her, a battle raged between the powers that belonged to her and the ones Thomas was controlling—and she was losing.

The spell took shape in her mind, an angry cloud that would swell until it burst into a cataclysm of destruction. She could feel its force gathering, tugging at the powers buried inside her, readying to wrench them from her at the moment Thomas plunged the sword into her neck. As her lifeblood spilled onto the earth, so would her powers flow into him, the final Pillar, joining with the powers of all the other Pillars that Llaw had killed, the powers Thomas had stolen from him as he died.

And then Thomas would be the most powerful being ever to walk the mortal realm—but he would not do so for long. As he ascended to take his place in the realm of the gods, time would splinter and space would fold in on itself and the earth would shatter into a million pieces, every life snuffed out, all of its history burnt to nothing.

The pull inside Klara broke into tiny crystal splinters and reformed into something hard and dense and molten, the force of it lifting her body off the ground, every cell of her being primed to meet the fight.

And then Klara *became* the fight.

Her senses vanished as the powers in her blazed, gathering into a wave as wide as time itself, swelling to fill the universe—and she was merely its passenger, gliding at the speed of light along its ridge straight for its target—

Klara ricocheted back into herself at the precise moment that Thomas slammed into the wall, the sword falling from his hand. It flew back to her, landing in her grip, and she was on her feet in a glorious rage, her senses not only returned but impossibly vivid. The room around her was made of brilliant colors, the smell of Thomas's fear and the awareness of Callum's helpless love overwhelmed her, and she watched Callum flex his arms and take back his strength in wonder.

Klara fixed her gaze on Thomas lying stunned and broken on the floor with his fingers twitching, feeling his heart pounding, his hatred trying to swallow her whole, his hunger for power and destruction overwhelming everything he had ever been.

She laughed, struck suddenly by the absurdity of it—a man made small by his resentments and envy, pretending to an eternal throne—and Thomas recoiled.

"All three of us in the Otherworld?" she mused, her gown billowing around her in some invisible wind, Thomas gaping at her in horror. "Wouldn't that get awkward at dinner parties?"

Thomas's face contorted in a hideous scowl and he started chanting again. And immediately Klara felt the danger, the mistake she had made.

She grabbed Callum's hand as Thomas's body started to rise from the floor, as if lifted by the invisible strings of a marionette.

"Run!"

CHAPTER THIRTY-ONE

CALLUM

By the time Callum slowed to a walk, he'd covered at least a dozen furlongs—and could easily cover another before tiring. But they were safe, for now.

"I'm sorry I ever second-guessed your superstrength," Klara said lightly as Callum set her down. He'd thrown her over his shoulder when they ran, knowing they'd make much better time that way. "It came in pretty handy today."

Callum knew she was trying to soften the horror of what had taken place in the old cottage, but the memory of Thomas's face contorted into a rictus of hatred was seared into his memory. He'd thought of little else as he ran, trying to remember when exactly Thomas had started to change. Because even before Llaw's depravity and evil flowed into him along with the powers of the other eight Pillars, the enchantments Arianrhod had conferred on Thomas had begun to twist and taint his soul.

"He was never like that before, Klara," he muttered. "You must believe me."

"I know," she sighed, putting a hand to his cheek. "For what it's worth, I think some part of him is still in there. I mean, I hate that he fooled me, too. If my sword wasn't enchanted, I bet he would have killed me that first day—but there were moments—he was kind sometimes, and funny, and I know he was just biding his time until he could figure out how to get the sword, but he didn't have to be so...sweet. He could have been a raging jerk and I would have had no choice but to go along with him."

Callum felt the return of his suffocating anger at Thomas's obvious attraction to Klara, and fear at the control he could've had over her. "You're a beautiful woman, Klara, and even a demon sees it. When I think of you alone with him—"

"You and me both," Klara said with feeling. "I can't believe I was thinking we should bring him back with us and have Dad give him a job around the manor."

"Please tell me you're joking," Callum said, the thought making him queasy. "Klara—now that he has lifted your sword's enchantment, nowhere is safe for us until he is defeated."

Klara shrugged. "Llaw had a sword, so I was in just as much danger then."

Then, as they rested in the shade of an ancient oak tree, he told her everything that had happened to him since he came to in the Ring of Brodgar, right up until the day before when they set out for the keep—and Klara did the same.

Callum could never have imagined that Klara's own story would prove even more fantastical than his own.

"But—*Anne and Aion*?" He shook his head in disbelief. "What are the odds that you would see the very story Aion told me play out in front of your eyes?"

"It might not be such a coincidence," Klara said gently. Callum was lying with his head in her lap as she rubbed his scalp and played with his hair. If it wasn't for the dangers that pursued them, he'd happily lie there for all of eternity. "Grams…knows things. She gave me the sword at the right moment. She knew when to find you. Plus, Arianrhod must have had her creatures keeping an eye on all of this while Llaw was hunting the Pillars."

Callum shuddered. "If you and Thomas hadn't killed him—"

"—then we'd both be dead," Klara said matter-of-factly. "You never would have met me, but you also would never have had to know what Thomas became."

Callum pushed himself up so that he could look at Klara. "That Tom is gone," he said. "He died the moment he found out about his powers."

Klara blew out a breath in frustration. "It's so frustrating. I never believed in any of this shit, but if I had, I would have expected it to follow some rules. Like why even have gods if they're going around undermining each other and blowing up the universe?"

Callum's headache pressed against his temples. He took Klara's hand in his. "You know things that are beyond my ken, Klara, but they cannae help us now. Let's go back to my father's castle. We need a meal and rest before we decide what to do next."

Klara bit her lip. "We don't have to go back there to rest," she said. "I'm sure we can find somewhere else."

Callum was taken aback. "But why? Father can help—just as he helped me to free you. Once I explain about Thomas—"

"You really think he's going to believe it?" Klara's lips flattened into a thin line. "I know it must be...tempting, to dive into this whole long-lost-dad thing. But this is a *lot*, Callum. And the stakes couldn't be higher."

Callum stared at her, trying to decipher the meaning behind her words. They'd become so close, so quickly, that he often could tell what she was thinking without her saying anything at all, but for some reason she didn't seem to trust his father.

But deep down, Callum knew she was right. There were moments...when the laird barked at a servant or showed off some detail of the castle's furnishings...when his arrogance was on display. And Callum still felt uneasy about the way he'd run from the battle in the clearing, leaving two of his men behind to die.

"You know what, ignore me," Klara said quickly, sensing his distress. "You're right, he's your dad."

"We dinnae have to stay, if he—if things are not as we hope," Callum said. "But he is planning to introduce us to Laird and Lady Westwood. Maybe they can tell us more about the sword."

"Like where the 'off' button is?" Klara said with a ghost of a smile. "Never mind. Twenty-first-century humor again."

Callum felt it before he saw them—the vibration in the earth followed by the appearance of a rider cantering toward them, leading a second horse. He wore the scarlet and purple of the Johnstone crest.

Callum leapt up, offering Klara his hand as the rider came abreast. He removed his hat with a flourish.

"My lord, Lady Klara, the laird is quite worried about your welfare. He sent myself and a good many others to search for you, we've been searching everywhere. He would like to bring you back to the castle."

Callum and Klara looked at each other—and she burst out laughing. "I guess that's decent of the guy," she told the guard. "But maybe next time he could call us an Uber before he gets the hell out of Dodge."

"Lady Klara is light-headed," Callum said hastily. "She needs rest and quiet."

"And a couple of Advil wouldn't hurt," she added, as Callum led her to the spare horse.

CHAPTER THIRTY-TWO

CALLUM

The laird seemed gratifyingly worried about them.

"We're only lucky William found you," he said, rushing out of the library as soon as a servant alerted him they'd arrived. "Two of my men are still missing." He cleared his throat and fussed with his cuffs. "I've instructed William to alert the sheriff to the presence of wild boar in the Elder Forest."

Callum and Klara exchanged a glance. His father obviously wanted to keep the true nature of the attack—monsters sent from the Underworld—a secret.

"Very wise, my lord," Klara said. "I would hate for another party to come under attack by those vicious beasts. We were lucky to survive."

The laird nodded vigorously, obviously relieved. "We'll

put that behind us, then. I suppose you'd like to bathe and have a rest now?"

"Oh, yes—this milkweed down is itchy," Klara said, brushing at the shreds of webbing that clung to her arm. "We got lost in a patch of it. I'm so sorry I've ruined this beautiful gown."

"The gown is of no consequence," the laird said, barely glancing at it. "All that matters is that you're safe."

"Father," Callum said. He and Klara had discussed how he could introduce the topic with the laird, but that was before the laird made it clear that the truth about what happened in the clearing was to be buried. Apparently magical creatures were as taboo a topic as fae matters. "Earlier you suggested a meeting with Lord and Lady Westwood. Klara is very interested in meeting them as soon as possible."

The laird blinked in surprise. "Er—of course. But surely you'll want to recover from your…exertions—"

"Not at all, my lord," Klara said, giving him a dazzling smile. "We're both as good as new, aren't we, Callum?"

"Yes," he blurted when she poked him in the ribs. "Why wait?"

"Well, in that case—" the laird rubbed his hands together in anticipation "—what about tonight? Lady Westwood hosts a salon each Sunday evening. All the best people in Rosemere attend and the entertainment is outstanding. I'll send word that we will attend tonight."

"That would be fantastic," Klara gushed. "Thank you, my lord."

"Your official debut will come later, of course," the laird continued, warming to the subject. "But you can start making some key acquaintances that will serve Callum well. However, we must find you something suitable to wear."

Klara looked down at her ruined gown. "I'm really sorry about—"

The laird waved her apology away. "And I've just the person to help. Callum has already met Mistress Drever, my wife's lady-in-waiting. She oversees the household staff now, but she'd be glad to help you choose one of my wife's dresses and have it tailored for you. She can help with your hair as well. As for you, Callum, you'll wear our colors tonight."

"Thank you, Father," Callum said uncomfortably.

He'd never been fond of flashy dress, preferring to blend into the background when out in public, and the scarlet and purple of the Johnstone crest would stand out in any crowd. But he could hardly refuse.

His father clapped his hands. "Right, then. I'll have Mistress Drever bring up a light lunch, Klara, and Callum, you'll come with me. We'll visit the hall of portraits and introduce you to your ancestors." He laughed at his own joke, obviously delighted with the way things were turning out. "Imagine, Callum—someday your own portrait will hang there, too."

Callum didn't miss the eye roll Klara gave him—but when the laird turned to her, she performed a somewhat clumsy curtsy. "You are too kind, my lord," she said, in a perfect imitation of the lady she would soon be pretending to be.

Several hours later, Callum stood next to his father in the grand entry hall, resisting the urge to scratch his neck where the stiff collar of his shirt tickled his skin. The woolen plaid belted over his formal trews itched even more, and the smell of oils his father's manservant had applied to his hair threatened to make him sneeze.

Still, the man he'd seen looking back in the long mirror in his father's dressing room had given him a shock. The first time Callum had ever seen his full reflection had been at Klara's aunt's house, and he'd had a good laugh at himself in the unusual outfit she'd loaned him.

But as the manservant made a last adjustment to his coat, Callum found himself looking upon a man of standing, of importance. Someone who would have inspired a mixture of fear and contempt in him in the past, when he and Thomas were always on the alert for the insults and worse that were hurled at them by the wealthy.

In fact, with his fresh shave and washed and styled hair, Callum judged himself...handsome. It made his face hot to think it, but after a lifetime in Thomas's shadow, the notion that his appearance might be pleasing to Klara filled him with pride.

He'd even summoned his courage and asked the manservant to teach him what was expected of him that night, saying he feared embarrassing his father. William betrayed no surprise at the request and spent several hours instructing him in etiquette. There was even a dance lesson that involved William playing the role of Klara with a perfectly straight face.

"I won't forget this," Callum told William with feeling. "I've nothing of value to give you, only my thanks."

It felt as though they'd come to an understanding. Callum was sure that William saw straight through to the rough, uneducated man at his core, but for some reason he didn't seem to mind.

William had gone to call for the carriage, and the laird was adjusting his plaid in a small mirror mounted discreetly near the door, so Callum was the first to see Klara descending the grand stairs. She was dressed in a stunning ruby satin gown and attended by a smiling Mistress Drever.

Callum realized his mouth was hanging open and snapped it shut just in time for Klara to see him and give him a brilliant smile. *Did she have any idea how beautiful she was?* Callum wondered, taking in the jeweled combs in her elaborately braided and twisted hair, the lace flounces at her wrist and hem, the way the dress nipped in her waist and did something to her breasts that made it nearly impossible to tear his eyes away.

"Good evening, Lady Klara," his father said formally.

Callum bowed and offered Klara his hand, a move he'd practiced over and over with William. Klara blushed as she slid her hand in his.

"Let us be off!" the laird said. "Rosemere awaits."

CHAPTER THIRTY-THREE

KLARA

The manor looked every bit as beautiful as when Klara's father and aunt had decorated it for the holidays, but in the place of the fresh pine garlands that had hung above the door and windows, fat candles flickered in iron sconces, and gold and scarlet silk decorated the walls. Warm golden light spilled from the windows of the ballroom that was used for weddings in Klara's time, and the soft music of a string quartet would have been just as at home then as now.

They were greeted by a servant who led them ceremoniously to the anteroom that Klara and her dad used as a combination broom closet/mudroom/lost and found.

"Laird Johnstone, his son Callum, and Lady Klara Spalding!" There was a smattering of applause as a dozen beautifully dressed guests watched them descend.

Callum took Klara's hand, his palm sweaty. Klara knew he was nervous about screwing up in front of his father. It annoyed her. Honestly, the laird reminded her of certain manor guests, the ones who wore too much jewelry and name-dropped and insisted on being upgraded to the best rooms.

"You'll do great," she whispered, squeezing his hand. Then she channeled Julie Andrews and walked regally down the stairs, ignoring the way her satin slippers pinched her toes.

She loved the gown she was wearing, but it was Mrs. Drever who'd chosen it. "If Catherine could see you now," she'd sighed, wiping at her eyes. Callum's mother had been a bit smaller than Klara and considerably shorter, but the seamstress had worked miracles, stitching lace to the sleeves and hem and doing her best to let out the bodice, though Klara still was having a hard time breathing.

A handsome older couple waited at the foot of the stairs.

"Lord Westwood," the laird said formally, bowing from the waist. Callum hurriedly copied him. "Lady Westwood. It is good of you to invite us."

"Oh dear, please let's not be stuffy tonight," Lady Westwood laughed warmly, instantly winning Klara over. "We've known each other for ages. Please call me Mairi and this is Arthur. And who are these enchanting young people?"

The laird puffed himself up as he introduced Klara and Callum and explained Klara's relationship to the Westwoods. Though they both were polite, it was Lady Mairi who took Klara's hand, her eyes sparkling.

"I'm going to steal your fiancée for a bit, if you don't mind,"

Lady Mairi told Callum. “It’s not every day I meet a long-lost relative. I must learn all about you. Arthur, you’ll simply have to do without me.”

Laird Westwood gave his wife a fond smile that reminded Klara of the way Grams looked at her wife, Laura. In fact she thought she could see a resemblance in his long, straight nose, the crinkles at the corners of his eyes from smiling.

Lady Mairi led Klara out into the hallway and down a long passage, at the end of which was a pair of handsome mahogany doors inlaid with a design of Pictish whorls and spirals. “These doors are beautiful,” Klara said, marveling at the doors. A shame that they weren’t the same doors they had in her time.

“Thank you,” Lady Mairi said, opening the door to a vast room lined with books and lit with candelabras on a half-dozen tables perfect for reading or studying. “But they were here long before my time. The library is the soul of this castle. I don’t tell many people this, but it’s protected by magic—or I should say that those with Westwood blood are protected when they are inside its walls. Not that I anticipate the need for protection from our guests tonight.”

Klara couldn’t tell if she was joking. “The castle is beautiful,” she said. “I hope it’s all right that Laird Johnstone brought me along tonight.”

“I’m delighted!” Lady Mairi said decisively. “Now, where shall we start?”

Here goes nothing, Klara thought, taking a deep breath. “I’m not exactly sure how to say this, Lady W—Mairi.” She paused. Klara knew that telling her information about herself could either be taken well or, most likely, go disastrously wrong. She hoped for the former.

Lady Mairi's expression didn't change as she interjected, "Actually, I know who you are, which is why I wanted to speak to you in private."

Klara's mind raced. How could Lady Mairi possibly know her true identity? "I don't know how much you know about me, but the worlds are in grave danger from the actions of the goddess Arianrhod and those who will stop at nothing to steal her powers."

"I know," Lady Mairi said, settling a cool hand on Klara's arm. "The Envoy alerted us. We are ready to assist in any way we can."

"The...Envoy?"

Lady Mairi raised an eyebrow. "You may know him by another name. There isn't time to explain just now, but I will arrange for you and Callum to meet with him after the entertainment. In my experience, it is easier to carry on unobserved when people have had a bit of wine."

Klara gave her a tentative smile. "I probably shouldn't say this, but you remind me of my grandmother, Adele Westwood. She was born in this house and now she lives in Edinburgh. Or, I mean, in 2022."

"How lovely." Lady Mairi beamed. "I wish I could meet her. It pleases me no end to know that the manor is in good hands all those years in the future. I wish I could talk to you all night, Klara, but unfortunately Arthur will become completely flustered if I'm not there to remind him who all these people are."

They returned to the ballroom arm in arm and rejoined Laird Westwood and Callum. Laird Johnstone was holding forth with a group of men at the center of the room.

"Do look at the portrait of my grandmother, Lady Agatha, if you have a chance," Lady Mairi murmured confidentially. "She wears a necklace very like your own. People always say that it was a gift from the fae."

"Lady Mairi!" a slightly drunken voice rang out, as a flushed woman in a bright saffron gown and elaborate feathered hairdo broke away from her group. "You've outdone yourself again!"

"But wait until you try the goose," Mairi said smoothly, giving Klara a wink as she went to join her guests. "Arthur had to have the Marquess of West Lanarkshire's cook kidnapped and tortured to get the recipe."

Two hours later, Klara was stuffed, and a bit light-headed from the wine the servants kept pouring into her goblet. She was seated between two noblemen whose names and titles she couldn't keep straight, and the effort of trying to answer their questions about her family was giving her a headache. Meanwhile, across the table, Callum looked like he wished he could disappear into the floor.

As the dessert dishes were being cleared away, Laird Westwood—who everyone called Arthur—got to his feet at the head of the table and cleared his throat.

There were a few good-natured shouts from the guests, who—as Lady Mairi had predicted—grew merrier as the evening wore on and the wine flowed. After thanking the assembled guests for coming, the laird asked them to retire to the far end of the ballroom, where chairs had been arranged in rows before a small podium.

Klara hurriedly excused herself to join Callum, her first

opportunity to speak to him in private. "Lady Mairi is taking us to see someone called the Envoy once the entertainment is over."

Callum didn't have a chance to respond before his father called out to him, beckoning them to join him in the front row. Klara had a feeling the laird was eager to be seen and admired, which would make it harder to slip away.

But there really wasn't much of a choice. There were so many rules in Callum's time, and she was on uncertain footing. If only her mother, an avid student of Scottish history and society, were here to guide her. As it was, Klara had simply copied what she saw other guests doing.

But Callum tapped into some previously hidden source of confidence. He offered her his arm and led her to a seat near the back with more dignity than most of the tipsy guests, giving his father an apologetic bow.

A stooped and wizened old man was hobbling across the stage, assisted by a servant carrying a heavy tome under one arm. As he helped the old man into his seat and placed the book on the small table in front of him, a hush fell over the audience.

Arthur ascended the stage, laughing at some private conversation. He struck Klara as the kind of man who was happiest in the company of others, always up for an adventure—like her dad's friend Craig, who was helping line up entertainment for the manor guests. *I ought to introduce them*, she thought before remembering that they were separated by five hundred years.

"Tonight's guest needs no introduction," Laird Westwood said, giving the old man a fond look. "Many of us have been listening to his tales since we were lads in knickers. So please enjoy the company of Claes the Elder of Pittenween, otherwise known as the Bard of Kingshill Manor."

There was a burst of applause, which the old man waved away. When he spoke, his voice was surprisingly clear and strong.

"I was reminded tonight, as I rode past Fearghus Cullan's flock, of the tale of the poor cotter from Jedburgh," he began. "He was on his way to the sheep market at Hawick…"

He went on to tell the story of the cotter, or farmer, happening upon a faerie birth. Hearing the attendants' lament that there was nothing to wrap the new baby in, the cotter threw down his plaid—only to have it snatched away by an invisible hand, upon which he heard shouts of joy.

He continued on to the market, where he bought a sheep at a remarkably good price. The cotter never regretted the loss of his plaid because from that day forward, his wealth multiplied and he died a rich and happy man.

"From this tale we might conclude that we should never hesitate to befriend a faerie," the Bard concluded, to applause and laughter. "And now I'll take your requests. The old stories live on through the telling, don't they?"

Klara glanced at Lady Mairi, who was seated at her husband's side, as riveted as the rest of the audience. There was so much she didn't understand about the gods, her sword, her powers. But this was supposed to be the location where so much of it started. She pulled at Callum's sleeve, and whispered a thought in his ear.

"I've a request," Callum said nervously after clearing his throat. "About the divergence of the human and fae realms."

The Bard raised his eyebrows. "That is an old, old story," he said, "one I don't often have an opportunity to tell—everyone in this audience seems a little skittish of talk of the fae. For all our advancements, we still are a superstitious lot, aren't we?" The audience tittered, a little nervous, and a little enthralled.

"In the beginning there were only the Creators, Breogan and Danu, and Mahoun, who some knew as Sathan. Breogan and Danu created the gods and gave them their own domain, the Otherworld. Mahoun could create nothing on his own, and he grew jealous and angry as Breogan and Danu continued to spin worlds and populate them with souls.

"The gods were their first creations, and they were innocent and beautiful. But Breogan and Danu grew bored after they had made the Underworld and mortal realm and fashioned humans and fae and all manner of magical creatures, and they decided to create new worlds in other dimensions, giving the gods provenance in their absence and tasking them with welcoming mortals into their realm upon their deaths. In addition, they gave each god a unique domain—the skies, the seas, fertility, time, justice and so on.

"Mahoun saw his opportunity in their absence to unravel what they had done, and began to sow discord among the gods. They were young and naïve then, easily distracted and manipulated, and he whispered lies in their ears and set them to squabbling and neglecting their domains. He lured both human and fae with trinkets and promises of power, and infected them with sinister appetites, until the peace that had reigned since the worlds were made began to splinter. Not all mortals were susceptible to his charms, so he concentrated on the weak and the damaged until there were enough of them to upset the balance.

"There were those in the mortal realm who were alarmed by Mahoun's interference and joined forces to defend against him. Leaders of fae and human worked together, the humans building fortresses and places of learning aboveground while the fae toiled underground to create spellcraft and try to tame the magical creatures.

"Mahoun's most faithful followers came from the *daoine síth*, the mound fae. Originally, you see, it was the nature of all fae to live in close community, sharing both the toil and rewards of the forests and burrows where they made their homes, raising their young and caring for their elderly together. The exception were the *clurichaun*—the solitary fae—whose magic was especially strong. They were celebrated as sages and artists and sometimes lived apart in hollow trees and caves.

"Mahoun targeted the *clurichaun* and attempted to poison them with suspicion and resentment. He rarely succeeded, but when he did, the fae developed a ravenous need for riches and power and sought to establish themselves in the shadows.

"While all of this was going on, the gods bickered and neglected their duties and stirred up trouble in the other worlds. They were like children who tire of their toys and leave them scattered about. They were distracted by sensual pleasures and loved freely, taking lovers wherever they liked but rarely experiencing real connection. Some say this is the fault of Breogan and Danu, that they failed to cultivate in the gods the conscience and wisdom that both human and fae aspire to. I cannae say, but as the eons passed the gods began to undermine each other and steal each other's powers and train creatures to do their bidding.

"In the mortal realm, the fae created spiritual centers—

'thin places'—so that they could travel between worlds and plead with the gods for reason. But Mahoun's dark fae—the *olc síth*—discovered the portals and used them for their own purposes, and formed alliances to strengthen their powers.

"It was around the year of our lord 1400 that Breogan and Danu returned to check on their creation and found it in a state of chaos and imbalance. Enraged, they threatened to destroy it all, but the *clurichaun*—the solitary fae who could not be corrupted—pleaded with them to give the worlds another chance. And so a Worlds Council was called, with representatives of the gods and fae and humans gathering at Rosemere, once a spiritual center of the mortal realm.

"It took place at a great castle on the site of what is now this very manor in which you find yourself tonight. In fact, it was Laird Westwood's ancestor who represented the humans at the Worlds Council and joined the king of the *daoine síth* in helping to establish a new order. The result was the Accords, a set of rules governing commerce and travel and the adjudication of disputes and all the other aspects of the two races sharing the same lands.

"Once the Accords were signed, Westwood Castle was torn down and Breogan and Danu built Kingshill Manor in its place in a single night. They charged Laird Westwood and the fae king with keeping the peace between the races.

"The fae king appointed the first Envoy, a *clurichaun* who would serve as an ambassador to the humans and live among them, and the laird's eldest daughter volunteered to serve as an ambassador among the fae.

"Once that was done, Breogan and Danu stripped the gods of certain powers and limited others. No longer could the gods travel to the mortal realm, except in the form of their animal familiars. They would only be allowed to communicate with mortals between worlds and in dreams.

"They were especially angry at Arianrhod, goddess of time and the skies, for bearing the child of a human and leaving him in the mortal realm while she took her lover back to the Otherworld to live out his natural life. They ruled that she should be denied her powers for a period of one thousand years as a punishment. In the way of the gods, they gripped her powers from within her soul, and cut them from her with a blade. They sent pieces of her power to ten mortals throughout time, so that her powers would slowly return to her over the course of history, as each Pillar of Arianrhod's power passed into the Underworld. The powers were hidden, so that no god might find them, and no unworthy mortal Pillar might abuse them. Then, they cleaved the blade in two and formed the pieces into two swords that might cut power from an undeserving creature: one for the humans of Kingshill Manor, and one for the *clurichaun* of the fae, so that mortals too might have the power to rein in the overstep of any god.

"That is the end of my story," the Bard concluded, taking a sip of wine. "There are many versions of the tale of what came after, of course. Some believe that the gods cut themselves off entirely from the mortal realm. Many people think the fae died off long ago or never existed at all, while others profit from twisting the old stories to their own purposes. And some believe that Mahoun is biding his time as he schemes to rebuild an army even more powerful than before."

The audience broke into hearty applause. Klara clapped along, but her mind was spinning at the things the Bard had said. Arianrhod, the dark fae, her Westwood ancestors, *the swords*—all of the pieces of a puzzle that was both too fantastical to believe in and too close to reality to ignore.

When the applause died down, the Bard winked at Callum. "I hope that satisfied your curiosity, young man. Now, who else has a tale they would like to hear tonight?"

"Tell the story of Johnnie Faa and the witch of Maybole," a man shouted, to laughter and cheers. The Bard launched into the risqué tale as more wine was poured, and no one noticed Lady Mairi leaving her seat and signaling to Klara.

"Now," Klara whispered, and she and Callum slipped into the shadows at the edge of the room where Lady Mairi waited. She led them out into the hall toward the back of the manor, through the kitchen where the staff was washing great stacks of dishes, and out the back door into the gardens where neat rows of pea vines and onions and aubergines grew.

Lady Mairi led them quickly along the path without aid of a lantern, slowing to allow Callum and Klara to catch up.

"We should have taken the tunnel," she said. "It's lit by faerie lights."

"What tunnel?"

"You don't know about them? There's a whole network of tunnels on our lands. They've been here for hundreds of years. Maybe they were filled in by your time. Here we are."

To Klara's surprise, their destination was the stables. Light spilled from a single window at the far end of the long, familiar building. In her time, that end of the stables served as the caretaker's quarters, but little else had changed.

Lady Mairi raised the heavy oak gate and entered the straw-covered corridor lined with stalls on either side. Horses snuffled and snorted, their sleep disturbed by the intrusion. Light leaked under the door at the end of the corridor.

Before Lady Mairi could knock, the door swung open and a tall, broad man with a full beard and a florid complexion greeted them with a bow.

"Imagine meeting you here, Klara," he said with a broad smile.

"Jockie?" Klara gasped. "Is it really you?"

CHAPTER THIRTY-FOUR

KLARA

"Me in the flesh, lass," Jockie admitted sheepishly. "And may I say you look very pretty tonight."

Klara was tongue-tied, trying to make sense of the fact that the caretaker that she and her father had become so fond of since moving to the manor, the guy who whistled tunelessly as he pruned the roses and mended the window screens, who'd put her bicycle back together after she wrecked it—that this same man was standing before her five hundred years in the past, dressed in a leather apron with a mallet in his hand.

Or rather, this was a younger version of Jockie. In Klara's time, she would have put his age at early seventies. The man grinning at her with a twinkle in his periwinkle-blue eyes was less wrinkled, his back straighter, his hair salt-and-pepper rather than completely gray. A man in his fifties, she would have guessed, a bit older than her father and every bit as enthusiastic.

"You're *fae*?" she blurted. According to Grams, faeries could live thousands of years. But there was a difference between knowing the lore and seeing it in living color right in front of her face. "And you've been living at the manor this whole time?"

"Aye, ever since the worlds diverged."

"You're the Envoy," Callum said, his eyes wide. "The one appointed by the fae king."

"Right again." Jockie stepped back and held the door. "Come in, come in—I'll put the tea on."

A thousand thoughts danced in Klara's head as she followed him into his workshop. It was remarkably similar to the way it looked in 2022, well-worn tools lined up in neat rows on the wall, stained ledgers piled on the desk. All that was missing was the mini fridge full of bottles of Irn-Bru and Beans, the little orange tabby who spent her days stalking mice when she wasn't snoozing on the wide windowsill.

As if reading her thoughts, Jockie scooped up a ball of white fur from his workbench, where it had been nestled in one of his work gloves. "This here's Snowflake," he said. "One of the house cats just had a litter and I took the runt off their hands."

The little kitten unrolled itself to stretch luxuriously in his big hand, yawning to show a tiny pink tongue. If Klara'd had any doubts, seeing Jockie's gentleness with the little creature confirmed for her that he was the same man.

She and Callum took seats at the small wooden table while Lady Mairi excused herself to get back to her guests. "I'll see you in the morning," she told Jockie affectionately. "I can show you the door that's sticking, if you're not too busy keeping the peace of the land."

"Aye, my lady," Jockie said cheerfully.

"I'm still trying to make sense of this," Klara said once she was gone. "The Bard told the story of Breogan and Danu tonight, but I'm still getting used to the idea that my ancestor was on the Council of the Worlds. And Arianrhod had told me that she herself transferred her powers to the Pillars so they wouldn't be taken away by jealous rivals, not that it'd been done in punishment to her. And *now* I've just learned that you're in charge of keeping peace between the fae and humans."

"Are you the first Envoy, then?" Callum asked in a tone of awe.

"Ah no," Jockie said, bringing a tray with three steaming cups and a pitcher of cream. "That was me dad, Aul' John Kennerty. I was but a wee mite when we left the mound. Grew up picking daisies in the same patch as your grandmother and snitching cakes from the same windowsill when Cook was looking away."

Klara's jaw dropped. "You know Grams?"

"Aye, I know her well. I was at her wedding, in fact. You won't remember, because you were just a wee little thing in that puffy dress, but I put you on my shoulders so you could watch your Grams and Alice have their first dance."

Klara *did* have a memory of a nice man lifting her into the air, one of Grams's old friends from childhood.

"But that's the future," Callum was saying, his brow wrinkled. "It hasn't happened yet. How—"

"A tangle that, eh?" Jockie said. "Let's just say that Cernunnos thought it wise to give me some insight. A temporary trade with my future self, if you will. Anyway, it's urgent business what brings you here. We best get to it."

"You already know?" Klara asked.

Jockie sighed. "It's a bad business about Thomas, but you lads got a rough start in life, Cal."

Before Callum could respond, Jockie nodded at Klara's necklace, the red stone shimmering in the firelight. "I see you're wearing Adele's Eye of Rose," he said, his smile a bit melancholy. "Have you looked for guidance there?"

"Do you mean this necklace?" Klara's fingers closed over the stone automatically, the faint thrum now as familiar as if it was a part of her. "I'm told it's been in my family for generations. Is it, um—enchanted?"

"I—I'd best say no more," Jockie said. "Adele must have her reasons for not telling you about it."

"But if it's magic," Klara pressed, "and it could help us, why won't you tell me? Grams would understand."

Jockie pursed his lips. "You'd have to know the spell. Which is why I'm not saying another word. Spells are at the root of the troubles coming around to plague us again, if you ask me."

"But fae use spells all the time," Callum said. "At the faerie market—"

"Bah." Jockie scowled. "That's the *olc síth*. They may share the same ancestors as me, but mark my words, they took a very malicious turn when they left the mound. The *daoine síth* have no need for spells—we have plenty of magic of our own. Just ask young Callum here." Jockie poked a finger at where

Callum's scar had faded nearly completely, where he'd healed unnaturally fast after his battle with Llaw and his hounds.

"Aye, it's true," he said. Then, remembering his own heritage, he turned his eye to the droplet of ruby hanging from Klara's throat. It seemed to shimmer with opalescence, and he felt it reaching out to him, like it was watching him, and with a flash, he had a vision of Grams at home in Edinburgh, gazing into her tea and muttering with concern over Klara.

"You've been tracking her by her necklace!" he said.

Klara's eyes widened. "That's what it's for, isn't it? Did Grams put you up to it?"

"Oh, aye, well," Jockie beamed, slightly flustered. "We always knew you were a smart lass, did we not? Well, it's true. It's not much magic, just enough to connect you to your Grams and her power, to her time. Can ye blame her for wanting to be your guardian angel?"

"And how did she get my dad to bring it to me?"

"Ah, Ethan, I've found the man open to the power of suggestion..."

"Oh my God," Klara said, scandalized. "You used magic on him?"

"Just the one time," Jockie said, "and only because she was worried about you. She probably used the stone to track your mom when she was your age."

"But that's an invasion of privacy!"

"Klara," Callum said, touching her hand. "Should we not worry about that later?"

Klara nodded reluctantly. She would only be able to scold Grams if they managed to save the world.

"So...where do we start? I'm about two years behind

Thomas on practicing my skills, and I've just been slingshotted into a past that I'm very uninterested in being a woman in, and now I feel like I've been forced to digest an encyclopedia's worth of Scottish folklore. How am I supposed to prevent the forces of darkness from destroying our timeline if I can't even keep the narrative straight?" It all came out in a rush, a flurry of aggravation and exhaustion. Klara hadn't even realized how *up to her eyeballs* she was in frustration until she was faced with someone she finally knew, who might know more than she and Callum.

She felt Callum's arm wrap around her shoulder, then curl around to stroke her hair. "Let's start with the sword, lass," he said. "It seems to be the thing that everyone is most interested in here, and your connection to it has grown tenfold since I saw you last."

Klara let out a big sigh and nodded. "Okay," she said. "Let's start with my sword, Jockie."

"Aye. Well, by now you've heard of the Divergence of Worlds, when Breogan and Danu created more separation from the realm of gods and mortals, and punished Arianrhod by stripping her powers." Klara urged him on. "Your sword is the human power cleaver: it holds the power of severing gods and creatures from their magical abilities. However, as you know, energy cannot just disappear, it must *go* somewhere. Once severed, the sword can either store the power in its enchanted jewels, or, when touched by blood, channel the power into those connected to it. It's not unlike an electrical circuit in your time, lass. Only, with magic."

"Okay, got it. So Llaw could steal Arianrhod's powers, because he had a sword like it."

"Exactly. The sword he carried was the fae version of yours—only he stole it recently from its safekeeper. It hasn't been seen since."

Callum and Klara shared an uneasy glance, wordlessly asking one another if they should tell him. Klara nodded. "Go ahead."

"I have the sword," Callum said. "I've been hiding it since Llaw died."

Jockie's eyes widened. "But that's wonderful news! It's out of the hands of those who would abuse it, and we can reunite it with its proper guardian!"

"Are ye sure they can be trusted? It's hard not to be skeptical after everything we've been through."

Jockie didn't deny it. "The lad's been through hard times. He was tricked by those he trusted and suffered great loss."

"It's Aion," Callum burst out, shocked. "I—just *saw* it."

Jockie tapped his forehead. "The Sight, lad. It's getting stronger."

"But I just saw Aion," Klara said. "His fiancée just died."

"It's true. I blame myself," Jockie said miserably. "He was bereft at failing in his duty of protecting the sword, I think, and turned to his love as a way to redeem himself. I warned him of the bean-nighe's duplicity, but after the sword was stolen, I should have kept better track of him."

"She is an evil witch," Callum muttered.

"She is like all of her kind," Jockie said.

For a moment no one said anything, each of them lost in the strange turns of fate that had brought them here.

Klara thought of Llaw, neglected as a child, growing up

with a hunger for love that got twisted into a ravenous need for power.

She thought of Thomas, a clever and mischievous boy with a big heart, cruelly used by a selfish goddess to carry out a task that slowly poisoned him until his very soul was consumed by rot.

Of Aion, whose loss of duty broke him, and who was capable of a love that would make him do something as dangerous as make a deal with the bean-nighe.

"Maybe Breogan and Danu were right," she said bleakly. "Maybe humans will always find a way to destroy each other."

"No." Callum's eyes burned with determination. "I won't allow the world to be destroyed, not while there is a chance to be with you in it. Jockie can help us find a way. But I need you at my side, Klara. I cannae do it without ye."

Klara took his hand, feeling his wrist pulse with the beat of his strong heart. "Okay, fine. Sign me up," she said with a weak grin.

Jockie looked at the pair of them, and seemed to come to a decision. "I will arrange a meeting with Aion. Come back tomorrow at the same time, and you can return the sword to him—it ought to buoy him, I'd wager. Perhaps he knows something that can help us stop Thomas and protect Klara."

"Of course. You're one of the kindest men I've ever known, Jockie. I'm glad Mairi brought us together again."

"Ah, ye flatter me," Jockie said. "But I'm just trying to do what my father did before me, and bring peace where peace is possible."

"As noble a purpose as any," Callum said. "I am honored to join you."

As they left, something frightening popped into Klara's mind, something so worrying she couldn't bear to tell Callum. "You go on ahead, Callum. I'll catch up."

She turned back to the Envoy. "There's one last thing, Jockie," Klara said quietly. "If the sword works as you say it does, then I should have the powers of eight other Pillars inside me, but I've barely been able to use my own time abilities since I arrived in Rosemere."

His warm brown eyes creased with worry. "Not at all?"

She shook her head sadly. "I tried, but I couldn't even save Janneth."

Jockie reached out, and held one of her hands between his two callused ones. "I dinnae ken, lass, but that's as strange a mystery as I've heard since you arrived in this time." He patted the top of her hand. "But do not stop trying. There's more to you, and these powers, than any of us know."

CHAPTER THIRTY-FIVE

CALLUM

The guests were starting to depart when Klara and Callum returned to the manor. Luckily, Laird Johnstone was tipsy enough not to have noticed their absence.

"A splendid evening!" he pronounced. "I saw you speaking to Lady Mairi, Klara. Well done—she is very influential."

Callum saw Klara bristle at the comment, but she gave his father a stiff smile.

"Klara is tired," Callum said. "She has had a long day. I'd like to take her home."

"Of course, of course, my boy." The laird led them a bit unsteadily to the entrance, where the Westwoods were saying goodbye to their guests.

"Thank you so much for coming, Arthur," Lady Mairi

said, taking his hand. "And for bringing your delightful son and his enchanting fiancée."

"I'll call on you next week," Arthur added. "I think it's time we draw up that contract."

As Callum was following his father out, he saw Lady Mairi put a hand on Klara's arm and speak quickly in her ear.

When she caught up, he said, "What was that about?"

"She said it was an honor to meet someone from the future," Klara said, "and that you're lucky to have a girlfriend like me." At Callum's raised eyebrow she added, "Okay, fine, she just said that she and the laird will help in any way she can."

Callum couldn't respond, because they had caught up with the laird at the carriage. "I think that went very well!" the laird announced once they were settled and the carriage began to move. "Now that the Westwood and Johnstone families will be joined by marriage, the old bastard had no choice but to give me that contract. Klara, you will have to call on their daughter as soon as possible. She was married last year, and would be the perfect candidate to host an engagement party. She and her husband are friends with all the best young people."

Callum took note of Klara's expression and hastily interjected. "Father, we haven't decided when we will wed. This is all very new to us, and—"

"But you must get married as soon as possible," the laird said, frowning. "It is one thing to host your fiancée for a few days, but people will talk if there is an unmarried woman living under our roof."

"That's fine," Klara said coolly. "We can find somewhere else to stay."

"I suppose we could prevail upon the Westwoods," the laird mused, "now that you've been introduced. They *are* family, after all."

"Can we talk about this later?"

"We can talk about this *now*, Callum," Klara said impatiently. "We don't have *time* for all this social climbing, remember?"

"There is a lot to do," the laird said, oblivious to her tone. "We shall have to bring in a dressmaker and make plans with the groundskeepers. We will need to send invitations as soon as possible, and that will require us to settle on a guest list, which means—"

"There's not going to be a wedding," Klara snapped. "Not until I'm good and ready. And I've got more important things to think about than what to wear, okay?"

The laird was taken aback. He looked to Callum, as if waiting for him to do something.

Callum was well aware that most men of his time wouldn't allow their wives to speak so freely—not in the humble part of town where he'd grown up, and certainly not at the upper reaches of society.

But most men weren't lucky enough to love women like Klara. Her fire and passion were among the things he loved best about her, and he wouldn't dream of silencing her. Perhaps they could come to an understanding…

"Are you going to allow her to speak to you like that?" the laird demanded, slurring his words slightly.

"She's tired," Callum said uncomfortably, "as I mentioned before, and I'm sure that after a good night's sleep we'll all—"

"I'm not tired." Klara's irritation was rising straight toward fury. "And I don't appreciate being talked about when I'm sitting right here. I appreciate your hospitality, Laird Johnstone, and the fact that you helped Callum get out of jail, but maybe it would be best if we all took a break from each other."

"I see," the laird said, his own voice hardening.

Callum tried to take Klara's hand, but she yanked it away. No one spoke for the remainder of the trip.

"I find that I am tired, after all," Klara said when they arrived, an obvious lie. "So I think I'll head upstairs."

"I'll see you to your room," Callum said. "Good night, Father."

The laird was handing his hat and coat to a servant and did not respond.

Callum had to quicken his pace to keep up with Klara as she hurried up the stairs. "Wait, please, Klara."

She turned abruptly, her long scarlet skirts swirling around her ankles. It was hard to believe this was the same girl who'd looked at him with such love in her eyes only an hour ago in Jockie's quarters.

"I'm sorry for the things my father said to you," Callum began. "He doesn't understand that—"

"Your father is a shallow, greedy man who only cares about himself," Klara said.

Her words stung more than they should have. "That's not true. He didn't have to get me released from jail or bring me into his home."

"Oh, *great.* So a few good meals and some nice clothes make up for *abandoning you at birth.*"

"I didn't say that, Klara," Callum protested, his face hot. "He only did that because of my eyes, because he was afraid people would think I was part fae."

"You *are* part fae."

Callum's retort died on his lips as, for the first time, he allowed the truth to sink all the way in. How strange it was to live nineteen years on this earth, only to discover that everything you believed about yourself was wrong.

Callum's earliest memories were of the only father figure he'd ever known yelling at him to stop crying…and of the boy who would become a brother to him comforting him afterward. Callum had spent most of his nineteen years of life believing that Brice was right, that he was little more than a gutter rat, worthless except for the moments in the ring.

But in the matter of a few days, Callum had discovered that he was actually of noble birth. As uncomfortable as he felt when the laird's staff bowed before him and the laird's wealthy friends greeted him warmly, there was a comfort to it that had little to do with fine clothes and splendid food, and everything to do with belonging.

And yet in the same space of time, Callum had also learned that he carried the blood of the fae, the race most spurned by the wealthy class to which he had been born. So tainted was this blood that his father allowed himself to be convinced it was better to give Callum away than to recognize him as his own son. That he forced his wife—Callum's mother—to hide her true identity every day of her short life so that she would not bring shame upon his name.

His father had been weak, and selfish, but he'd also experienced great loss. He was far from perfect, but so was everyone Callum had ever known. He himself was so flawed that sometimes he'd despaired of his right to the little he had. The thought of rejecting the father he'd yearned for all of his life, a father who clearly wanted Callum now regardless of mistakes he'd made during a terrible time, was unimaginable.

Callum longed to go somewhere alone to think about everything, to pray for the wisdom to know the right course. But that was impossible, given the fact that the future of the worlds rested on him and Klara.

"You don't need him, Callum," Klara was saying. "He's not better than you just because he's rich."

"That's easy for you to say." The words carried the force of his anger. "My father is my only living relative. He's all I've got."

"All you've got?" Klara grabbed his hands. "You have me. You will always have me."

Callum lowered his head. "I'm sorry..." he said as he realized his mistake.

"Hey," she said, lifting his head with her finger under his chin. "Save your sorrys for when you don't put the toilet seat down."

Callum let out a breath, the air warming her hand.

"Thank you," he breathed. "I love you."

"I love you, too."

CHAPTER THIRTY-SIX

KLARA

Klara had barely touched her breakfast when the servant returned to take the tray away. A few minutes later Mistress Drever arrived with an armful of gowns.

"Callum tells me you'll be visiting Castle Udne again tonight to meet the Westwoods' daughter," she said, hanging the gowns from hooks in the dressing room. "You'll be needing something suitable for evening. I'll have the seamstress get to work as soon as you choose."

Klara was surprised that Callum had revealed their destination until she realized that it was the best way to avoid raising the laird's suspicions—and keep him from making other arrangements again without consulting with her. She only hoped that the next time he saw the Westwoods, they'd be quick enough on their feet to go with the story.

Getting into and out of heavy, tight-fitting gowns was getting old, especially since Klara wasn't sure she'd even be able to manage on her own. She tried to stand still as Mistress Drever busied herself with the laces and pins and hook fasteners, but by the time she'd tried on three dresses in a row she no longer cared which of them she'd be stuck in for the rest of the day.

"I agree," she said when Mistress Drever told her that the russet taffeta suited her, even though she'd give anything for her sweats. "Exactly what I was thinking."

After that followed what seemed like eternity having her hair washed, braided, and twisted on top of her head.

"We'll just need to take a look at Catherine's jewelry and choose something to go with the dress," Mrs. Drever said, "and then you can relax until it's time to leave."

"Oh no—I'll wear my own necklace," Klara said, her hand going to the smooth stone.

"Of course. Was it a gift from Callum?"

"It belonged to my mother, actually," Klara said—and out of nowhere she felt the sort of pang of grief she hadn't experienced in a long time.

Perhaps sensing that she'd touched a nerve, the housekeeper excused herself, and Klara was finally alone. She couldn't understand how anyone could live this way, like a fragile doll on a shelf, spending their days being pampered and coddled, but not allowed to go anywhere without raising eyebrows.

Except for Lady Mairi. She was the only woman Klara had encountered who seemed to have a mind of her own. It wasn't the other women's fault that they lived in such a repressive society, but she was still glad to know that she was descended from women with backbone.

Her husband, Laird Ewan, seemed like a decent man, too… unlike Grams's father, who she rarely spoke of and only in negative terms. That Laird Westwood was the reason Grams had fled to New York as a teen. "Better to be disowned than forced to live like that," she'd once said.

It dawned on Klara now that Jockie had been Grams's true father figure. If she ever managed to return to her own time, Klara was going to demand that Grams tell her everything—the fae lore and magic that Jockie had taught her, and why Grams had never told Loreena the truth. Klara smiled at the thought of Grams giving her the necklace the way parents in her time tracked their kids with their phones.

Good one, Grams.

Klara's anger had subsided by the time they had to leave for their appointment with Jockie. She missed her mother terribly, but she was still lucky to have a loving family, something Callum had never had. It would take time for him to trust that Klara wouldn't leave him the way his parents had… wouldn't betray him as Thomas did.

When a footman brought a note with her dinner, Klara scanned the heavy inked lettering and realized it was the first time she'd seen Callum's handwriting.

Please meet me at the west entrance. I've found a driver to take us to Kingshill Manor. Yours, C.

Yours. Such an old-fashioned way to sign a letter, but also… kind of lovely. Klara folded it carefully and tucked it into an inner pocket of her gown before going to meet Callum.

He was waiting for her with an anxious look on his face.

"I'm sorry for last night," he blurted. "You were right. You are the most important person to me, Klara."

"Hello to you too," Klara said, kissing his cheek. "Um…I think I'm sorry too, but we're okay. We already settled it last night. This thing with Jockie—"

Callum was nodding with relief. "Yes. Of course. The carriage is ready."

The road was empty at this hour, and the driver left them at the footpath that led to the stables with a promise to wait. Jockie greeted them at the gate, holding an oil lantern to light their way.

"I've got the tea on. Aion's already here. You should know that he's…well, he's unsettled. Traumatized, I s'pose you'd say. That kind of loss, mixed with that kind of sinister magic…" Jockie looked at Callum. "But I don't have to tell you that, do I, lad? The strength you traded for, it came at a cost. When you use it, remember that it has two faces. It can be used for good, to protect you and those you love, but if you are not careful it can be turned."

"Like what happened to Thomas," Callum murmured sadly.

"Indeed." Jockie put a heavy hand on Callum's shoulder, and neither said anything for a long moment. "I believe Cernunnos shared with you the vexing truth that none of us are purely good or evil. I cannot say why some mortals master their evil impulses and some succumb. After two thousand years of life, Breogan and Danu's design is as much a mystery to me now as ever."

"Are they coming in, or standing there all night?" Aion's impatient voice floated out, and Jockie gave a sheepish grin.

"Come on, then. Cook sent over some cakes. Can't 'ave ye starving."

To Klara's surprise, Aion wasn't alone in Jockie's quarters. Lady Mairi was seated near the fire, serenely sipping tea from one of Jockie's chipped mugs while Aion paced.

"You know each other?" Klara asked.

"I visit the *daoine síth* now and then," Lady Mairi said. "I like to know what's happening, you might say."

"Eh, she's bein' modest," Jockie said. "The Westwood ladies have always liked to stir things up. If there were more like her, the fae wouldn't have to become almost invisible in your time, Klara. In fact Lady Mairi would probably be pesterin' the ministers at Parliament."

"I'm sure I don't know what you're talking about, John Kennerty the Younger," Lady Mairi said primly—but the sparkle in her eyes told another story. She squeezed his hand and said her goodbyes, promising to visit Klara and Callum soon.

"Can we get on with this?" Aion demanded.

Klara gasped as he moved into the light. Aion had aged decades since the last time she'd seen him up close, five hundred years in the future, his pallor a sickly gray, his skin loose around his shrunken flesh, his eyes burning in their sockets. It was strange to know that he would survive this grief, but that he looked like a dying man now.

"I'm...so sorry for your loss," Klara said, her heart breaking for both Anne and the purposeful, caring man Aion must have been.

"Yes, well. I suppose it was inevitable, a fae falling in love with a human—she was always going to die before I was ready." He frowned. "But that isn't why we are here. Where is the sword?"

Callum pulled the ratty, wrapped blade from his belt, and Aion eyed it with distaste. "You couldn't stand to handle it with more reverence?"

"I couldn't stand to let it be discovered by someone with ill intentions, sir." Working quickly, Aion unwrapped the stained leather from around the pommel and hand guard, then inspected the stones and blade for nicks or damage.

"To think of what this sword has been through since I last held it, the evil committed with it..." he murmured, and then looked up with fire in his eyes. "I'd enjoy crushing Arianrhod and her monster under my boot and listening to them scream."

Klara stepped back, surprised at his vitriol, and suddenly nervous about returning the sword to him. Surely he wasn't so damaged that he would use it for ill?

"The bean-nighe?" Klara asked.

Aion's lip curled. "That accursed sack of rot and bile, yes. I'd love to be the one to snuff out her dying breath."

She smiled nervously, gently. "But surely that wouldn't bring Anne back?"

Callum stepped closer. "Klara, if the same had happened to you, I wouldn't feel any different than Aion feels now. Ye cannae blame him for his grief." Aion stood a little straighter, looked Callum in the eye, and nodded his thanks.

"Yes, but the sword—"

"Did you hear that?" Jockie said, suddenly alert.

Klara strained her ears, nothing. "I don't hear anything..."

Jockie's eyes darted around, and she glanced at Callum who had the same unnerving look on his face.

"Callum?"

Jockie grabbed a wooden staff from the corner and started toward the door—but before he reached it there was a loud crack and brilliant flash of light followed by the sound of splintering wood.

"Run!" Jockie yelled. "Take the tunnel. Under my bed. I'll hold him off as long as I can."

Callum seized Klara's hand, but before they could run, Thomas burst into the room, a huge serpent slung around his neck. Another twisted around his feet, hissing with its jaw open wide to show its forked tongue, its bloodred eyes flashing. Half a dozen more snakes slithered in over the wreckage.

Thomas held his sword, grinning. "Surprise, surprise," he said cheerfully, jabbing it in Klara's direction. "You know I shan't give up anytime soon, Klara. And now, you've revealed to me the location of both copies of what I seek!"

She ran for the feed room, Callum on her heels, and he slammed the door behind them and pushed a heavy barrel of grain against it while Klara lifted the door in the floor. Only then did she notice that Callum had dragged Aion along, too.

"You go first!" she urged. Callum picked up a lantern hanging from the wall and handed it to Klara who hurried into the darkness below.

Klara could hear crashing and grunting and a terrible chorus of hissing from the other room, and prayed that Jockie's fae magic would hold off Thomas and his monsters. The lantern's glow illuminated the mouth of a tunnel carved from the earth, roots protruding from its walls.

The light bounced dizzily off the tunnel walls as they hurried through the tunnel, stopping only once they heard a mighty splintering from above, and then continuing their path at a jog. When the tunnel ended at a set of rough wooden steps leading to a heavy oak door, Callum rammed the door with his shoulder. It gave way in a hail of splinters, and they entered a chilly, dank-smelling chamber that Klara recognized as the old larder.

Klara froze as a snake zoomed out of nowhere and launched itself at her ankle, almost wrapping around it before Klara kicked it out of the way.

"Nice try," Thomas shouted triumphantly, coming around the bend behind them amid a horde of snakes. Callum grabbed Aion's arm and dragged him out of the chamber and into the hall, and Klara sliced off the head of the closest snake. She was alone in the chamber now, half a dozen snakes between her and the door, Callum yelling for her to hurry.

She closed her eyes and concentrated on the feeling of the sword vibrating in her hand, her powers gathering like a raging storm. She let the sword guide her, slashing and jabbing at an impossible speed, feeling the blade sever dense flesh.

When she opened her eyes, Thomas was coming at her with fury in his eyes. She parried his strike, the clash of metal accompanied by what felt like an electric shock. Klara gasped and nearly dropped her sword—

And then strong arms swept her up and carried into the hall and through the library doors, which banged shut behind them.

Callum held her tightly. "Were you bit? Did they hurt you?"

"I'm fine. But is Aion—"

Something slammed into the library doors. They shuddered, but held.

"Still here." Aion sagged against the wall, looking as if he'd run a marathon.

Another thud, and this time the hinges pulled from the wall. Klara's heart hammered in fear. One more blow and—

The doors crashed open. Thomas stood before them in a writhing mass of snakes, his sword raised in triumph.

CHAPTER THIRTY-SEVEN

CALLUM

Thomas took a step forward—and instantly flew backward against the wall of the hallway. He hit it hard and rebounded with a look of shock on his face. The snakes turned on each other and formed a writhing mass pressed against the wall next to him.

Thomas gripped his sword in both hands and roared as he rushed toward the entrance to the library, and once again was repelled.

"The library's enchanted," Klara yelled. "No assholes allowed."

Callum moved in front of her, not trusting the spell to protect her, and watched Thomas figure it out.

"The Accords," he muttered, his intelligent eyes dark with

fury. "You damn Westwoods—why should it be you? Why should you and that pathetic brute back there be in charge of this world?"

"We aren't," Klara shot back. "That was the whole point. No one is supposed to be. Jockie's the Envoy because he believes in peace. His father and my ancestors were chosen because they were *good* and *fair.* Something you'll never understand."

Callum's mouth went dry at the thought of having left Jockie behind with Thomas and his snakes. "What did you do to him?"

Thomas tsked, regaining his composure. His eyes were as dark as shale as he flicked his palm in the direction of the snakes. Instantly, they dissolved into pale dust.

"Less than he deserved. You know what's wrong with you, Klara? You're attracted to weakness. To men who will never amount to anything. With Jockie's powers, he could have done anything. He could have taken over the manor, Rosemere, all of Scotland centuries ago. And you would never have been born."

Thomas turned on Callum with a hate-filled smirk. "You're nothing but a pathetic bastard born to a whore. Brice should have let you die. I can't believe I wasted so much time on you. I taught you everything I know and you still let yourself get beaten."

"Because I won't cheat," Callum said grimly. His face was hard, his shock quickly giving way to fury. "What happened to you, Tom? You never cared about power and wealth before. You always said we were lucky not to be rich because we were free, that we could go anywhere we wanted and that was better than all the treasure in Rosemere."

"I was a fool." Thomas's teeth were bared in a snarl. "The difference between us is that I grew up and saw what the world is really like. When are *you* going to learn?" Callum couldn't believe what he was hearing. This couldn't be his oldest friend—his soul had been crushed by Arianrhod and Llaw and Malabron. But surely he was still in there, somewhere, and Callum just needed to find a way to speak to him.

"In, the name of everything we shared, please stop this," he pleaded. "I know you, Tom."

"Do you?" Thomas's face changed, softening. He looked at Callum imploringly. "Do you know me, old friend?" Callum took a step forward and Klara grabbed Callum's arm and pulled him back.

"Don't!" she muttered urgently. Only then did Callum realize he had been about to step across the threshold.

"Would you kill me?" he asked. Thomas dropped his gaze…but not before Callum caught a fleeting glimpse of something like shame.

"You *are* in there," he said. "Please, Thomas, dinnae let this destroy you. It's not too late." He prayed that it was true. "Think of everything we shared, all the good times we had. We can have them again if you'll only—"

"What we shared was *hell*." The ferocity of Thomas's contempt nearly took Callum's breath away. The dark, mocking gaze was back on Thomas's face. "Stop deluding yourself. Both of us would have given anything for a different life, and I finally got smart enough to make it happen. I'm done with suffering, done with settling for scraps, done with being scammed and used and lied to, and done with taking orders from the likes of Brice. You and I have gotten nothing but raw deals our whole lives. Cheated of our mothers, our fathers, our livelihoods, our respect. But you and I have *power*, Callum. We're strong, we know how to fight—why haven't we ever just taken what we need? Why do we have to accept the raw deals? I know I won't, but take a good look at yourself," he said disgustedly. "You traded with a woman notorious for bad deals that rob mortals of years of life, for what? Strength you barely use because you're chained to *her* like a whipped dog. You let a *woman* tell you what to do."

Callum felt Klara stiffen beside him. "Don't go there, buddy," she warned him.

Thomas didn't even look at her. "No more raw deals for me. That stopped the moment Llaw failed to kill me. In fact—" he paused to lick his lips, cherishing the moment, all eyes on him "—I even used the demigod to lead me to you, the last Pillar."

"That cannot be true, Thomas."

"Jumping in time is hard, but tagging along in someone's wake is easy. Llaw left a trail as obvious as a bear in a berry field. I saw you, at the faerie ring, I saw you, on the Isle of Skye. And I knew that the Ring of Brodgar would be my moment, to kill Llaw, to kill Klara, and step into my full power. I only wish you hadn't gotten involved, Callum."

"But you didn't succeed, humble yourself," Klara growled. "Sounds like an inferiority complex to me."

"Oh but I will succeed," he said, drawing a figure as if writing on an invisible wall. A pale, shimmering halo formed around him, and he started to fade, as though he'd been made of smoke. "Where I'm going, I won't need friends. I won't need anyone at all."

"No!"

But Callum was speaking to empty air, the only sign that Thomas had been there at all a trail of dust where the snake had fallen from his hand.

"Where's Aion?" Klara had turned away from him and was scanning the room in confusion.

Callum joined her in searching, but Aion was nowhere to be found.

"He can't have just vanished!"

"*He's got the sword*, Callum." She ran out the door of the library, Callum right behind her.

"Where are you going?"

"We've got to find Jockie!" she said as she disappeared into the larder. She was tugging at the heavy door when Callum caught up. He nearly pulled the door off its hinges, and they were plunged into darkness.

"Klara, let me get a lantern!" Callum said, knowing that nothing would stop Klara. In the next instant he heard her sharp cry, and his blood went cold.

"What happened?" he said, feeling his way along the wall.

"Nothing. I fell. But I think I found Jockie."

It couldn't have taken Callum more than a few minutes to run back to the library and return with a candle, but Klara had managed to drag Jockie into the light near the end of the tunnel. He was starting to come around, rubbing his face and attempting to sit up.

"I'm sorry, lass," he said. "I tried to hold him back."

"You were amazing," Klara said, kneeling next to him and taking his hand. "Is this from the snakes?"

Callum knelt beside her and saw that Jockie's broad face and meaty hands were covered with punctures, tiny pairs of jagged blood-crusted dots.

Jockie snorted. "Never mind that," he said. "Those creatures are nearly harmless. No more dangerous than the wee snakes in the garden. That spell was but a child's amusement."

Callum gaped at the Envoy. "You mean we could have stayed and fought him? If he was trying to kill us, why would he use that spell?"

"That's what I was tryin' to tell you back there," Jockie said. "The other monsters he summoned—the ones who killed your father's men—those came from between worlds. It's not like time traveling in this world, or using a portal to go from one place to another. He would have needed more than a spell."

"But if he was able to before—"

"Malabron must have compelled one of the gods' creatures to help him. It wouldn't be the first time he lured magical creatures to the market with a shiny bauble."

"Wait—do you mean Malabron?" Klara asked.

Jockie's eyebrows shot up. "None other."

"There's something else," Klara said. "Aion's disappeared."

Jockie was instantly alert. "What do you mean—disappeared?"

"We looked all over the library, and he's just not there. We're not sure if he slipped out a window, or why."

Jockie said nothing for a long moment, tugging at his beard, his acorn-brown eyes troubled. "He just wasn't the same," he finally said, "but I don't see why he'd turn. Even in his grief, he's always had a good sense of right and wrong."

Klara paled. "Tom—" She cleared her throat. "I bet it was Tom. Aion already seemed on the cusp of morality, but Tom made this big speech about how life had cheated him, given him a raw deal, how he wouldn't take it anymore. What if…"

Jockie pressed his hands on the table, gazing at the wood like the grain held a clue. He looked up and his eyes held pain. "What if Thomas's speech spoke to the dark part of Aion? We'll have to move forward imagining it's so. As long as Aion doesn't give Thomas the sword, we should be all right for now." He sighed. "Meanwhile, I think it's best if the two of you go back to the library. Mairi's sure to be only delighted to bring your dinner. You'll be safe there until morning."

"I still need to get to Udne Castle," Callum said miserably.

"I know you do, lad. But all that rich food will surely give you indigestion. Good, simple fare is what you'll need for what's coming next."

CHAPTER THIRTY-EIGHT

CALLUM

When Callum left the stables, carrying a loaf of brown bread wrapped in a cloth that the Envoy had insisted he take with him, he lingered in the garden staring up at the window that he knew to be Klara's in the future. There was no reason to think that she was in the same room now—hundreds of years before she was even born, something that still made his head feel thick and cottony—but that didn't quell his faint hope that she might sense that he was looking for her, that his vow to protect her was as strong as ever.

At least Callum knew that Klara was safe in the manor for the night. Laird and Lady Westwood seemed to understand even more about the state of the worlds than he did, they were under the protection of the Envoy, and Klara could get to the library quickly if Thomas came back.

And she had her sword. As Callum trudged back to the castle, memories of the day he'd taught her to use it came back, her long hair flying as she gave it her all. Now she was at least as skilled as he, the sword becoming like a part of her as she leapt and spun and slashed. Klara fighting was a beautiful, graceful thing, unlike Thomas's trickery and Callum's brute force which were meant only to win.

This one night—it was all Callum was willing to spend apart from Klara. Which brought up something else Callum had no idea how to discuss with Klara: her assumption that he could return to her time and start a new life with her there. He'd be willing to do so; he'd live anywhere, in any time, to be with Klara, especially now that Thomas was lost to him.

If only he hadn't made the deal with the bean-nighe prohibiting his return. But if he tried to travel there, he would die. If Klara ended up going back without him—if he were to have any kind of life in his time—Callum could not bear to lose his father.

When he reached Udne Castle, the servants had all gone to bed but the light was still burning in his father's office. Callum tried to walk silently past the door, unprepared to confront his father now; much better to wait until the morning when he'd had time to collect his thoughts.

But just as he thought he'd made it safely past, he heard the laird clearing his throat behind him. "I see that sleep eludes us both this evening."

With his heart sinking, Callum turned to find his father rise from his desk. "Hello, Father."

"Come, come, sit with me awhile. When I was a lad of your age, I ushered in the sunrise in every tavern in Rosemere at least once, usually with a pretty barmaid for company."

Callum smiled uneasily, wondering what point the laird was making.

"But then my father grew ill and my responsibilities seemed to grow every day. I had to learn the business and supervise the staff and balance the accounts. At first I missed my friends, the carefree life of a bachelor."

The laird seemed to be waiting for a response. When he didn't get one, he plowed on. "But soon I came to appreciate the life of a member of noble society. Callum, I'm sure it will be hard to say goodbye to your old friends, but if you think about it, you'll be doing them a favor."

"A…favor?"

The laird swept his hand around the room with its fine appointments. "I can only imagine how different your new life will be from…your past situation," he said delicately, as if he couldn't bring himself to refer directly to Callum's poverty. "If you were to bring your friends here, it would be terribly awkward. You've benefited from Klara's experience with certain…social customs. Your friends wouldn't know how to behave, and that would embarrass them."

Now it was Callum's turn to narrow his eyes. Did his father think he'd grown up eating from a trough?

"And you couldn't return the visit," the laird continued, steepling his fingers. "It won't do for you to be seen in that part of town in the future for any reason other than the family business. I realize that men your age from some of the better families do occasionally seek entertainment in the rougher custom houses, but the Johnstones have always been above that. And now that we will be linked by marriage to the Westwoods, protecting our family name will become even more important.

"Besides," he said with an indulgent smile, "your Klara is already making friends with excellent people. Soon she'll keep you so busy squiring her from one party to the next that you won't have time for anything else."

Callum was now so uncomfortable he slid to the edge of his seat. "I don't think Klara will take to that well, Father. She is interested in science, in the study of the stars. She plans to continue her studies—and as she told you, we've no plans to marry anytime soon."

The laird's face hardened, and he drew himself up in the chair. "And as *I* said, that is unacceptable. Klara is a lovely girl, but she must be aware of her liabilities. She has no money and while the Westwoods have welcomed her, everyone knows that they only recently made her acquaintance. Tongues will wag, I promise you that. I do hate to be blunt, Callum, but if Klara hadn't been fortunate enough to attract your interest, no eligible bachelor would give her a second look. She'd be lucky to marry an old widower with a dozen children needing to be looked after."

"Klara won't marry anyone she doesn't want to. And she doesn't care about wealth."

The laird raised his eyebrows, then barked an ugly laugh. "Every woman cares about how and who they marry. Don't be a fool."

Anger was catching fire inside Callum, made worse by the

fact that Klara had warned him about his father, but he'd refused to listen. Then, the rage turned into anguish: his father wasn't wrong, not in this time. How was Klara supposed to study the stars in this time, when all a woman *could* do was marry for wealth, or die alone, without a means for a living. An overwhelming sadness overcame him; to love Klara as she was, to be who she was, he would have to allow her to return to her time, and never see her again.

Still, his father's cruelty in saying it stung. "You may think that because you can't see past your own vanity and greed," Callum said. "But I shall love Klara for more than her connections, and she loves me for more than wealth. It's not something I can imagine you would understand, since you cared more about what people would think than about your own son. You *abandoned me*."

It wasn't until Callum heard his own voice break that he realized how much pain he'd suppressed, just because he wanted his father to love him. All the years he thought that his mother gave him up because she was poor and struggling with no way to feed him, he'd resented her for it—when the truth was so much uglier. A man who could have fed and clothed a hundred children wouldn't keep his own just because he carried his mother's secret.

The laird's shoulders sagged, his pompous expression fading. "I've admitted I made a mistake. I would never have done it if it weren't for Mistress Drever, anyway—she is the one you should save your anger for."

Callum felt sickened. His father was so callous that he'd blame an old woman—one who had faithfully cared for his wife—for his own sins. "If you hate the fae so much, why did you ever marry my mother?"

For the first time, his father looked unsure of himself. He drummed his finger on the arm of the chair, finally giving an extravagant sigh. "I fear you will make too much of this, son, in your current state of mind. Trust me that everything will look different once you've had a chance to consider."

"Tell me."

The laird compressed his lips. "I never intended to," he said. "I didn't know her nature when I—" He sighed and began again. "I didn't lie when I told you that she came to the castle. But she did not come from across the sea, and there was no courtship. Her father sent her because his worker was sick that day and..." He shrugged and gave a weak smile. "It was one afternoon's amusement, but when she became with child, her father came to see me. He, er, made it clear that there would be consequences if I didn't marry his daughter. And all my men put together would have been no help if he'd brought fae curses upon me."

Callum thought his jaw would hit the floor. His father had never loved his mother; he'd taken advantage of a poor common girl, stolen her virtue and only married her under threat.

"I can see what you're thinking," his father said, his irritation returning. "You think I'm the one in the wrong. But what you don't realize is that you can never trust a fae. They're conniving, lying, deceitful—"

Callum got up from the chair with such force that it toppled backward, shaking with fury. He loomed over his father with his fists clenched as the laird cowered in shock.

"*I'm* a fae, damn you," he said. "And you are no father of mine."

CHAPTER THIRTY-NINE

KLARA

Well past midnight, Klara couldn't fall asleep. She had been given what her father had christened the Muriel Spark room—he'd named all the guest rooms after Scottish authors—a room that Klara had cleaned dozens of times. Just last week she'd found a guest's earring under the bed and mailed it to her in Louisiana.

Sometimes living in different centuries messed with Klara's head.

When Klara finally did drop off, she dreamed that Finley was trapped in the tunnel under the Kingshill grounds as dozens of snakes slithered and hissed, coming closer and closer. She was running blindly in the direction of his frantic barking, tripping over roots and brushing against thick cobwebs, but the tunnel seemed to go on forever—

"Klara."

Someone was shaking her shoulder. Klara's eyes flew open and she fumbled for her sword, blinking in the sunlight streaming through the window—only to come fully awake to see Callum crouched next to her with a serious case of bedhead.

"I'm sorry," he said. "I didn't want to wake you but I think you were having a nightmare."

Klara launched herself at him, throwing her arms around him and nearly knocking him onto the floor, and Callum held her tightly.

"You came back!" she gasped, pulling back to take a good look at him. There were creases on his face and his eyes were bleary, and the woolen blanket that had been folded over a chair was twisted around his legs. "Were you sleeping on the *floor*? Why didn't you get into the bed with me?"

"I didn't want to disturb your sleep." He blushed a deep pink. "And…it isn't actually common for men to sleep in the same room as lasses they aren't married to."

Klara laughed, more relieved than she could have imagined to see Callum. "At least you should have taken some of the covers. You must be freezing."

She pulled the coverlet from the bed and slid down onto the thick carpet next to Callum, draping it over them both. Callum put his arm around her and pulled her close, and Klara nestled against him and tried to forget everything but being together, if only for a moment.

But Callum needed to talk. "I'm so sorry," he kept repeating. "You were right about the laird. He is not a man of honor." And then, finally, "I'm never going back there."

Klara pulled away from Callum and stared into his eyes. "You don't have to say that, Callum. I shouldn't have judged him—like you say, things are different in your time, and I don't even know him. I'm incredibly lucky to have a dad, and I should have—"

"Hush," Callum said, and kissed her softly, his lips barely brushing hers. "It wasn't your fault. I wanted to believe my father was good—I wanted it so much that I couldn't see what was in front of me."

Klara stroked Callum's stubbly cheek. "Does this mean I don't get to hang with the girls at Lady Esibell's tomorrow afternoon? Because we were going to work on our pouncing and couching." Honestly, Klara couldn't think of a place she'd rather not be. At a noblewoman's house where she'd be making up conversation to fit a sixteenth-century narrative.

Callum's eyebrows knit together. "What does that mean?"

"I think it has to do with embroidery. Oh, and Esibell thinks you're 'right braw' which I'm pretty sure means hot," Klara said, remembering their passing conversation. "But then I overheard her friend in the shiny yellow dress tell Esibell I'm too peely-walley so…"

"You are *not*," Callum said. "I mean y'are, but it's lovely. It means pale, and you have skin like cream." After a moment he added, "I'm glad we dinnae have to be friends with them, Klara."

"We'll find better friends. We've already got Lady Mairi

and Jockie, but maybe we can find a few people our own age…"

Klara let her eyelids flutter shut and concentrated on the delicious feeling of Callum's big hands idly rubbing her back.

"Klara…"

"Mmm?"

"There's something I need to tell you. About the bean-nighe."

Klara opened her eyes, reality flooding back, and leaned up on her elbow. "This doesn't sound good."

"I told you I went to her to come here," he said, not quite looking at her. "But she does not grant more than one wish. There was a condition. If I go back to your time I'll…die."

Klara stared at Callum in horror. "No," she whispered. "*No.* Tell me you're joking."

"I wish I was. I didn't know if you were alive, or dead, and in that moment I would have traded literally anything to come and make sure you were safe."

Tears gathered in Klara's eyes. "I can't lose you, Callum. We have to find a way to get around it." Something occurred to her. "When Arianrhod appeared to me in the tower, she wanted me to report to her on Thomas. I was never going to do it, but maybe I could strike a deal with her—"

"No," Callum said firmly. "She cannae be trusted. And I dinnae think even she can fix this. I don't regret what I did. If I hadn't, I can't bear to think of what Thomas might have accomplished by now."

Klara nodded and wiped her eyes. She wasn't going to waste time on what-ifs and regrets. "My powers are getting stronger, Callum. I may not have been a match for the bean-nighe or

Llaw or Thomas before, but don't count me out yet. We just have to stay alive long enough for me to fix this."

Callum took her hand and pressed it flat to his chest, over his heart.

She felt its steady, familiar beat. It was as if her own matched his in every way. She was his and he was hers, no matter what happened. They would fight for this love because it was worth fighting for.

"I will protect you," he vowed, "as long as I still draw breath."

Klara smiled weakly. "That's settled, then. Now let's go kick some traitor ass."

They found Jockie seated at his workbench carefully applying oil to the blade of a curved hand saw.

"Lookit what the cat dragged in," he said, beaming.

Klara set down the pan she was carrying, lifting a cloth off a dense brown pudding. Callum caught a whiff of a delicious, spicy aroma.

"The cook told us to bring you this," Klara said,

"Clootie dumpling!" Jockie exclaimed. "My favorite."

"Being the Envoy has certainly skewed your tastes to the human side, Jockie." Klara startled and looked into the shadows toward the voice, surprised she hadn't seen the woman when she first walked in.

"How did you—"

"It's a fae thing, wee one," she replied in a voice like honey and silk. The irony of the moniker wasn't lost on Klara, for the woman was much smaller than she, perhaps only four feet tall and lithe, with blue-tinted skin and long colorless hair.

"Klara, Callum, I'd like you to meet Siofra. She's a scarp pixie." Jockie sighed. "I'm afraid she came to me bearing bad news. Why don't you tell them."

Siofra's cool gaze landed on them, and she paused before she began to speak, as if deciding if the two human youths were worth her time. Then, she began, her voice low and sonorous. "I enjoy a livelihood at the faerie market," she began. "Providing for the pleasures of others. Hand massages, dances, conversation. I specialize in aromatic scalp massage. Yesterday, I was beckoned by a fae named Malabron—" Klara and Callum exchanged uneasy glances "—to tend to his most recent fascination, a human boy with an outsized sense of luxury and entitlement."

"Let me guess," Klara interrupted. "He's got red hair, blue eyes, a bad attitude, and his name is Thomas?"

"Exactly so. But he is not the purpose of my visit." Siofra paused dramatically.

Klara waited until an awkward amount of time had passed before finally interjecting, "And your purpose was…?" *The fae are so weird*, she decided.

"There was another there, one well known by my kind, but twisted. He was thin, with angry eyes, and he huddled in the corner clutching a sword to his chest." Callum grabbed her hand and squeezed, and Klara's sense of dread grew. "The sword had a unique hilt—filigree of leaves and stems, encrusted with emeralds and amethysts in the shape of a thistle."

"It's Aion!" Klara gasped.

Only Jockie looked unsurprised. "I prayed it would not come to this. His alliance with Malabron and Thomas is the worst news we could get," he said grimly. He stood and went to the window, staring out at the cold mist. "Ah, but the gods are shortsighted. Not all of them—there are those, like Cernunnos and Cían and Aengus Óg, who unselfishly devote themselves to their mortal charges. But others manipulate humans and fae for their own amusement, as though they are mere playthings—dollies and toy soldiers that can be put back on the shelf when they're tired of playing with them."

"Are you saying that Arianrhod deliberately destroyed Aion's life for *fun*?"

Jockie turned back from the window. His face seemed to have aged in a matter of seconds. "I'm saying that when Arianrhod gave her creature free rein to do as she wishes in the mortal realm, she opened the door to disaster. To the gods, a broken heart is inconsequential. They love as they wish, their affections as fleeting as their tempers. They have never bothered to understand that mortals—humans especially—can love so completely that two souls can become entwined until they cannot survive without each other."

Klara exchanged a glance with Callum, touched by Jockie's words despite their terrible implications.

"You saw Aion," Jockie continued wearily. "He is but a shadow of a man now. He was always a jolly lad, with a joke and a smile for everyone. As a child he used to follow me around begging me to make stars shoot from his fingers."

At Klara and Callum's confusion, he gave a sad smile. "It's just a silly trick. The Envoy is really not meant to waste time on such nonsense, but I can't resist the wee ones."

A memory came back to Klara of her birthday last year. Her father had grilled corn and burgers, and Jockie and Grams and Alice and Aunt Sorcha had come, and Craig brought his guitar. When Sorcha brought out a sugar-dusted almond cake with a single candle, it suddenly burst into a fountain of sparks.

Sorcha swore it wasn't a trick candle. But maybe the trick had been Jockie's.

"Aion loved with all his might, and he took his duty as keeper of the sword seriously. His parents, his friends…but when he met Janneth, everyone could see that here was the great love of his life. And I can see now that when she was taken from him because of the deception of that banshee, all that goodness turned to bitterness."

"He wanted to punish Arianrhod. To destroy the bean-nighe," Callum said, his face going pale. "And Thomas is determined to destroy everything. Aion wants to be there when he does, is that it?"

"I fear 'tis so."

"But…then how was he able to enter the library?" Klara asked. "I thought it was protected."

"Indeed it is," Jockie said. "It was meant to be a shelter for human and fae of pure heart."

"Which Aion was," Callum said, the terrible truth dawning on him. "Right up until he decided to join Thomas."

"This changes things," Jockie said worriedly. "Thomas alone is one thing, even with Malabron's help. But Aion…"

"What can he do?" Callum asked.

"And all he wants is to destroy the bean-nighe," Klara added. "Which is fine with me, by the way."

"You don't understand," Jockie said. "Killing the bean-nighe isn't our problem—it's that Malabron has an interest in him. Unless there's something in it for him, one more or less dead fae makes no difference to him. But if Aion had something to offer—something that could increase Malabron's power—"

"The stolen sword," Klara said, the pieces falling into place. "The bean-nighe is known for negotiating for years off mortals' lives to extend her own. If Aion borrows it to kill the bean-nighe, her powers and life will flow into him, including the life she's stolen from every poor fool who made a deal with her. Aion will live for thousands of years, serving at Malabron's pleasure—and with all of the powers that the creature has stolen. Then, once that's done, he has no need for the sword. But Thomas and Malabron do, and now they have a powerful ally."

"Dear God," Callum breathed, a look of horror on his face. "We have to warn Arianrhod. Maybe she can call her creature back."

"That's not the answer," Jockie said. "The bean-nighe is clever and Arianrhod is not at her full power. I doubt she can control her creature anymore."

"What if we get to the bean-nighe first?" Callum said. "If Klara kills her with her sword, the powers will flow into her. If Aion is angry but appeased by it, he has no reason to help those two scoundrels."

"I'm not sure I want the powers," Klara said. "Maybe you should kill her…then maybe you could come back home with me."

"'Tis a good plan, but we must hurry," Jockie said. "My guess is that they'll kill the bean-nighe first and then—once Aion absorbs her powers—Malabron will send both him and Thomas to kill you, Klara. With Thomas's fighting skills and the bean-nighe's magic, no one could survive their attack."

Klara seized Callum's hand. Suddenly the original quest—a mere swordfight against the best fighter in Rosemere—seemed like a walk in the park. "How can we find her? And what if we don't get there in time?"

"Don't worry," Jockie said, patting her hand as if she was a child. "I've still got a few tricks up my sleeve."

CHAPTER FORTY

KLARA

They returned to the tunnel and turned when it branched off, then followed it much farther than they'd gone before, until they reached a huge, wooden door carved with a series of knots and set into the tunnel wall.

"You've brought us to the mound, haven't you?" Callum asked Jockie.

"Do you recognize the door?" Klara asked.

"No. But there's…a feeling. A familiarity."

"Your blood knows," Jockie said approvingly. "If I didn't know better, I'd say you were more than a quarter fae."

He made a looping gesture and the door seemed to disintegrate into dust, then re-formed after they walked through.

They were in a large chamber that smelled of the first shoots of spring and was lit with amber faerie lights.

The sound of hoofbeats was followed by the Stag God entering the room. In the form of his familiar, Cernunnos was a large, noble creature with beautiful antlers and shining eyes.

"Prynhawn da," Jockie said, and the stag bowed his head in greeting.

"I asked Cernunnos to meet us here," Jockie admitted. "I didn't want to tell you in case he refused. Come, come. We don't have much time."

He put his hand on the great stag's back and motioned Klara and Callum to join him. Callum held Klara's hand tightly, and the moment they touched his stiff, soft fur, Klara felt the familiar sensation of the swirling tunnel of brilliant mist transporting her.

They were in the clearing again, the one that Cernunnos always seemed to use for such dreamlike meetings. This time the sensation of spinning, the silvery mist, did not frighten her; nor did Cernunnos's transformation to his human form.

"You must help us, Cernunnos," she blurted. "We've got to get to—"

Cernunnos raised a hand and Klara found herself silenced as if he'd turned off her voice with a remote. "I sense your discordance, Klara," he told her. "It will not help. Jockie was right to send word to me. You are headed into a perilous confrontation. You must be ready."

His grip on her voice lessened. "It doesn't matter if I'm ready, if Thomas has discovered what he's after, it's over for all of us." Cernunnos's golden gaze landed on her, and suddenly her heart slowed, her breathing became deeper, and the urgency leaked out of her like a deflating balloon. "Am I wrong?"

Instead of answering her question, he danced around it, like usual. "A boar sharpens his tusks daily. Does the boar live a life of battle? No. So why then does he sharpen his tusks every day, if he lives in a peaceful forest? Because on the day that he does need to battle, he will be ready."

Klara barely resisted rolling her eyes, even with the relaxing force of the god's gaze upon her. "Ho-kayyyy...and what's that got to do with racing to prevent time from splintering into a million pieces and the earth going up in a blaze of confused time bombs, or whatever?"

"These last days, you have used your sword often. It has spoken to you, guided you, and you've honed your ability and connection with it. Why have you not honed your time powers, Klara of Kingshill?"

Her snark evaporated and was quickly replaced with shame. "I—" it came out creaky, so she cleared her throat and said more forcefully "—I haven't been able to. It hasn't been coming to me. I'm worried—I'm worried they're gone." From behind her, Callum slipped his hand into hers and squeezed. She squeezed back, but was too afraid to look at him, to see fear in his eyes before they went into their own battle.

The god was unmoved. "Why?"

"Thomas and I tried when we arrived, and we couldn't, neither of us, and he said... He said he wondered if they returned to Arianrhod as they always should have."

Cernunnos just gazed at her, but she was sick of the guessing games, she was done being a pawn in someone else's game, no matter how small or large. Her stubbornness became her strength now and she glared back.

Jockie cleared his throat behind her. "Ah—" he began, gently. "If I might?" Cernunnos nodded. "Klara, what makes you think that Thomas was being honest with ye?"

That's not fair, Klara thought. She'd tried and tried and they'd never come back to her, not once. She wasn't lying. Why would she lie?

"Just because they didn't come then, Klara, doesn't meant they aren't still within you," Callum began. "Think of it, Klara. Every time you used your powers in your time, they exhausted you. Twice I had to carry you unconscious to somewhere to rest." His hand touched her cheek, and turned her toward him. Ashamed, Klara realized he would see that she was crying, but he just thumbed the tears off her cheeks. He brought his lips so close to hers, without breaking their gaze. His breath was hot against her lips, welcoming.

"I believe you, Klara, and I believe *in* you."

He then kissed her with passion she could only describe as the kind she felt when they made love. All of him within her, his strength and soul entwining itself into hers. Bonded.

She swallowed, took one last look in his eyes for strength, and then turned back to the god. "After all this time and all my worry, you're saying they just needed to reboot? Like a freakin' OS update?"

A small smile appeared on his face. "You did just receive the powers of eight other Pillars, Klara. Is it so much to imagine?"

Klara brought the palm of her hand to her forehead and closed her eyes. "Of *course* I get the bulk of the powers of the goddess of time, and the owner's manual is the same as my ever-loving *iPhone*!" She looked up, her gaze steely now. "All right, then, I have the powers. What next?"

Jockie gave a little cheer. "Och, we get your bahookie to the bean-nighe and give 'er a skelping!" Klara couldn't help but laugh.

Now, Cernunnos sighed. "As I have told you both many times, I cannot meddle in mortal affairs. But the bean-nighe is different, because she—and all magical creatures who serve the gods—straddle two worlds at once. They are not gods, but they are marked by gods. And though most of the time they deal only with the one who chose them, the truth is that they serve all of us gods."

"Braw, then stop her, damn it!" Callum said forcefully. "Klara is ready for Thomas. For once, Cernunnos, dinnae give us your riddles and excuses. If you don't act quickly—"

Jockie put a hand on Callum's shoulder. "He knows, son. You don't need to explain it."

"I know this is not what you want to hear," Cernunnos said calmly. "But no matter how much I might wish it to be different at the moment, I cannot meddle—"

"—in the affairs of mortals," Klara said impatiently. "We get it. How can you help us, then?"

"I can tell you where to find her."

The bean-nighe was lying low, according to Cernunnos, in her hideout, and had been ever since Llaw's death, coming out only when the washerwoman sensed one of her souls near a waterway—she could never resist the madness she drove men to.

"Arianrhod knew Llaw had to be stopped," Cernunnos

had told them, "but that didn't mean she relished his death. She was still his mother, and no matter what he had done, that love endured."

When the news of his death reached the realm of the gods, Arianrhod had been wild with grief. Her wailing had disturbed the celestial realm over which she ruled, shifting the tides and causing unexpected eclipses of some of the distant planets. She'd retreated to a distant corner of the realm and wasn't heard from for days; the other gods decided not to go after her, remembering the violent moods she was prone to when punished.

The gods weren't the only ones to tread lightly. The bean-nighe, who'd witnessed the goddess's tantrums in the past, feared for her own safety; though the goddess could only appear in her familiar form—an owl—in the mortal realm, she wasn't above plucking monsters from between worlds to carry out her vengeance when she was angry. (The bean-nighe's predecessor, a foul-tempered *fachan*, had been crushed in an avalanche after failing to carry out a task.)

It was Jockie who guessed where the bean-nighe was hiding. "It's a ghost portal, innit."

"Okay, sorry to be dense, but what's a ghost portal?" Klara asked.

"It's sort of a holding cell, invisible to the other gods." Cernunnos did not look happy about it. "Llaw took one when he found you in the faerie circle. You've even taken it, Klara, when you came to this time."

"But I came straight here, there wasn't any holding space in between," Klara said.

"You may not have known it, but you passed by one. With

practice, you could learn to linger between worlds. It can be dangerous for mortals like yourselves because of the magical creatures there—but the bean-nighe is one of them."

"Then we must go there at once!" Callum said, already rising.

"I cannot protect you there," Cernunnos warned.

"There's something else," Jockie said worriedly. "Malabron has eyes all over Rosemere. He will soon reach the same conclusion, if he hasn't already."

"How do we get to the portal?"

"We can do better than that. Cernunnos has already brought us between worlds—we can get there from here."

CHAPTER FORTY-ONE

KLARA

Klara held Callum's hand tightly as Cernunnos transported them through the vortex. When the mist cleared and the whirling stopped, the first thing Klara noticed was a terrible stench, a mixture of rot and burnt plastic and cheese left in the sun. As her eyes adjusted to the dim, flickering light she saw that they were in a huge, windowless room the size of a big box store with damp walls rimed with efflorescence, the floor covered with a thick layer of dust and littered with broken bricks and rags and what looked like animal bones. There was a sound of water dripping, and wet sludge seeped into her shoes.

That's when she felt it, a pull from within her. She turned toward the source of a light, a small fire giving off sickly greenish flames. Crouched above it, a small figure blew on the embers. Callum started toward her with purpose, but his feet kicked the debris, sending it skittering through the dust.

At the sound, the bean-nighe leapt up and Klara had a glimpse of glowing yellow eyes and pitiful rags before she let out a shriek like nails on a chalkboard and dashed across the room away from them.

Jockie chased after her, Klara and Callum hot on his heels, but they weren't quick enough. The bean-nighe slipped between a long crack in the wall, much too narrow for the rest of them to pass through. Callum put his shoulder to the wall and shoved at the stone as debris started to rain down from the ceiling. Jockie joined him, grunting from the effort.

The walls were cracking all around them now, and Klara realized that if they didn't get out soon they'd be buried alive—she had to do something. Klara raised her hands and thought about her powers, thinking about pushing Llaw away from her, about propelling Thomas off her, only now, concentrating on the stone that Callum and Jockie were trying to dislodge.

She felt the stirring inside her, stronger than it ever had been before, expanding more and more until, with a rush she experienced with every molecule of her being, the force shot out of her fingertips and slammed into the wall.

The stone toppled, sending Callum and Jockie sprawling. More stones fell from the ceiling, one coming dangerously close to Jockie's head, but Klara gritted her teeth and they just…stopped.

"Let's go!" Callum called, and Klara found with a jolt that

she couldn't move. Holding the ceiling from avalanching down on all their heads was all she could do.

Her voice came out in a whisper. "Callum…I can't move."

"Could you keep it up if I carry you, lass?" She nodded, barely. Callum rolled up to his feet and picked Klara up, slinging her over his shoulder while she continued to hold her eyes closed and her hands aloft. He grabbed Jockie's arm at a run and dragged him through the opening just as, with a deafening boom, the ceiling fell.

Dust swirled in the darkness, filling their nostrils, and Klara coughed and staggered onto a slippery surface. She blinked dust from her eyes and gasped.

They were surrounded by stars, a vast night sky filled with unfamiliar constellations above and around her. She looked down and let out a cry, because there was nothing beneath her feet, only the night sky in every direction.

"What is this place, Jockie?" Callum asked, nearly losing his balance. It would have been comical in other circumstances, watching him slide on nothing as if it was an icy street.

"We're still between worlds." He seemed to have no trouble navigating the space as he walked toward them. "Just a different part of it. The natural laws are different here. Don't think about it or you'll get tripped up."

She was about to ask where the bean-nighe had gone when the space in front of her shimmered and seemed to fold in half. There was a groan like icebergs colliding underwater and then the air ripped open, scattering nearby stars, and something came at her at a gallop. It was three or four feet tall.

Klara's sword was in her hands before she was even aware she'd moved, but the creature raced by her, followed by another, then three more. She was reminded of a herd of startled, pale ponies, tripping over each other as they grew smaller and smaller in the distance.

"Shopiltees," Jockie said. "They're no threat to us. Probably got spooked when we came through the portal."

"But I thought you said that violent creatures got banished here."

"They do, but they're not the only ones. When Breogan and Danu returned and found that the Underworld had been taken over, they opened a gateway between worlds. Now all kinds of creatures wander there."

"How do we find the bean-nighe?" Callum said impatiently. "This place is as big as our night sky."

"I think it *is* our night sky," Klara said, wondering how to explain the vastness of the universe to him. "Just very far away, past everything we can see—our planets and stars and sun."

"You're almost right," Jockie said. "It is like what you describe, but separate. And though no one has ever reached the edges, it can also seem very small, because you can easily find whatever you like if you know how. Remember I said that things work differently here? If I used the right summoning spell, I could fetch beasts too—it's how Llaw and Thomas brought back all those monsters."

"Then summon the bean-nighe!" Callum urged.

"It won't work on her," Jockie said. "She's too smart. She'd feel the call but she wouldn't respond. Only the dumb beasts can be compelled."

"Then how—"

"We can't bring her to us—but we can find her with a dowsing spell. Just as Cernunnos conjured a clearing for you, the bean-nighe will conjure a stream or lake so she feels at home. Grab hold of my shirt, now."

Jockie began to chant, and the space around them folded again, enveloping them like great, soft clouds. When it unfolded, they were standing on a hillock next to a cloudy stream rimmed by dead stalks. At the water's edge was a small hunched figure dressed in rags, poking at the stream with a stick, already whirling around to face them with her sickly yellow eyes.

"You did not surprise me!" she shrieked, pointing at Callum triumphantly with a crabbed and bent finger.

She thinks we're here for Callum, Klara thought.

Something whizzed by her ear and slammed into the bean-nighe, catching her in the shoulder and knocking her to her knees. She looked up in wonder and rage, her hand going to the wound, an ugly hole in her flesh from which viscous yellow bile leaked.

"Imagine," an all-too-familiar voice called, "meeting you here."

CHAPTER FORTY-TWO

KLARA

Thomas strolled down the hill toward them at an almost leisurely pace. Behind him, Aion sprinted toward the bean-nighe with the power sword in his hands.

"Callum, you must stop him!"

But Callum was frozen, his eyes going from Aion to Thomas. "But—"

"Go!" Klara screamed. She knew that Callum was desperate to protect her—but if she could not stop Thomas it wouldn't matter. If Aion managed to kill the bean-nighe, all of her powers and lifeblood would flow to him, and—

And he'd be nearly unbeatable, together with Thomas's powers.

Jockie had the same thought. "You must fight like you never have before. Callum, you must trust Klara now."

Aion had reached the bean-nighe, tackling her so that they rolled into the water.

"I can keep her from escaping," Jockie muttered through gritted teeth. His fingers were painfully twisted as they traced designs in the air, his skin was pale and clammy, and he was beginning to tremble. "But not for long. You—*must*—*not*—"

Callum ran toward the water and Klara's heart flipped in fear. Even with the strength of ten men, what chance did he have against a power sword and the banshee bean-nighe?

Callum, you must trust Klara now. Jockie's words echoed in her mind, and the answer slid into place like a key into a lock: *she* also had to trust Callum to fight his own battle.

It was now, after she'd given her heart completely, that Klara finally understood that neither of them could stand in the way of the other's destiny. Instead, they each had to trust themselves enough to fight their own battles, and only then could they be together without the encumbrances of the past.

And *that* was worth fighting to the death for.

Klara spun around to face Thomas. It seemed to happen in slow motion, her skirts swirling around her, the sword slicing through the air as she raised it with both hands. She felt its energy flowing into her, melding with her, and then it multiplied a thousandfold as soon as she thought of the Pillars and their powers, also somewhere inside of her, innocents whose lives were cut short by a power-hungry demigod. And with that, the voices of her ancestors, every generation of women who came before her, began chanting a chorus in her mind, and while she could not understand their words, she was filled with their purpose and power.

A hard, bright scream split the air and Klara knew it was her battle cry.

"Impressive," Thomas said sarcastically, raising his own sword. "For a *girl*."

Klara's eyes blazed. *Oh, it's on*, she thought, *you arrogant, misogynist* chad.

Red sparks glinted off the hilt of his sword as he began chanting, and when Klara attacked, it was as if her sword struck a powerful waterfall that nearly ripped it from her hands.

Thomas laughed and slammed his sword sideways into her arm, knocking hers to the ground. Klara looked down to see blood pouring from the wound above her elbow, bright white bone showing.

She looked up at Thomas in shock. Her arm was useless now. Klara dove for the sword with her left hand, knowing she'd never be able to fight with it, when she felt a huge pressure behind her eyes, heard the rushing of voices in her mind, the voices of all the women who had ever held the sword, and the outrage of the lost Pillars.

Go back go back go back go back

She closed her eyes and opened herself. *Show me*, she thought, faces of women flashing through her mind, glimpses of her mother and Grams and women she'd never seen before. *Show me how.*

Klara was suddenly in the blinding vortex, turning back time as the voices awakened her powers. And suddenly she understood that they had never been hers alone, that what had been unleashed in her the day she traveled back in time with Callum were the powers of her ancestors, that she'd struggled to learn to control them because they were hers not to master, but to honor and protect for every generation that came after her, for every Pillar in Time who had fallen to Llaw.

Her eyes flew open and she was staring at Thomas, her arm unhurt, in the moment before he attacked. Her mouth was open and screaming and this time she let the scream propel her as she leapt into the air, impossibly high, flipping over in a blur of flapping skirts as Thomas's thrust met nothing.

He landed on his feet, easily recovering his balance. "Well, that's annoying. The little kitten has grown claws," he sneered. "I was rather hoping you wouldn't figure out how to access those."

Her eyes widened. "You felt me do that?"

"I'm a Pillar, too, Klara. Or should I say, *I'm nine Pillars, too,* little kitten."

"No!" she ground out. And now they fought as equals. Klara's powers held, a tight thrum like the string of a cello reverberating inside her, and the blade of her sword danced and flashed as they circled each other. The few times she made a mistake, slipped up, lost the advantage, all she had to do was think of the women who had come before her, and *fwiiip,* they showed her how to right her mistake, and she'd carry on fighting like a harpy. But so did Thomas, and each time *he* made a mistake, she could feel her mind being yanked back through a vortex, her body retracting its last steps until he restarted time again. It was an eerie feeling, and it only made her angrier.

Behind them the sounds of another battle raged, a dark

symphony of shouts and hissing and a banshee scream, water splashing and rocks grinding against each other and thuds and grunts. *Trust Callum.*

Klara struck Thomas in the thigh, a glancing blow that drew blood but failed to slow him down. Thomas missed her neck by a fraction of an inch when Klara dove beneath his blade. They were beginning to tire, but they fought on. Klara's lungs were screaming for air, her muscles exhausted, when the chorus escalated in warning, a deafening scream in her mind—

And just as she found an opening and slashed at Thomas's side, she realized her mistake: he'd feinted and hooked her ankle, sending her slamming onto her back, the sword ripped from her hands.

The breath was knocked from Klara, and for a moment, the voices were silenced. Gasping, she looked up at Thomas grinning above her, blood trickling from a flesh wound where her blade had glanced off him. Klara clawed at the ground, but the sword was just out of reach, glimmering in the dirt.

CHAPTER FORTY-THREE

CALLUM

Callum raced down the hill, Aion churning up a froth as he fought to restrain the bean-nighe. Being a spirit, she kept changing form: twig-like hag, robust young woman, nearly insubstantial wraith, but somehow Aion held on to her, though he couldn't raise the sword into position. Behind him, Jockie worked his spell to keep Aion in a cloud of illusion and shifting visions, but still, the old fae persevered.

"Don't!" Aion yelled as Callum charged. "Not until—"

His words were cut off as Callum slammed into them.

He bellowed with rage, getting an arm around Aion's sword hand as he tried to kick at the bean-nighe. But Aion grabbed his ankle and twisted, forcing them both under the water.

Whatever sinister magic Malabron had summoned had given Aion strength to match his own.

He came up sputtering, the bean-nighe writhing in his grip. "What did you do?" he demanded, keeping a distance between them.

"He gave it to me freely," Aion said. He looked even younger than when Callum had first met him, in the prime of his life—strong and vital with flashing dark eyes and thick black hair tied back. "I don't want to kill you. I want no blood on my hands but hers." The bean-nighe surfaced, and she let loose a piercing wail that scraped along Callum's eardrums, nearly causing him to lose his grip.

He could hear the clash of swords up on the bank but didn't dare take his eyes off Aion. "But if you and Thomas succeed, the worlds will be destroyed—"

"We all die," Aion said bleakly. "But I'll have my vengeance first."

And then he lunged.

Aion drove his fist into Callum's gut before he could land a blow, and as he doubled over Aion raised the sword above his head. Before he could strike the banshee, Callum managed to grab a fistful of her hair and wrapped it around his wrist, pulling her behind him, while she shrieked with rage. He felt her shift into her wraith form, the hair going delicate, gossamer-thin, and tickly under his palms, but he held. The bean-nighe shifted again, wiry and skeletal, and began trying to bite Callum with her rotting teeth; it was taking all his strength to hold her away from him.

Aion got a hand around Callum's neck and began to squeeze. With his free hand Callum tried to pry it free but

Aion was stronger. All he could do was wedge himself between them so that Aion couldn't use the sword on the banshee.

A scream filled the air—not Klara's, but a hundred deafening voices in unison. Startled, Aion loosened his grip for a fraction of a second—and it was enough.

Callum ripped away from him and brandished his dirk. He watched Aion's eyes fill with understanding and the agony he saw there took his breath away—

But it didn't stop him from plunging his blade deep into the bean-nighe's heart, taking all chance of vengeance and a deal with Malabron away. She made a hideous sound as she died away, the wailing of a thousand widows, the screech of hawks, the scream of a skulk of foxes.

He released her into the water, a soiled rag floating on the surface that soon sank into the depths.

CHAPTER FORTY-FOUR

KLARA

There was a noise like a dozen screeching cats and Klara tried to twist her head, but Thomas put his foot on her chest, pushing the air from her lungs as he picked up her sword from the dust out of her reach.

"What have you *done*!" he roared.

Then Callum came into her view, water dripping from his body, his face and hands scratched and bleeding, a look of murderous rage in his eyes. Jockie followed behind him with Aion in his arms—the Aion of yesterday, pale and haggard and dying.

Callum stopped a few feet away when Thomas put Klara's blade to her neck. She could feel the sharp tip of it pressing against her and fought against the terror as their eyes met. *Stay strong,* she willed him, seeing his agony.

He tore his eyes away from her. "The bean-nighe's powers flowed back into the earth," he told Thomas. "Where they belong. They were stolen, just as you stole the sword."

"You *idiot*!" Thomas bellowed. He no longer looked like the mischievous, handsome young man Klara had met, his face contorted in hatred. "You could have ruled with me, Callum. You could have power like you never imagined!"

Callum's eyes filled with sadness. "We never wanted that, Tom. Remember? You used to say we lived like kings, going anywhere we liked while rich men choked on their own arrogance. You said the city was ours—don't you remember?"

There was a moment—a fraction of a second—when Klara thought she glimpsed the old Thomas behind those veiled ice-blue eyes, the boy who'd looked out from rooftops and eaten stolen bread with his best friend, ruling the only domain that mattered.

And then the light blinked out and she knew that boy was gone forever, overtaken by the twisted powers of the dark fae and the goddess and the tainted hunger that would never let the worlds be truly in balance.

But in that tiny break in Thomas's concentration, Klara felt her powers pulse through her and out through her fingertips, sending a blue, shimmering current arcing toward the sword's jeweled grip. It flew out of his grip and into her hand—

And Thomas stumbled back, while Klara was lifted into the air and set on her feet.

She'd only surprised him, but it was enough. The chorus had become a part of her now, and as Thomas gripped his sword she could feel them fighting with her. Thomas was strong and she could tell he was bringing every bit of fight he had to this moment, but he was up against centuries of courage and steadfastness and devotion to peace, even when that peace had to be won with blood.

But there was one thing she hadn't counted on. As her strength began to flag, Thomas's did not. Klara had truth and valor on her side but her body was still mortal, while he was fueled by evil magic. She could feel herself tiring, her movements unsteady, her balance slipping.

Just a little longer, Klara told herself desperately, trying to ignore a gash in her hip, blood trickling into her eye—

But then Thomas maneuvered her up against a huge rock and she was trapped, gasping for air, exhausted to delirium. She tried to dodge but each time Thomas jabbed, almost playfully, keeping her trapped like a lightning bug in a mason jar.

And Klara knew she was done. She was too exhausted to even try to reach for her powers. She would not get out of this, not this time. Thomas would deal the killing blow and the last of the powers would leave her as she died, and he would—

The chorus of her ancestors swelled one last time and suddenly Klara understood. Her body would die, but she would join those who'd gone before her, who'd defended Kingshill and everything it stood for. All she had to do was let the sword do its work one last time.

She turned the hilt, taking the blade in her hands, and willed the sword to do the rest. Thomas watched in confusion as she held the tip above her heart. She locked eyes with Callum and telegraphed her love as she—

But he became a blur, a force that knocked the sword from

her hand just as Thomas's own blade arced down, straight into his chest.

Klara screamed as Thomas gripped the sword tightly, holding Callum upright with it as blood poured from him, a look of shock on his beautiful face. She kept screaming as her vision blurred and the powers seized her from within, spinning her into the blinding vortex, and she was once again lying on the ground with Thomas's boot crushing the breath from her body.

She twisted her head to see Callum running toward them and willed time to slow, something she'd never done before. Her hand rose of its own volition, palm out, and held time at bay. There was no time to marvel at the sensation, no time to understand, only the chorus—wordless now, a harmony in a minor key at once melancholy and beautiful.

Everyone and everything was frozen, even Thomas, though his eyes followed her still—except for Klara, rolling to her feet and grasping her sword in hand, leaping into the air, bringing her blade high above her head. It was balletic, the grace coming from deep within her, choreographed by the multitude. She saw the fear in Thomas's eyes, suddenly unable to grasp his own control of time even as he could see it pass. She measured the fraction of an inch by which she would miss colliding with Callum, a split second of mortal time, a gift of her ancestors.

Her blade drove into Thomas, catching him just below the ribs, slicing through bone and flesh. As he fell to the ground she struck once more, impaling his wrist to the earth, his fingers twitching as the sword fell from his hand.

"How?" Thomas whispered, blood bubbling at his lips. "I am stronger."

"*Love* is stronger," she snarled. "And I've been practicing."

Death in movies was quick compared to the reality of it. On screen, the plot must move forward. But in real life, right now, death wasn't swift.

It took its time with Thomas.

It was patient.

The bubbling of blood that once foamed at his lips was now a flowing stream, increasing with every gasp of breath he tried to inhale. Suffocating him slowly, pooling around him in a gory aura.

What was once ichor in his veins now only held iron and death.

The power he once had was no more and instead, death took its place and the life drained from Thomas's eyes.

As abruptly as they'd awakened inside her, the powers of her ancestors slipped away, just as Thomas did. Klara fell backward, into Callum's arms.

"Klara! Klara, are you all right?"

He was holding her upright, covering her with kisses, and Klara wanted to kiss him back but she was too weak, and there was something—something was happening and she had to be there, she had to witness—

"My children." Jockie was staring at something else. Emerging from the mist were figures dressed in white, four, then six, then more, moving gracefully across the earth without seeming to touch it. At the center they carried a limp, pale Arianrhod, her golden curls dull and lank, her arm trailing listlessly. Only her eyes were alive and bright and looking directly at Klara.

CHAPTER FORTY-FIVE

KLARA

The gods, ten in all, arrayed themselves in a semicircle before Klara and Callum and Jockie, Aion's body at their feet. Cernunnos was among them, resplendent in his robes, standing with the gods he'd summoned to the clearing.

Dechtere stepped forward and began to speak. Klara wasn't sure how she knew all of the gods' names, but they came to her like a dream she suddenly remembered.

"After Breogan and Danu left for the second time, there was harmony among us. We all intended to follow the Accords, and never to let our petty disputes and selfishness upset the balance of our worlds again.

"But, though we meant to keep our own realm in order, some of us feared that the mortal races could not live in harmony, and thus would ensure our destruction. Lugh, Eostre, and I decided to work in secret to pit them against each other until only one of the two mortal races survived. In this way we hoped to preserve our worlds at the cost of the sacrifice of the vanquished."

Lugh came forth to join Dechtere. "We three gave the fae the tools to destroy the human race, but most of them refused. Those who were persuaded worked in solitude and so it took many centuries for them to achieve what they could have done together, but we had infected them with distrust of each other. And so their campaign languished."

Now Eostre came to the front, pausing to lay a hand on Arianrhod's shoulder for a moment.

"We did not anticipate the bitter shadow that Arianrhod's behavior had left over us, one that came to oppress us in time. We began to resent her for the limits Breogan and Danu placed on us, for curbing our pleasures and stifling our freedoms, forgetting that none among us was innocent.

"We made of Arianrhod our scapegoat and took pleasure in her suffering. We saw her anguish in being separated from her son, but we refused to help him. We turned away and had no pity for her."

"We were wrong," Dechtere said forcefully. "We thought that a second chance was all we needed, but that wasn't true. *We* had to change, to learn the lessons we pretended to. To understand that we were on the path to destroying everything once again, it took almost losing our sister. Arianrhod was also wrong. She used you mortals for her own purposes. She traded in malicious commerce and risked all of our worlds.

But we had allowed her suffering until it was too great for her to bear alone."

"No more." Eostre's voice rang out clear and strong. "We *are* changing. We will care for our sister Arianrhod and share our powers with her until her own are restored. We will settle our disputes among ourselves and make no decision affecting our worlds without reaching concordance."

"I wish to speak," Arianrhod said timidly, her voice a thin husk. "I harmed you, Klara, and all the Pillars. I am to blame for the loss of Thomas and for the deaths of eight innocent mortals. And I did not understand the power of love until I lost..."

She faded in that moment, shimmering between life and something else, before finding the strength to continue. "And because I have come to understand the pain of loss, I need to confess to something else, Klara. It was not your mother you saw at the Ring of Brodgar, but an illusion that I conjured. I...am sorry. If it helps, she is at peace in the Otherworld."

Klara was caught up in a swirl of conflicting emotions. "But...I hear her, sometimes. Not a memory, but she *speaks* to me."

Arianrhod came toward her, tottering painfully, and gathered Klara into her embrace. Klara stiffened, still too angry at the goddess to welcome her touch. But the other gods had forgiven her, and besides, it felt like being enveloped in the softest down, perfumed with the scent of a wintry night.

When Arianrhod pulled away she left a dusting of silver on Klara's gown. "I do not doubt you, Klara, but I have nothing to do with that. You possess powers you have only begun to tap."

Klara didn't respond, searching for the inner knowing that was still nascent within her…but she was too exhausted, too spent. She squeezed Callum's hand, suddenly tired of the gods, of their excuses and promises. They'd prevented the destruction of the worlds without their help, and Klara needed rest. She wanted only to be with Callum, away from everything but each other for a while.

"There's one last thing," Cernunnos said. "The bean-nighe's curse she placed upon you, Callum, is one that cannot be reversed." She paused. "Unless it is granted by the bean-nighe, and that, I am certain, won't be possible. She is known for her trickery and for never breaking a deal."

"My brothers and sisters helped me to do what I could," Arianrhod said, casting them a grateful eye. "Callum, you may never return to Klara's time. But Klara—we can grant you passage for a short time, on the days when the veil between worlds is thin."

A whirl of emotions soared through her in an instant. The unknown swirling like a vector through her mind but it was the possibilities of a future with Callum that rooted her to this moment and the moments they could have in the future to come.

"You mean—like at Samhain? And Imbolc and—"

"All of the sacred festivals." Arianrhod nodded. "But if you stay even a second too long in either time, the portal will forever close."

Callum and Klara exchanged a look. It was a lot to take in—but it was also a spark of hope, and a choice. A choice between staying in this time with the love of her life, whose cool dancing eyes kindled such warmth in her body and soul, who supported her and protected her and made her feel whole, powerful, invincible, and whose time was quiet, wild, beautiful, and rustic. Or to return home, to her sweet, bumbling father, and her snuggly dog, Finley, to a time when she could pursue not one but multiple degrees in astronomy, in modern science…but only see Callum for a few hours, a few times a year.

No…this feeling was not a mere spark of hope, it was a roaring fire of it. So bright that it would fill even the darkest of nights in a glow.

"I guess I should thank you," Klara told the goddess. "But honestly, right now, all I want is to never see any of you again."

Then she turned to Jockie and took his hand, so that he and Callum and she were joined. "I think we're done here, Jockie," she said. "Let's stop by the castle and see if Cook made you another cake."

EPILOGUE

KLARA

TWO MONTHS LATER

It had been a while since Klara had attempted to use her powers, but the trip might have been their smoothest yet: twenty seconds in the vortex, no stomach churning, and the mist felt refreshing after leaving an unseasonably sunny and warm December day in 1568.

The moment they landed in the faerie circle in the Elder Forest, though, it was unambiguously winter. Slate skies met bare branches, the temperature had dropped by at least twenty degrees, and she was glad for the fur-lined jacket topping her gown.

"I can't wait to put on a pair of sweats," she said, shivering. "Just you wait, Callum, you're never going to want to wear anything else."

In the months since, they had been able to find a loophole to breaking the bean-nighe's curse on Callum. With thanks to Aion killing the bean-nighe in the twenty-first century. Klara wondered sometimes what Aion had said…or *done* to get the bean-nighe to break her own deal, an act that had never been done before. Sometimes, Klara found, it was better to not know.

"I am more interested in seeing these secret undergarments of yours," he murmured wickedly, pulling her close and kissing the top of her head.

"*Victoria's* Secret!" Klara laughed. "And they're not secret, they're just—"

She broke off at the sight of an old truck lumbering into the clearing.

"He's here!"

Now Callum laughed. "You saw him only this morning, love!"

"I saw sixteenth-century Jockie—not this one."

Klara had wondered if she would see Jockie differently now, but it was the same beloved caretaker she remembered, wearing a new red down jacket and sporting a fresh haircut. Even his beard had been neatly trimmed.

"You look fantastic!" she said as he got out of the truck. She threw her arms around him and inhaled faint traces of cologne. "Jockie! Do you have a new girlfriend?"

"Ah no, lass," he said, embarrassed. "Just spruced up a bit for the *Alban Arthan* bonfire tonight. And you look very nice yourself! Did you ever find the Eye of Rose?"

Klara's hand went automatically to her neck, where the necklace had become a comforting presence. She'd lost it on the day of the battle, and though she'd looked everywhere, it hadn't turned up. "I haven't. I'm afraid it's somewhere between worlds now."

"Ah, well. Maybe your Grams will find something even better in the bottom of another old box," Jockie said consolingly.

Callum extended his hand, smiling broadly, but Jockie pulled him into a full-on hug. "It's 2022, lad. We men can be right sensitive now."

"Are Dad and Grams freaking out?" Klara asked. It was the one regret she had about staying in Callum's time—she had no way of letting them know what had happened and that she was okay.

Jockie shot her a conspiratorial grin. "Not a chance. They think you've been staying with your aul' pal Brittany in New York City, workin' as a waitress, like. And this fine lad works construction in Brooklyn. I had to send a few texts and whatnot and do a little messin' with their memories—oh, and I told them you were comin' dressed for the festival."

Klara laughed. "You're a genius, Jockie. And don't worry, we're going to tell them everything tonight. They deserve to know the truth."

"Is that all for *Alban Arthan*?" Callum asked once they had piled in the truck and were heading through town. He was captivated by the holiday decorations in the shop windows and hanging from lampposts, the blow-up snowmen on the lawns and reindeer on the roofs.

"Ah, lad, no. Christmas is a much bigger do here…but Ethan's gone all out for the celebration tonight. He's got it in his head to feature entertainment and special packages at the manor for all the festivals. They're very popular—your Grams tells me there's a waiting list for the next two years."

"What a *coincidence*, Jockie," Klara said, certain he'd had something to do with it.

She'd been looking forward to this visit for weeks. The days following the battle between worlds had been both busy and wonderfully restorative. Laird and Lady Westwood offered Klara and Callum the use of the caretaker's house on the grounds of the manor.

In exchange, Callum went to work as Jockie's apprentice. He had a talent for carpentry and had already joined the guild and started taking jobs with local smiths and masons. Klara had decided there was nothing sexier than watching Callum carrying lengths of lumber, his well-defined biceps and shoulders straining the fabric of his shirts.

Meanwhile she and Lady Mairi had begun a genealogy project, charting not just their own family but assembling all the records of Rosemere dating back to the Worlds Council. With Mairi's help, she'd commissioned a few copies of *Magic and Mystic Centers* and records of the Accords, to be put on public display both at the manor and in the faerie mound. She was determined that history would have a harder time repeating itself on her watch.

As Jockie pulled in, Klara spotted Finley galloping toward them, ears flapping and short legs a blur. Aunt Sorcha was a few steps behind him, wielding a batter-covered wooden spoon.

And there at the top of the drive was her father, flanked by Grams and Alice, all three bursting with excitement.

Klara was happy in her life in Rosemere—but she couldn't wait to see her family.

"Look out!" Callum exclaimed.

As they reached the bottom of the drive, Jockie abruptly hit the brakes. Finley was jumping at the passenger side door, yipping like a puppy. A few moments from now, they would all be embracing. There would be laughter and tears of joy and everyone talking at once, good food and wine and music, conversations that would last long into the night and begin again in the morning. Klara would love every minute, and their parting would be hard—but the festival of *Imbolc* was only seven weeks away.

"Are you still nervous, Callum?" she asked as Sorcha corralled Finley and dragged him out of the road.

"Not anymore," he said, taking her hand. "I thought it would be strange, comin' here to your time again. But I feel..."

"Like you can get used to it?"

"Like I belong," he said. "Just as you belong with me."

They kissed, and Klara could hear applause break out, Grams whooping and her dad whistling.

"Ready?" Klara said...and together they got out of the truck and walked into their future.

★★★★★

ACKNOWLEDGMENTS

First and foremost, I want to thank my incredible agent, Joanna Volpe. It is wild to think you have other clients when I feel like the only one. Without you, I don't know where I'd be, and your attentive care, friendship, and all-around beautiful nature have fueled me throughout our years together. I adore you!

Alongside Joanna, I want to thank the immaculate team at New Leaf Literary and Media. You are all a powerhouse that is fueled by love. I am beyond grateful to be a part of such a nurturing and beautiful agency.

Kate Sullivan, my absolutely brilliant editor. You and I have been on countless FaceTime calls, text chats, and email threads this past year, and even though we are thousands of miles apart, thank you for holding my hand and helping me believe in myself when even I couldn't do so. You are a rarity in this world and I am grateful to have you.

Bess Braswell, you are a massive reason why this book is in the hands of readers today, and for that, I am immensely grateful. I adore Inkyard Press, and being a part of the Harper-

Collins family for six beautiful years has been an absolute honor and privilege.

To my parents, Joan Zielinski Alsberg and Peter Alsberg. Even though you both aren't here, I will forever feel your presence in each word I write and every book I publish. You supported me when even I couldn't see the strength in myself. For that, I am beyond grateful. I love you both so much. Forever and always.

To my godmother, Marcia Longman (aka Mama Marcia). In a world of uncertainty, I know I can always rely on you to be a beacon of light that helps guide my way through the darkness. I love you.

To my friends and family: my twin, Marisa Alsberg Hanebrink, and my sisters Anna Camilla Rosenfeld, Stephanie Alsberg Stafford, Jennifer Alsberg, and Nikki Alsberg. To my cousin and my twin flame, Sarah Alsberg.

To my found family: JD Netto, Laura Sebastian, Hanna Hakkarainen, Alison Jensen, Jenna Houston, Tom Rainford, Gabby Gendek, Natasha Polis, Elizabeth Sagan, and James Trevino. I couldn't have done this, or life, without you. I am so lucky.

To my Joffe Books family: working two jobs at once is no easy feat, but the support I have had from you all has been the crutch I have leaned against since day one. I cannot thank you enough. To Jasper Joffe, Emma Grundy Haigh, Kate Lyall Grant, Nina Kiscul, Steph Carey, Jasmine Callaghan, Najma Haji, and Laura Coulman-Rich.

To my fur babies, Fraser and Fiona. I love your floofy booties and infectious smiles!

To my amazing online family. I am so grateful to have had

us all grow up together, and I wish I could give each one of you a hug for all you've done. I adore you and appreciate you all more than you know.♥